Count On Me

Count On Me
By
Melyssa Winchester

Copyright © 2014 Melyssa Winchester

For information regarding the cover and the models within please visit prochkailo at Fotolia

Isabella Rose. It is my hope, as you grow older that you find all the happiness and acceptance you deserve, as well as your very own Kayden. You deserve nothing less than the best. Never give up, never give in and never believe that you're not good enough. I'm so blessed to have you call me Mommy.

"We've all been hurt by words before. So before you speak, think about how your words might affect someone else." – Naya Rivera

Prologue

Kayden

I need to keep walking.

Just keep my head down and walk to my car. Go home. The one thing I've been dying to do since Coach finished giving me the weekly after practice speech.

I don't need to be getting involved in this even though it's my friends that are the ring leaders. I need to pretend I can't hear or see any of this and keep walking until I'm safely locked away where none of them can get to me.

That would be the smart thing to do, but let's face it; I never do the smart thing. I do the one thing that's sure to land me in the most shit once my brother Dean gets wind of it.

"Hey Kayden, you want in?" Dillon yells, motioning toward their latest project.

"Nah man, this one's all yours." I say, forcing a laugh so he gets the idea that I'm cool and not bothered by what they're doing.

I am though, bothered by it. It's one thing to pick on some nerd walking the halls with their nose in a book, but Isabelle? Everyone knows the girl has issues, so why do this stupid game with her?

"Your loss bro." he calls back and I start walking again, more determined than ever to just get to my car and get the hell out of here.

It's a game to us. We take one kid every couple of months and torture them in a bunch of different ways until they break under the pressure. I say us because I've been part of it before, more than a few times actually. It's not that I think it's right, but it beats turning them down and becoming the one they attack.

I don't want to be a part of this though and not because when Dean finds out he'll kick my ass. Truth is, he'd do that anyway. This time I don't because of who it's happening to.

Isabelle Reagan.

The blonde haired, blue eyed Senior I've lived across the street from since we were in diapers. Before my mom split, we used to spend a lot of time over at their house. She used to call it tea time, but I swear with the way they used to act, I'm pretty sure there was something other than tea going into those cups.

Isabelle was always super quiet and I remember thinking it was kind of creepy, the way she'd almost look through you, yet never say a word. When she did manage to interact, it was always in really weird ways too, like she wasn't normal. Mom took off, leaving me with Dean and I was happy about it. It meant I wouldn't be forced to spend any more time with the weirdo next door.

Yeah, I know, I'm an asshole, but that's not exactly news.

I won't be in on this because despite the way I used to look at her and maybe still do, I know things now. Dean ended up explaining a lot to me a few years back when he had to pick her up from school because she had an accident and the school couldn't reach her mom. Attacking her didn't hold any appeal for me.

It's when I hear her cry out that I stop. It's not the cry of someone being bullied like we've done before. This is different. It's almost like it isn't human at all, but the cry of a wounded bird.

Keep walking. Don't look back. Just keep walking.

I don't do it. Instead, I turn around and take in what's going on around me.

Her backpack is on the ground ripped apart, judging by the papers and books spilled out all over the place. Her hair, which was in pigtails earlier, is now half hanging out, which only made the knot in my stomach tighter.

It's hard to tell from here, but it looks like she's got tear stains under her eyes, which means Dillon and the others are getting exactly what they want. I'm about to turn around again, but before I can, Dillon gets one of the girls to hold her arms and her eyes lock on mine.

Shit.

Why did they have to grab her and turn her in my direction? Don't they realize I can't handle the emptiness I see staring back at me?

Fuck.

"Look at this Amy, she's crying again. What a freaking baby. Is the little retard scared? Is she gonna piss her pants again?"

The minute the words come out of his mouth, I'm done. I'm a first class asshole, but I'm nothing like Dillon right now. What he's doing, the things he saying, there's no way in hell it's right. Everything about this is just wrong.

"Maybe she wants you to kiss it better Dillon. I've seen the way she looks at you when she doesn't think anyone can see. She totally wants your lips on her."

"I think you're right, Ames. Maybe I should give her a little something to remember me by."

I watch as he moves closer and Amy drops the hold on her arms. He reaches out and grabs her. As I try to get my legs to move, Isabelle struggles against him and her shirt rips. Before any of the idiots I call friends can say anything though, it gets worse.

It's happening again.

The way it looks as it makes its way down her legs to the ground does something to me. Where I couldn't move before, in either direction, now all I can do is move and it's not in the direction I wanted only minutes before. No, this time I'm moving straight for her.

Dillon shoves her away from him before I can get to her and she falls to the ground, right in the small puddle that's accumulating at her feet. Hearing her sobs, either from pain or embarrassment is more than I can take.

Fueled by a rage like I've never felt off the field, I switch directions at the last second, turning my attention to the asshole that did this to her. Grabbing his shirt, I yank him to me, so close that there can be no confusion about what's about to happen.

"Say sorry."

"Fuck you, Kayden. It's not like I'm doing anything you haven't done before!"

"I don't give a shit." I snap, positioning my body so close to his that he's blocked in like the animal he is. "She doesn't deserve this shit. Apologize. Now."

"Oh, I'm sorry man. I had no idea this was your girl. You should've warned me."

I'm not exactly sure what pisses me off more; the arrogant way he says it or the words he's saying, but I'm bored with it. My fist connects with his face and as he reacts to the impact, I hit him again. He falls backward, catching himself at the last second, attempting to mount a defense. Too bad for him that there's nothing he can do.

See, that's my secret. This isn't the first time I've been in a fight and I'm pretty sure it won't be the last. I live with an alcoholic brother that enjoys beating on me at least five nights out of seven. After having it happen for the last eight years, I've learned how to fight back and now, no one can take me. Not even Dean.

I slam my fist into his face again. As he stumbles, I land another hit to his stomach and finally he falls to the ground. Lifting my leg up, I kick him and keep on kicking until blood pours out of his mouth. I don't even stop then.

It's only when I hear the wounded whimper a few feet away that I force myself to stop and back away. Turning, I walk toward her and it's only when she starts backing away that I get what she's seeing.

I'm filled with rage and she can see it all over my face.

Moving forward, I bend down slowly and whisper. There's no guarantee it's gonna work, but I gotta try to calm her.

"It's okay, Isabelle. It's over now. You're safe."

I reach my hand out, hoping she'll get the hint so I can get her up and out of here. As she places her small hand into mine; I'm shocked by what happens next.

"Kayden."

One word.

My name and just like before, I'm completely frozen in place.

It's the first time I've heard her speak in almost eight years. Despite my reputation for being a total jerk and not giving a shit what anyone thinks, the way my name sounds rolling off her tongue makes me feel pretty damn special. It's like to this girl right now, I'm her savior.

I find myself liking it, though I'll never admit that to another living soul. Just like I won't admit how badly I want to hear her say it again.

Shaking off my thoughts, I take her hand and pull her up until she's safely nestled in my arms. As I turn around to grab her backpack, I feel someone shove into me. I grab on to her tighter, balancing my body off of hers while at the same time, protecting her from falling again.

Turning around just enough to see the person who pushed into me, I come face to face with the very person I just sent to the ground.

"I don't know what's gotten into you man, but you're gonna pay for that shit. Maybe not right now, but you will pay for it."

"Anytime—anyplace—anywhere." I seethe as I turn Isabelle in the direction of my car and start walking away.

The further away we get from everyone, the more the reality of what just took place sets in. I just kicked the living shit out of my best friend for Isabelle Reagan.

What the hell have I gotten myself into?

Chapter One

Belle

It's always been this way.

People think that because I'm quiet, I don't hear the names they call me. Retard is the most popular, but there's a ton of other ones. They assume because I don't talk that I must be deaf, so I'm called deaf mute a lot. It used to bother me, but I guess after you hear the same names repeated for so long, eventually they lose their impact.

If they paid attention, they would know that I'm not a retard, I don't ride the short bus and I'm not a deaf mute. I'm just autistic.

My mom says that I *'started acting funny'* right around my fourth birthday. She took me to the doctor and after a little bit of a wait, there were even more doctors. There's been so many since then that I've lost count, but it doesn't change anything. I'm still autistic and there's no quick fix for it. I'm going to be this way for the rest of my life. I think I'm the only one that's okay with that.

My mom kept taking me to all of those doctors because she didn't understand me and honestly, I think she wants them to put me back together, like I'm broken or something. I'm not broken, I'm just different.

I'm okay with the way I am, except when I get into situations that are too much for me. It's only then that I hate it and wish they could fix me. The worst part has to be the accidents. I know how to go and I know what it feels like, it's just a lot of times, I get overloaded and can't control it. I hate that part because it's embarrassing. It's when that stuff happens that I wish my life was different.

Sometimes I even wish I was dead.

Those kinds of thoughts, I don't talk about them. I know if I told my mom how bad it is for me, she'd only worry more and take me to another doctor. I know she means well, but I'm tired of it all.

Most kids, when they walk into their class don't get freaked out by the lights. They go to their seat and move on like nothing is wrong. I can't do that. I'm in a lot of classes with other kids like me, but there are some I wanted to be in that I have to take regular classes for. It's those where my issues are hardest to handle. Turning down the lights is minor compared to what else happens.

If too many people are moving around real close to me, it makes my heart almost beat out of my chest and breathing is hard. The blood rushes to my head and I get overloaded which sometimes means I scream out or shake. For the kids at school, that's what makes me a retard.

I've gotten control over a lot of it. I know my triggers and I do things in order to redirect, but it still gets me sometimes, which is what the bullying is about. This time is different though because normally, they just call me names and push me around a little. That's not what happened in the parking lot and I'm scared it's not going to be the last time it happens.

My mom homeschooled me until I started high school. She wanted to continue it, but I ended up telling her no. It's not that I enjoy being picked on, pushed around and treated like a leper. I just can't stand being more of an outcast then I already am.

Kayden Walker is my next door neighbor. We used to play together when we were babies. Well we did, until his mom took off and left him alone with Dean. He's the only friend I've ever had even though I'm pretty sure he doesn't feel the same. Kayden's mom made him hang out with me, I know that, but it doesn't change anything for me. Spending time with me the way he did when we were younger made me feel special and not in the bad way.

I'm not sure why he didn't join in with his friends today. I've seen them do it before with other kids and he seems to enjoy it. Enjoyment is the last thing he felt today. I saw it in his eyes before he bent down to help me up. The last time I've seen someone look like that was when Dad fought with Mom.

I don't like anger. It scares me. Whenever my mom raises her voice around me, I completely shut down and hit myself. I've been doing it since I was four. She tells me that anger is a natural part of life, but I just don't see it that way. Why be angry when you can be happy? It's why even now, walking toward his car; I'm still scared of him. I don't want to do something and have him get angry at me the way he did with Dillon.

"Isabelle."

He says my name so easily that I'm jealous. When I said his name earlier, it had taken every bit of strength I had to get the sound to come out. It caused me physical pain to do it, yet here he is saying mine like he does it all the time.

"Why didn't you get on your bus?"

I have to answer him. I can't let him stand there wondering. I just don't know if I've got it in me to get the words out. When I'm home with my mom and Tristan, it's easier to speak because they understand me, but here, now, at school and in front of Kayden, it's too hard.

So I do what I always do when I can't speak. I motion with my finger toward the school as if all the answers he wants are going to be answered with the simple motion.

"You stayed after school for something?" he asks, his eyes never once leaving mine as he tries to figure out what I'm trying to say while saying nothing at all.

I nod my head and he smiles. It's not a big one, but considering the way he looked a couple of minutes ago, it's a nice change.

"Do you want a ride home?"

I nod and he walks me around to the passenger side of the car. Holding up one hand, he jogs quickly around to the driver's side, slides in and reaches across to pop the door open on my side. Then, using his other hand he motions for me to get inside.

It would be so easy to slide in the way he did, but I can't do it. I know he's only trying to be nice and take me home, since it is on his way and all, but I think he forgets exactly what happened to me out there with his friends.

"Get in the car, Isabelle. I don't care about that."

Once I do as he says and slide into the seat, doing my best to keep my jacket over the wet spot, I close the door and wait for him to drive away. After about two minutes of him not doing anything but staring straight ahead, I clear my throat. The sound breaks him out of his trance and he turns, his lips lifting until he's full on smirking at me.

"I'm sorry. I know I need to take you home, but I can't. Not yet. I need to ask you something first."

Considering how one sided this conversation has been so far, I'm kind of surprised he wants to ask me anything at all. I expected him to want to get rid of me as quickly as possible.

"You have your notebook?" he asks me, motioning toward the remains of my broken backpack. "I know you have trouble talking, so, how about I talk and you write?"

His voice is low, soothing even, as if he knows my issues with loud noises and is trying not to spook me. The way he's acting reminds me of the way he was when we were kids. It's a time I miss more than I want to admit. He was so patient with me back then. It's the complete opposite of the way he's been lately. He's like the old Kayden again. It's nice.

I pull the notebook out of my bag and search around with my hand for a pen. When my hand finally lands on one, I pull it out and yank the cap off; creating a loud popping sound that makes me jump in my seat. I brace myself for the laugh that's sure to come, but after a few seconds, I realize he's not doing anything but staring ahead again.

"How long were they doing that with you before I came out?"

I scribble on the paper quickly, the answer easy.

I guess it was fifteen minutes.

"Why did you go with them?"

Staring at the paper in front of me, I take a minute to think over my answer. I want to tell him the truth, but I'm afraid that when I do, he's going to laugh and think I'm pathetic.

Amy said that Tim wanted to ask me to the dance, but he was nervous and she wanted to help him out.

"Fuck!" he yells, banging his fists off the steering wheel, the sound making me jump and throw my body even closer to the passenger side door. His anger is startling. Noticing my reaction, he sighs before allowing his body to collapse into the seat. "Isabelle, I'm sorry. I forgot."

It's okay. I write, adding a smiley face at the end to let him know it's okay. I have issues, but it doesn't mean he should feel bad for reacting. After years of my mom doing the same thing, I feel like an old pro, at least with telling people it's okay.

"You know," he says. "You can just smile; you don't need to write the happy faces."

I lower my head and out of the corner of my eye I see he's frowning, which makes me sad. This is probably why the doctors think I've got social anxiety, but it's not that at all. I just have the uncanny ability to make people feel bad because I don't know the proper way to act. No matter how hard I try to learn it, it never sticks.

"What did they do to you?" he asks, shifting the tone of the conversation again.

Pushed me around a little bit, yanked my backpack off and ripped it open. Tim and Dillon did that part. They grabbed me pretty hard on my arms. You know the rest.

I can see his attempt to calm his breathing and again, I just feel sad. I actually debated whether or not to tell him what they did because of the reaction he'd have and seeing it now bothers me. He shouldn't have to worry about this.

"They won't do that shit to you again, okay? I swear to you, no more. If it happens, they're dead."

I'm not sure how I'm supposed to answer so I pick up the pen and do the one thing that I hope will get him to smile again. I can sense the tension rolling off of him and it's making my stomach uneasy thinking about it. I want him to be okay.

Holding up the notebook, I turn it in his direction and the minute his eyes catch what I've done, they soften and he smiles. It's a real, genuine smile. One I haven't seen him wear since we were seven. It makes me happy knowing that I was right.

"One more question and I swear I'll take you home."

Ok. I print out quickly.

"Why do you draw the happy faces instead of just smiling?"

Because I don't smile, not ever. I answer easily.

"I hate to be the one to tell you this Isabelle, but you just did."

Before I can question what he means, he takes the notebook out of my hands, placing it between the seats until its laying perfectly flat between us. Lifting a finger and bringing it back down on the paper, he points to the face I drew and then looks up at me.

"It's a nice smile, Isabelle. Don't let those assholes take it from you."

Kayden

I have no idea why the hell I said that to her, but it isn't like I can take it back so I let it sit there between us. The only thing that bothers me about what I said anyway, is I told her not to let the assholes take it from her and I'm one of them. Maybe she'll see it that way and steer clear of me.

I can hope anyway.

When she told me what they did, it took every bit of restraint I have not to smash my hand through the windshield, that's how angry it made me. It's even worse because we've done that same thing to a bunch of other people and I've never once given a shit about it.

Maybe it's because I know there's something wrong with her that makes me like this. It makes her more vulnerable than the others or that's the pretty picture I'm selling myself to push away the guilt I feel.

Hell, I've dunked heads in toilets, stolen underwear during PE and run them up the flagpole and laughed the entire time I did it. Add to that, pushing kids around, tripping them in the halls and then all the name calling and I really am king of the assholes. I'm the one that taught Dillon all he knows and what he used on Isabelle less than a half hour ago.

As I pull into her driveway, I look over and notice she's frowning. I immediately want to know what caused it because it doesn't seem like it should be there. If the girl can't smile then she shouldn't be able to frown either.

Since when am I this worked up over the way a girl looks? I should be more concerned with getting her out of my car so I can get it cleaned, not with the frown that seems even deeper across her face.

"What's wrong, Isabelle?"

Before she can reach over to grab the pad, I pick it up and tear the paper out. I have no idea why, but I can't let her write on it again. I want to keep it the way it looks right now.

The damn happy faces have obviously messed with my brain.

I pass the pad across to her as I put the car in park and she immediately starts scribbling across the page furiously. It's obvious that whatever she's frowning about is pretty big. Even when I'm in class with her, I don't think I've seen her write quite this fast.

My mom's car isn't here, which means she's not home and I don't like being home alone.

Is this girl kidding me? What teenager doesn't like being home alone? Man, I'd kill for Dean to get his ass out of the house once in awhile so I could have peace and quiet. Trust me, there's nothing more I want to do in the moment then trade spots with this girl.

"Why?" I ask, curious. "I thought everyone liked having the house to themselves?"

She shrugs before writing on the pad again, this time slower than before.

Serial killers enjoy coming for people that are home alone. Like that one Scream guy, except he likes calling first.

I read what she wrote and I laugh. Loud. I really tried to keep it in, but I couldn't. I wonder if that's part of her thing, blending fiction with reality. Focusing on that made it easier not to focus on the first part. I didn't want to think about how much truth there is to her serial killer comment.

Wexfield, Ontario is a pretty small town, but that doesn't mean we don't have crime. In fact, we had a couple murders a few years ago that still weren't solved.

Yeah, this is definitely not a place I want my mind going right now or I'm not sure how comfortable I'll feel leaving her alone. Shaking it off, I look up and catch her eyes locked on me. Shit, did I wait too long to respond?

"I think you're pretty safe here. Serial killers only come for the really dumb blondes anyway."

It was supposed to be a joke but the way her eyes well up with tears, I know she took it the wrong way. Damnit, even when I think I'm doing the right thing, it still turns out wrong. I really am the fuck up Dean says I am.

"Isabelle, please don't cry. I don't know how you took what I said, but it's wrong if it's making you cry."

She wipes at her eyes before turning back down to the paper in front of her and writing away again. After a couple of minutes go by and she's still going, I lean over and try to catch some of what she might be trying to tell me. Just as I'm able to catch a few words, she lifts her head and it smacks clear into my nose.

I feel the burn immediately, but as I wipe at it with my fingers, I'm happy to see there's no blood. She's got one hell of a head butt, but not one that can beat my made of steel nose.

Making out the paper in front of me, I see the words *'I'm sorry'* first. In an effort to make sure she knows she has nothing to be sorry for, that it was my dumb ass idea to bend over her, I reach out and touch her hand.

I don't know how she reacts to touch. It's been too long since I've spent any real time with her, but she doesn't jump and that makes me feel pretty good. I don't understand this. I'm not supposed to give two shits about this girl, so why is it that the simplest things she does and the way she reacts get to me this way?

"It's my fault, I was being nosy."

You're a nosy walker.

Again on the paper in front of me is a happy face. It's almost as if the damn smile has some kind of spell over me, because I'm smiling again. Even her cheesy joke has the desired effect. Instead of being a nosy parker, I'm a nosy walker. I think I've smiled more since getting in the car with her today then I have in the last ten years.

"Now that you've officially made me never want to be nosy again, can I see what you were writing?"

Nodding, she passes me the pad and as my eyes run down the page of things we've said, I stop dead the second I see what it is she was so furiously writing before the head butt.

If they come for the really dumb blonde girls like you say, then it means they're sure to come for me. I'm retarded and that's even worse than being dumb. I want to be like Super Girl and fight back, but I would probably just get scared, pee my pants and cry like the big, stupid baby I am.

I don't know much, but what I do know is, the minute I get to school tomorrow and see Dillon; he's a dead man. The problem is, if I blame him then I have to blame myself too. The guys on the team aren't the only ones that called her all those names and thought things about her. I have too. I'm just as guilty as they are, maybe even more so because for the first ten years of our lives, we were sort of friends.

"None of that is true, Isabelle. Shit, I'm sorry. We never should have said those things about you. We're all just a bunch of dicks."

She sits still and silent for so long I start to worry. Before I can ask her, she turns to me, the tears from earlier present in the corner of her eyes and I'm left with the horrible feeling that I'm the cause and there's nothing I can do to fix it.

You said those things about me?

The way I see it, there's only two ways I can handle this. I can lie to her, tell her I just worded things wrong, or, I could do the right thing and tell her the truth. I didn't just say those things about her like everyone else.

I'm the one that got everyone saying them to begin with.

I'm a complete pussy though, so I go with a third option, one that I know almost as well as I do lying. I evade the question and change the subject.

"Isabelle, look. I think you should get out and go home now. I know you're afraid to go in alone, but you need to get cleaned up."

It's a dick move, but it's me, so it really shouldn't come as a surprise. I can't answer her questions because I can't hurt her, at least not this way. If I tell her the truth, I will break her, so being a mean asshole is the only way I can go now. Better she hates me for making fun of her then learning the real reason she gets made fun of at all.

She picks up the pad and quickly scribbles out one final statement before undoing her seatbelt, opening the door and sliding out, slamming the door behind her. It's only when I've watched her make her way across her lawn and inside her house that I dare look down at her final words to me.

The circle of pain has been completed as I read it. I've done exactly what I set out to do. I've made her believe me to be the dickhead I already know I am.

It's only two words and a sad face, but it's the impact of those things that makes everything that much worse. Scribbled on the paper I can't seem to pull my eyes away from, is the simplest of statements yet the hardest at the same time.

Goodbye Kayden.

As I pull out of her driveway and peel forward into my own, it hits me. If I'm the bad person I think I am and I want her to stay away from me, why does the sad face hurt so god damned much?

Chapter Two

Belle

I'm such an idiot.

When he was asking me questions in the car, I really thought he might be one of the good guys. Despite knowing it was his friends that did everything to me earlier, I thought by saving me and taking me out of there, he was proving he actually cared.

Kayden Walker is no better than the friends that lied to get me in the parking lot. He just did a good deed for the day by taking me home; otherwise, he's the exact same way he's always been, at least for the last eight years.

I watched out the window a little and he stayed parked there. He's probably calling up Dillon and the others, apologizing for what he did to them. Letting them know that next time they wanted to come after me, he wouldn't stand in their way.

He never should have stepped in back there. He should have kept on walking when Dillon called to him. They could have done anything they wanted and no one would be fighting. I could have gotten home some other way then his car, where it was warm and for a little while, comfortable.

I don't think he realized just how close I came to speaking to him in the driveway. I wanted to say things because I was feeling pretty comfortable, at least until he said sorry for the names people call me. Everything changed after that and now I don't know if I'll ever be able to speak in front of him again.

It's probably better that way. Come tomorrow morning, everything will go back to normal. We'll pass in the halls and ignore each other just like we always have. It's been that way for years, but now it upsets me and I don't want it to. I don't want Kayden and his stupid words to affect me.

I know what I need.

The first time I came home from school in tears, baking had been my mom's way to make me feel better. She's pretty short, so she grabbed one of the kitchen chairs, hopped up on it and grabbed all the stuff we'd need to make cookies. We sat in the kitchen, putting it all together and making some of the best cookies I've ever tasted. She dished out advice while we waited and by the end of the night, I went to bed with a smile on my face and a full belly. The kids and their taunts were behind me, at least for another day.

It's one of the only times I can remember eating them. Mom never bought the packaged ones because I had issues with food or more specifically, with processing foods with harsher textures. Up until about a year ago, she would mash up everything I ate because anything chunky I couldn't eat at all.

I feel pretty bad about it. She works so hard to make sure that Tristan and I have everything we need, and because I'm the way I am, she has to bust her butt that much harder. Sometimes, when I think about all the things she does for me; it's easy to see why she might blame me for the way things turned out. I'm not sure she signed on for this when the doctor told her she was pregnant.

The front door opens as I slide myself off the counter, but before I can get my bearings; I feel arms wrap around me, spinning me around and the high pitched giggling is a giveaway to exactly who's behind it.

I love my little brother. When all of this starts getting to me, Tristan is the one bright spot. I can't help feeling happy whenever I'm around him. If I wasn't happy, he would definitely find a way to fix it. That's how amazing he is. Tristan is a miracle baby. After they had me, my parents were told they couldn't have any more kids and then six years ago, along came my little brother. I love him more than anything.

With the way he's hugging me now, I'm starting to think I don't need the cookies after all.

"Belle! I painted the coolest picture in art today! You totally gotta see it!"

Tristan is what doctors like to call Neurotypical, which in human speak means, he's pretty normal, but when he talks about art, it's like you see a whole other side to him. He fixates on it, which makes him a lot more like me than anyone wants to admit.

"Well, what are you waiting for? Show me already!" I say, jumping up and down with him to show how excited I am. It's acting like this now that everything from earlier fades away. I'm me and I'm okay again, but more than that, I'm back where it's safe.

He races off in what I hope is the direction of his backpack and almost slams into my mom in the process. She's doing it again. She went to the store, grabbed a whole bunch of groceries and is trying to carry them all in herself, instead of just calling ahead and having me meet her.

Grabbing two of the bags off the pile that are stacked over her head, I place them on the counter and watch as she follows suit.

"Thanks honey. I really wasn't trying to buy out the store."

"I figured, but you just can't help yourself."

"This time, it's all on your brother. When did he learn how to pout to get his way?"

"The day you brought him home, I think. He's just smart about when he uses it."

She laughs and the room goes silent as we both set to work unloading the bags and putting everything away where it goes. That's another thing that we do because of me. We have every area in the kitchen labeled. Three years ago, my Uncle Joe gave me a label maker and I went around making labels for everything until eventually it became so obsessive that everything had to be put away exactly as it's labeled.

My mom calls them Belle quirks, but that's because she's too nice for her own good. It's clearly evident that I'm crazy. I don't have the heart to correct her though, so quirks it is.

"Honey, where did that bruise come from?" she asks as she points to my shoulder.

Crap. I knew there was a reason I liked wearing my jacket so much. Now I'm going to have to tell her everything that happened today, something I don't want to do.

"I bumped into something at school, no biggie."

"What kind of something? Those look like fingers marks."

I'm getting nervous. I can feel my heart starting to pick up under the scrutiny of her gaze. I really don't want to talk about this, not when it's still so fresh. Tristan bringing his picture in right now would be perfect. I need a distraction.

"Isabelle Reagan, tell me what happened right now and don't even think about lying."

"Some of the kids…"

"The kids at school did this to you?" she asks, cutting me off before I can tell her everything despite my very strong urge not to.

"Yes, they did, but it's okay. They were just goofing around. Kayden got me out of there before it went too far."

This stops her in her tracks. I haven't mentioned Kayden's name since he stopped coming over. For me to bring it up now has to knock the wind right out of her.

"Kayden Walker?"

"There's only one Kayden, Mom." I answer before turning back to the groceries, putting them away, hoping she'll drop it now that she knows Kayden brought me home.

"Are you sure it was nothing?"

"Yes. Just kids goofing off. They grabbed me a little too hard, but I'm fine Mom, I swear."

She's gonna fall for it because she truly believes that if something were the matter, I would bring it to her.

"Okay well, I'll finish up in here and start making dinner. I was thinking Irish stew tonight, that sound okay?"

"Yeah, sounds fine." I say backing out of the kitchen and going in search of the artwork a certain little brother promised me. As long as I keep myself focused on that, then the events of earlier and more importantly, the ones that happened with Kayden can finally leave my mind once and for all.

Kayden

The minute I step through the door I can tell what kind of night it's going to be and it puts me even more on edge.

Littered all over the room are beer cans, some of them crushed to bits, others tipped over and laying in place. There's an assortment of liquor bottles placed on the bar, looking more drained than they did this morning before I left. The worst part is, the person passed out on the floor in the middle of it.

Dean Walker, my brother. The man that's well on his way to earning the proud title of town drunk. Sadly, this is a scene I've come home to more than once and nothing good ever comes of it.

I have to admit lately, Dean's been doing better, if there is a better for my brother. He managed to land himself a full time job, even cleaning up his act for it, which if you know Dean, is a big thing. For the first time since our mom split, I started to believe things would even out again. That instead of coming home to a passed out drunk brother, I'd come home to a real house, with someone who actually gave a shit.

It's not that I don't think Dean cares because I know somewhere underneath all the mess, he does. All of this shit is just what happens when you're twenty-five and get left to raise your kid brother alone, but is it so wrong that just once I'd like to come home to a clean house? To have a brother that's awake and smiling instead of passed out or angry?

I'm gonna have to wake him up, but I really don't want to. That's how it always starts. I wake him up, try to sober him up by tossing him in the shower and getting him something to eat, but instead of being thankful, he starts to tell me what a piece of shit I am. It doesn't take long after that for the beating to start, but that's not all Dean. He usually pisses me off so bad that I push back, just not with words.

Yeah, I definitely don't wanna wake him up right now.

I figure the reason he's home now, instead of at work the way he has been, is because he lost his job and I definitely don't want to be on the receiving end of the rage he's got over that.

Leaving him in the mess he created, I head down the hall, closing his door as I pass on the way to my own. It's a rule that his door is supposed to be shut all the time, so if he wakes up and sees that in his drunken haze he left it open, I'm the one that's gonna pay for it.

I push my way into my room and don't even bother shutting the door behind me. I don't have the same rule, so right now, all I wanna do is lie down and get the stench of this stupid day off of me and out of my head.

Problem is, I can't do it. Even walking in and finding my brother passed out in his own filth isn't enough to get her and what happened out of my head. So what do I do? I pull the damn paper out of my pocket, unfold it and start reading.

There scrawled across the pages are her words to me, answers to my questions, but even more than that, jokes and things that still make me smile. Standing out like neon lights, are the happy faces and even though I turned on her, treating her like shit before kicking her out of my car, I'm still smiling every time I see one of them on the page.

Those happy faces remind me of the way things used to be and despite not wanting to focus on the past because of everything that happened with my mom, I can't help it. It's not my mom I remember though. It's her.

She used to talk to me when I was over at her house. It wasn't much because her mom said she was a little slower than me with her speech, but the words she did say, I always understood. I actually remember the first time she spoke to me and the way her voice sounded. It had taken so long for it to happen that I actually believed back then that she didn't have a voice at all.

Guess I know where all the deaf mute comments came from.

Dean told me things about her before, but I can't remember much of it now, other than that she's got some issues. I want to go back out there, wake him up and ask him about it, but his rage kills that idea quick. He's the only one I can ask though, so maybe when he screws his head on straight and lays off the booze, I'll bring it up.

My phone vibrates, so I stretch out across my bed in an effort to get it out. There's this part of me that hopes it's her so I can try and fix what I did, but I know it won't be. She doesn't have my number and even if she did, I'm pretty damn sure I'd be the last person she'd want to talk to. As I look at the screen, I see it's Amy.

Have a nice time with your girlfriend? I bet the smell was a real turn on huh?

Tossing my phone across the room after reading the words, it smashes up against the wall and I hear sounds from the front room, which means Dean's up and moving. It's always easy to tell when he wakes up because it sounds like a herd of cattle moving through the house. How one person can make that much noise is beyond me, but it's Dean, so of course I don't get it.

It doesn't take long for him to stumble down the hall and appear in the doorway. As I watch, he leans his body on the door in an attempt to stay steady, a snide looking smile on his face.

"I got a funny call earlier about your dumb ass."

Indulging Dean when he's like this is never a good idea, but since I've already managed to screw my entire day up just in the span of a couple hours, I go for broke. If he wants a fight then I'm more than willing to give it to him.

"Oh yeah, what did I do this time?"

"Word is you fucked up Dillon's face pretty bad and that it was because of the freak across the street."

"Don't call her that." I seethe, not understanding where the sudden urge to protect her comes from, but running with it. "She's not a freak. She's just got issues, something I figure you both got in common."

"What are you trying to say boy? That me and that crazy bitch are the same?"

"She's not a crazy bitch. You're the one that told me that remember?"

"I don't like your tone."

"Well I don't like that you smell like a brewery, so I guess we're even."

He stumbles across the room and the thing is, I could easily have cut him off at the pass considering how utterly wasted he is, but I don't do it. I want him to hit me, in fact I want him to do to me what I did to Dillon a couple hours ago.

He grabs me and it's not long before I'm back up on my feet and being tossed across the room. That's another thing about my brother. It seems that while the liquor makes him unsteady, it also gives him superhuman strength.

I feel the pain shoot through me the minute my body crashes into the wall. It's almost like a script with us. The location is the only thing that changes. I should be thankful he's doing it in here instead of out where all the bottles and cans are, but I'm really finding it hard to care about much right now. I just want it over with.

"You're a disrespectful son of a bitch, you know that, Kayden? I fucking bust my ass, going to work every day so we can keep living here and all I get for thanks is your smart mouth. No wonder Mom took off and left us."

Again, this is not something new to me. He says this every single time we get into it. I'm always the reason mom bailed, even though I'm pretty sure it was the dude at the strip club that's actually the cause. I don't bother telling him this though. My smart mouth has already gotten me into enough trouble today.

"Yeah I know Dean, I'm an asshole. You gotta knock some sense into me, yadda, yadda, yadda."

His fist connects with my face before the last syllable can fall, but I don't make a move. He hits me again and I slump even more into the floor. I feel the blood rising to the surface on my lip and instead of handling it, I just sit there, letting it come. It's easier this way. I let him get his anger out and he'll screw off again. I just gotta make it through the next few minutes until he tires himself out.

"You're the fucking king of the god damned school and you're gonna blow it all to save some retarded girl that you can't even stand? You're damn right I gotta knock some sense into that dumbass head of yours."

Punch. Kick. Punch. Kick.

He repeats in a cycle one after the other and as I sit there and take it, the only thing I really want to do and can't, is tell him not to call her a retard again. My anger is rising now, but it has nothing to do with the beating and everything to do with the names he's calling her. The names I've called her.

God, I deserve so much more than this with everything I've done.

As the room starts to spin, I focus on the one clear thought in my head that I'm determined to use to get through this. It's not even a thought, but a picture and it's so damn beautiful, I want to hold onto it until this entire moment passes.

Clear as day, I can see myself smiling. Something I haven't done since the day my mom left us and this stupid ass town behind. A smile Isabelle gave me, wanting nothing in return and one that even in my haze is turning into something more with each passing second.

It's not my own face anymore, but hers I see and it's what I grasp onto as I feel the world start to spin and go dark. A clear picture of Isabelle finally doing what I wanted her to do while I was driving her home.

    Smiling.

Chapter Three

Belle

My night turned out pretty great considering the way it started. I finally got to see Tristan's painting, even getting permission to put it up on my wall because I liked it so much. I didn't get to make the cookies with my mom, but I did get to make them, which is better than nothing.

The bus is gonna be here to pick me up soon. I'm not looking forward to that. Even though I was able to let it all go last night, it doesn't mean what happened yesterday is gone completely. I can't escape it, no matter how much I want to because the problem lives right across the street. We're bound to see each other and it's all going to come flooding back.

It won't be any easier at school. The girls that were there yesterday, helping Dillon and Tim do things to me, will haunt me in the halls. They'll call me names, push me around and do everything they can to make sure my day is that much harder. I've seen them do it with the other kids before, so I know what I've got waiting for me.

I wanted Mom to call in sick for me this morning, but I chickened out asking her. I really don't want to go today, especially if Kayden is going to be there, but hiding at home isn't an option either. Mom always tells me its best to face things head on. So that's exactly what I'm gonna do.

I just hope the fear I feel doesn't end up making everything worse.

That's the thing no one gets. The accidents I have, they happen when I'm scared. It starts with my heart racing, which I hear is normal for other kids too, but with me just builds and builds until I can't control my body's response.

"Isabelle! Your bus is here!" I hear my mom call up the stairs and I swallow the awkward lump in my throat. It's time. There's no turning back now. I've just gotta remember to keep breathing and get through this, no matter how bad it gets.

That's harder to do as I get on the bus and see the faces of the other kids like me. All of them have their own challenges they have to face, just like I do. I just hope that by knowing me, that Dillon and his friends don't turn on them next. I'm not sure if I deserve it or not, but I know they don't.

I had this dream last night, about the way things would be when I got to school today. Everyone just forgot about what happened and things went back to normal. I faded into the background like I've always done and no one pays me any attention. It was such a great dream. It's too bad that isn't at all what happens.

The minute I step off the bus, the name calling starts. I can hear the words 'retard' and 'moron' being coughed out in whispered tones, coming from all different directions, so I can't even say it's one person doing it. I take it all in as my feet pick up speed, but it's what I hear next that hurts most.

"Did you hear she pissed herself in front of everyone?"

"I heard she really thought Dillon wanted her."

"Like there's anyone who would go to the dance with that reject."

"What was God thinking when he made her? She's defective. Her mom needs to return her."

Tears are building in the corners of my eyes and I don't want anyone to see them, so I start running, pushing past the kids that reached the door first and speeding up even more as I run for the nearest restroom. All I need is a stall with a door that actually locks and a few minutes to collect myself. I'll be fine if I get that.

I know what's coming if I don't make it in time. The very thing the kids were all talking about seconds ago. I can't let that happen. I can't let everyone see me break. I need to be stronger than this.

The girl's bathroom comes into sight, but before I can reach out to push the door open, I'm swept off my feet and spun around by a strong pair of arms I can't place. I start to struggle against them, wanting to break free and hide before everything comes crashing down, but I'm powerless against the person holding me.

"Isabelle," the voice says, quieting me as he pulls me against his chest. "It's okay. I'm not gonna hurt you."

I know that voice. The low, melodic rumble. I heard it yesterday when just like now; he'd rescued me from everything his friends had done.

Kayden.

I need to tell him to let me go, warn him that if he doesn't, things are going to get a whole lot worse, but I can't get the words to come out. It's constricted, like something is lodged there preventing me from even making the smallest noise.

This is definitely not the right time to be mute.

I keep struggling against him because it's the only way I can let him know to let me go, but he doesn't. If it's possible, I think he's holding on tighter and even though I don't want it, I can't help but admit that it's comforting.

"I'm gonna let you go but don't run, okay?"

I nod my head and I feel his arms relax, allowing me to move. I don't do it though. I do exactly what he asked me to do and I stay still, my eyes drilling holes into the floor with the intensity of my stare.

I can't look up. I can't look into his eyes and see pity. For whatever reason, I've become his pet project and I don't want any part of it. So despite my body responding to his words, I won't give him the satisfaction of letting him see just how much he gets to me. Especially since he's probably doing it so he has more material to make fun of me for later.

"What's your first class?" he asks, as he leans in close, other students now passing around us.

I don't know why he's asking me this. He has to know by now that I won't answer.

"Shit. I'm an idiot. You're upstairs right?"

I nod again, thankful that he's finally catching on. Just like a minute ago, he sweeps me up into him, moving ahead, pushing through the throng of students that are now filling up what had been a near empty hall a minute ago. I'm not sure if it's so busy because of everything being floated around or if it's because Kayden's here now, but whatever the reason, I hate it. I just want to get to my class and away from him, so I can calm down.

"Ignore everything you hear okay?" he speaks down to me as he continues moving toward the stairs.

I do as he says and instead focus my attention on the woodsy smell that seems to be wafting off of him and directly into my nostrils. It's a scent that even with the help he gave me yesterday; I don't think I've ever smelled. It's strong but not heavy. It's like a mixture of freshly cut wood and the way the grass smells after it's been cut in the summer time.

Turning the corner once we've reached the top, he stops and turns until he's directly in front of me. The smell still lingers between us, but it's more distant now, not nearly as overpowering as it was a few seconds before.

I turn toward the classroom, prepared to move myself around his body in order to go in and take my seat, but before I can take a step around him, his arm comes out and brings me back, startling me.

He did his good deed for the day so what else can he possibly want from me?

"When class lets out, I want you to wait for me here, alright? Promise me you won't leave and go on your own."

He sounds like my father with what he's asking and if I could smile or even laugh, I would do it now. Just who does he think he is? Babysitting the autistic kid is not a job he wants, he must know this, so why is he doing it?

I don't nod or make any other motion to let him know that I'll do what he says, instead making my way around him, practically running until I'm in my seat. It's only when Ms. Taylor makes her way into the room, Kayden right on her heels that I realize he's not going to give up that easily.

I watch as they whisper to each other, both of their eyes landing directly on me more than once and I feel sick. It's obvious he's trying to get the teachers help in making sure that I don't leave the class. Pushing them and their stupid conversation out of my head, I start pulling my books out of my bag, putting my full attention into making sure I keep my breathing steady so my heart can finally stop racing.

A shadow comes across the desk just as I'm about to start reading and looking up, my eyes lock right on a pair of the lightest green eyes I've ever seen. These are eyes I haven't looked into since we were ten years old, at least not this closely. They're eyes I've missed.

There's no rage in them this time, they're soft as they look into my blue ones. Despite the softness, I know I'm not going to like what has to say and thinking about it makes me nervous and uneasy.

"She told me that you get out at 11:15. So I'm gonna come back and be outside the door at 11:10."

Grabbing the paper off the desk, I grab a pen from my pencil case and start writing. He might have gotten his way in the hallway earlier, but now he's on my turf. He isn't going to push me around. His friends have already done that enough already.

Just go, Kayden. You're not wanted here. I don't need your pity. Just go.

His eyes turn icy as he reads my words, his lip twitching, almost as if he's angry with what he read and is trying to control it. He doesn't break though and the next time he speaks, he makes his point loud and clear, leaving me even more confused.

"It's not pity, Isabelle. It's survival. I'm not letting you go through this alone. I'll see you at eleven."

Kayden

When I heard the stuff people were saying this morning, it took everything in me not to turn around and punch the living shit out of every one of the people saying it. Apparently Dillon wasted no time spreading yesterday's garbage around and by the looks of everyone talking, it seems to have spread pretty quick.

It all rolls off my back even though a lot of what is being said has my name attached. I might be one of the popular kids and might even like the perks that being it affords me, but I really don't give a crap what they say about me. I don't need the social standing the way most people do.

Isabelle on the other hand, deserves none of what she's getting. She isn't like me. The stuff people say about her affects her whether she's able to show it or not. Hearing what these idiots are saying about her, about us, while she's running across the campus to escape it bothers the hell out of me.

This girl, who has never done anything bad in her entire life is being torn apart by a bunch of mindless drones and it's unfair. That's why I chased after her the way I did, even though I promised myself I wouldn't go anywhere near her. I couldn't stand the way her face scrunched in as the words being spread sunk in, hating even more the water pooling in her eyes, clear as day, even though I was pretty far behind her.

When she struggled against me in the hall, it did weird things to me. I wanted to let her go because I knew I was scaring her, but I also wanted to hold on tighter. I don't know what the hell is going on with me and this girl, but every single time I'm around her, it's like I lose my shit. I stop thinking about myself and how all of this is gonna come down on me. All I can see is her and how she's affected.

I'm not that guy. I'm not the one that protects the girl, shielding her from the typical high school bullshit. No, I'm the one that's creating it and making as many lives as possible horrible for my own personal amusement. As much as I try to remember that though, it seems around her, I can't. All I want to do is be that guy. The one I can never be.

I'm aware of the fact that standing up for her the way I am is only going to make them go harder at her, if the texts I got last night are any indication. I'm going to be the one making her life worse, but I don't care. I need to protect her from this since it's my fault it's happening at all.

Her movements are predictable. Whenever something happens, she runs for the bathroom. It's her safe place. She did it this morning, just like I knew she would and I couldn't let her. I probably should've, but I couldn't.

It's selfish of me really because she's not the only one with problems. I've got a Mac truck full of them myself and there's only one person on the planet besides Dean that knows.

Isabelle.

She's seen the cops pulling up to my house at all hours of the day and night. She's seen the ambulance coming for Dean when he drinks so much he gives himself alcohol poisoning. She's seen him and even me carted away in handcuffs. The difference is I took her issues and exploited the hell out of them, while she holds onto mine. Her doing that means no one knows the truth about the way my life really is. I'm not sure if it's because she's just that nice of a person or her social issues, but whatever the reason, she's never let it slip and I'm grateful.

It's not that I care if people know, because I don't, but I've built myself a pretty good back story here and I don't want to have to start over when people find out. I don't want to deal with the looks I'll get and the change that'll happen when the truth comes out. It's a waste of time and energy. She knows though and because of that, I want to keep her as close as possible. I'm securing my place even though I'm pretty sure I don't want it anymore.

"If I didn't see it with my own freaking eyes, I wouldn't believe it. Kayden Walker, the king of Wexfield High, cuddling with the retard."

I've been expecting this. With the way I pulled her to me and dragged her up the stairs, it's inevitable.

"If you know what's good for you, you'll shut your mouth right now."

"Or what, Walker? You gonna go postal on my face again?"

"It crossed my mind," I snap as I take in the group of people around me. "Wonder if this time your girlfriend will come to your rescue."

Tim moves toward me, but the minute his eyes lock on mine, the urge to fight building, he takes a step back. It's good to know that at least one of these jackasses is smarter then he looks.

"I don't know what's gotten into you man, but you better snap out of it. People are talking and it's not good for you if it keeps up."

If I didn't want to knock the smile off his face so bad, his words might have gotten to me. I know exactly how it works here. I know it will only take one or two more times of me being seen with Isabelle for everything I've achieved here to come falling down around me. The thing is though, I just don't care. They can take their little clique and shove it.

"Awe, Dill. I didn't know you cared."

"Man, the girl's really gotten to you hasn't she? You're willing to throw away everything for some stupid girl that can't even talk to you."

I ignore everything he says because I don't think I'm ready to admit to myself, let alone them, that there actually might be some truth in it. I'm just trying to do the right thing, it's that simple.

"Just leave her alone Dillon. You want someone to harass, you've got a whole school full of people. She's off limits."

I watch as he seems to consider my words, a first for him considering how idiotic he can be. Just as I'm about to push my way around them and head to my locker, he speaks and the minute he does, I know that the peace I thought I might have been able to broker, isn't going to be happening anytime soon.

It's going to get a hell of a lot worse.

"You want me to leave her alone, then you've gotta pick someone to take her place. You want us to believe you don't have a thing for this girl, well here's your chance."

Chapter Four

Belle

"Isabelle, I don't think he's coming. I'm sorry."

I want to turn and tell her thanks for pointing out the obvious, but even if I could say the words, I still wouldn't. With the way she's looking at me right now, her eyes full of the same pitied expression I see every day, I just want to get as far away from her as possible and enjoy what's left of my lunch.

By the time class let out at 11:15, I'd completely given up on trying to calm myself. It was easy for the first little while to forget about Kayden and his promise of coming back for me, but the more time that went by, the harder it was to ignore. I started sweating first and then my heart started racing and no amount of movement or other coping mechanisms seemed to help.

When Ms. Taylor said that we could go, I took my sweet time. If he was outside the door waiting for me then I was gonna make him wait as long as possible, even if it got him in trouble. As it turns out, the time I wasted didn't seem to matter because he didn't show anyway.

I don't know why it bothers me that he's not here. I guess I hoped that the look of determination I saw in his eyes this morning was true and he would be different in some way. That he wouldn't be the same Kayden I've known him to be for the last eight years. He would be better somehow.

With a quick glance down at my watch, a pink Hello Kitty one Tristan picked out for me, I realize that I've wasted twenty minutes of an hour long lunch waiting for him to show up. I'd be lucky now if I even had enough time to inhale my food before having to go to my afternoon classes.

"It's okay Ms. Taylor; I sort of figured he wouldn't anyway."

"If you want, you can come to the lounge with me and have your lunch. It's just me and a bunch of stuffy teachers, but at least you'd have some quiet."

It's not the first time I've done what she's offering me. When things become too much, certain teachers will offer up their small sanctuary in order for me to get control of myself. At least they do unless I'm too far gone and they have to call my mom to come get me. As tempting as it is to take her up on it now, I won't. I told her the truth a minute ago. I expected this, so I'm more than okay dealing with it on my own.

"Thanks, but I'll just go eat at my locker."

"If that's what you want, dear." She answers, again the pity written all over her face as she looks me over. "But if you have any issues, you know where to come."

Little does she realize, that's all I am, one big ball of complicated issues.

I've almost made it down the stairs and to my locker without being made fun of when it hits me. The way things were earlier isn't happening now. There are students spread out all over the place, but none of them were even looking in my general direction, much less at me. Was it really going to be that easy? Have they moved on already?

It wasn't until I turned the corner to where my locker is that I see the reason why things have been so quiet. On the stretch of lockers directly across from my own, I see Tim, Dillon and Kayden and they're surrounding someone I know. In fact it's someone that was in class with me only a few minutes ago.

Eric Carmen is new to Wexfield. He has Asperger's, which is how he ended up in Ms. Taylor's class. We're the same, yet different. He's a year younger than me, but with the way the class works, we're there for the same help so we all go through it together, regardless of our age.

He's completely pressed up against the lockers and there's a frightened look in his wide eyes that I recognize instantly. It's the same look I was wearing when this all happened to me.

Keeping my head down, I make my way to my locker as quietly as possible, not wanting to alert them any sooner to my presence. Swirling the numbers on my lock around, I tune everything else out and focus on the voices, their venom all directed at the only other person in the school that actually understood what it was like to be me.

"What's with the stutter, Eric? D-D-D-Do we scare you?" Kayden mocks before laughing. "Are you gonna be like your girlfriend and piss your pants?"

The second the words come out, my entire chest seizes up and I find it hard to breathe. Of all the people to say that, I really didn't expect it to be him. Tim and Dillon yes, but with the way he'd been with me this morning, I thought Kayden would've been different. Guess he hasn't changed after all.

"Y-Y-You shouldn't t-t-talk about Isa-belle that way." Eric stutters, which makes my heart break. Even with these three surrounding him, breathing down his neck, he's still trying to stick up for me.

Eric's better than me. I couldn't even open my mouth, let alone do what he did.

"Look at this guy Kay; he's got some balls talking back to us!" Dillon says and my blood runs cold. I know what's going to happen now. It's the same thing that always happens when someone stands up to them, but can't follow up. Eric's gonna pay for it. "You know what that means, don't ya Eric?"

The smooth way he asks the question gets to me. I can't let this happen, not to Eric. I might only end up making things worse, but I have to do something. Someone has to stand up to them. I didn't do it yesterday because I'd been scared, but hearing the way they're all going at him and laughing at his stutter, I'm not scared.

I'm just angry.

"STOP!" I scream, surprising myself with the forceful sound of the word.

All three guys turn around, their eyes locking on me, Dillon smirking the minute he sees me.

"Awe, the retard can speak after all." He laughs as he shifts his elbow into Kayden's side. "Why didn't you tell me she could yell? I could definitely get used to hearing her scream my name if it sounds like that."

There's a moment while we're all standing there, none of us moving or even looking away from each other, where I see what looks like a flash of rage pass through Kayden's eyes. Just as quickly as it appears though, it's gone and I start to think I imagined it. There's no way this guy that had been so nice this morning, actually gave a crap about me now. I'm just a retard to him, same as I've always been.

"Come on man, this is about Eric, not her." Kayden replies, turning his back on me and focusing again on the scared boy that's still frozen up against the lockers.

Not sure where it comes from, but not willing to stop and let whatever they're about to do happen, I start walking toward them, pushing myself in between Tim and Kayden until I'm standing directly in front of Eric.

"Let's go." I say, my voice coming out in a whisper. I hold out my hand to him, kind of like Kayden had done with me the day before and I prepare myself for the fight that's about to happen once I feel him take it.

"What do you think you're doing retard? You're not going anywhere with him. He's ours."

I want so badly to tell him what an asshole he is, but the words won't come. Whatever surge of strength I had to get me to this point is gone and I'm back to being the mute they all believe me to be. It doesn't change the fact that I can still move though, so I push my body forward. Before I can get around Dillon, he steps in front of me. With as big a guy as he is, I know there's no sense trying to get around him. He's like a brick wall.

"Please let us go." Eric pleads. He's scared of saying something to make it worse and I don't blame him. Dillon has always been a hot head and there's no telling what he'll do if we try anything he doesn't want us to.

When his words seem to have no effect, I turn and look at Kayden. I know it's a long shot, but he was nice to me once. If we want to get out of here without having a repeat of yesterday, he is literally my only hope. Problem is, the minute my eyes lock on his, he doesn't make a move to help. He just smiles and it's not the way he did in the car with me. It's worse.

"Get out of here, Belle. Dillon's right, this is between us and Eric. No one wants to get pissed on today."

Eric's hand slides out of mine and as I turn back to him, I see sadness in his eyes. He feels bad for me. He knows how it makes me feel and by releasing me, he's giving me an out. Before I can force the words up to stop them, Tim rushes at Eric and grabs him, throwing him over his shoulder so fast, I almost don't catch it. By the time I blink, they're all running off down the hall away from me.

It's watching them running away from me; becoming small shadows in the hall the farther away they go that I realize it. I'm really as helpless and pathetic as they all think I am and now one of the only people in the school that has ever been nice to me is paying for it.

Chapter Five

Kayden

I am the world's biggest chump.

When Dillon said he would leave her alone if I chose someone else in her place, I didn't even hesitate, I took the bait. As long as she was protected from them, from me, it was the right call. Except, it wasn't the right call and now I'm being forced to watch as this Eric kid is repeatedly slammed into the stall door because he doesn't have what Tim and Dillon want.

What went down a couple of minutes ago is why they're so angry. Dillon didn't like that she screamed at him to stop, especially when he spends all his time referring to her as the deaf mute, but it's not as if I've done anything to stop him. In fact, with everything that just happened, I only made it worse.

I saw the look in her eyes when she wanted to get Eric out of there. She really thought that turning to me would give them the out they deserved. Even after everything I've said about her over the years and how I left things when we were kids, she still thinks I'm better than I am.

This happening to Eric, I hate it. I know who he is and what he means to her. He's the only kid here that gives her the time of day. They're in the same class and I can tell by the way she is with him that he's earned her trust. I want to stand up and say something right now, but these guys won't listen to me. Even if they did and by some bit of luck they let the guy go, they would only turn it back around on her the next day. It's how we work.

Bailing on her was such a dick move, but necessary if I want to keep her safe. I'm still not exactly sure why I'm going out of my way for this girl; I just know I can't let her go through what she did yesterday. She deserves better than that. Hell, we all do. I know she told me earlier she didn't want me to come back for her, so she probably didn't even care that I hadn't shown up, but it still didn't help me feel like any less of an ass.

I'm really no better than my brother, my mother and even my dead beat father. None of us could ever keep our word. I suppose it's the Walker family trait. It's not exactly the one thing I'm looking forward to being known for, but it's the way it has to be.

"The deal was, I'd leave your little girlfriend alone if you picked the next target and got involved. Seems to me that Tim and I are doing all the work. What's up with that, K?"

I absolutely loathe when people call me K. The last person that did it got their face smashed into a locker. It's irrational I know, but my mom used to call me that and ever since she split, it's been a sore thing for me. I already want to pound the shit out of Dillon; calling me K is just making me homicidal.

"I'm letting you guys have your fun first, and don't call me, K."

It's already too late when I realize I didn't refute the girlfriend comment. Sometimes being a hot head can be a real pain in the ass. Just like expected, Dillon catches what I didn't.

"Not even gonna try to deny the other stuff huh?"

"Watch it man, spending so much time around that girl, he's probably all hormonal and shit." Tim jokes, making me want to beat the hell out of them and bail on this whole thing.

Except, I don't. I never do.

"I picked him, didn't I? So do whatever you're gonna do so we can get on with this. It's boring."

"I gotta admit, it was kinda fun hearing her yell at us over this guy. Maybe she likes him. Looks like you got some competition Kayden."

I catch the way he says my name differently and I can't help smiling. He might be the big man here, but he knew his place against me. I guess yesterday taught him something after all.

"He's as much of a loser as she is. Figure they're a match made in heaven."

Even I have a hard time stomaching the way the words come out. I have no problem accepting that I'm a total jerk, trust me, I've earned it over the last eight years or so, but the words now, they feel so wrong.

Tim turns to Eric and he's got this sick looking grin on his face. I know what's coming. It's something I've done before. Putting fear into people isn't enough for us. It's like going physical, we're getting the complete rush of it all and I flinch and turn as Tim's fist lands square in Eric's gut. Yeah, this really doesn't do a damn thing for me anymore.

I find myself wanting to find Isabelle. The way it felt yesterday in the car, before I had to go and turn it all to shit was nice. She's not the only one that doesn't smile. I mean, when you don't have a reason to do it; it's not that shocking when it doesn't happen, but with her it did, more than once. Hell, the girl even managed to make me laugh.

Right now I want nothing more than to laugh again because I can't take watching Eric's face as he crumples to the floor like a wet rag. The sound coming from him reminds me of the way Isabelle sounded yesterday before I got her out. It's another reminder of how wrong this is.

They're all just wounded animals and we're here putting them out of their misery.

"Let's get out of here. Amy's been talking about some surprise she has for me and well, we all know about Amy and her surprises."

The way Dillon talks about his girlfriend is revolting, but it's not something I haven't heard a million times before. Shit, the girl used to be mine before she was his and I wasn't any better. Though to my credit, I wasn't vulgar around her. I was just disconnected.

I have to keep up with what Dillon wants from me. It's the only way I can make sure she stays safe. I can't walk into another situation with her like I did yesterday; I don't think I have it in me.

That's when it hits me. I can't deny it anymore. What she thinks, what she's feeling, understanding her, it all matters to me and it's because of one seemingly simple fact.

I like her.

Belle

Six.

That's how many times I tried to open my mouth today, trying to let teachers know what I'd been a part of earlier. Six times that I failed at it because the minute my mouth opened, the words wouldn't form.

This shouldn't be all that surprising, but it is. This isn't about my own comfort level anymore. This isn't about social awkwardness or autism, though I'm pretty sure if I could talk to my mom about this, that's exactly what she would say it is. No, this isn't about me at all. I need to do the right thing by Eric, even if with the way he's acting as I pass him in the halls tells me otherwise.

He won't look at me or at least he tries not to. He caught my eye in the hall twice and both times, he looked down and shuffled away from me. Maybe he knows that he's taken my place and he hates me for it. Either way, I don't like it.

It's no surprise with the way things keep happening that I think I'm better off dead.

My mom would have an easier time because it would be her and Tristan and he's normal. She'd be able to get out and enjoy herself more, instead of always worrying about what I need. She wouldn't have to run to my rescue. Hell, she'd be able to date again and finally move on from my dad. I know she wants that, but her support of me stops her every time.

If I was gone, Eric would still be floating under the radar. They didn't pick on the special needs kids. It's only since what happened with me that they've started. I could save the world a whole lot of trouble if I just went home, took a bunch of pills and went to sleep forever.

Just as I see the bus rounding the corner, I hear my name being called. Turning from side to side slowly, I see where the voice is coming from and just who it belongs to.

It's Kayden and he's jogging toward me. I hate that I have nowhere to run. That I have to stand here and wait for him to reach me because even though the bus is here and it's super close, it's not close enough. I really don't want anything to do with him, so what he's doing running toward me makes no sense.

"I need to talk to you..." he says, his voice winded as he finally reaches me.

I shake my head. I don't need words to let him know just how much I don't want to talk to him right now. I'm sure I can get my point across loud and clear with the look on my face and the slight movement of my head. Even if I didn't have troubles speaking, I still wouldn't want to say a word to him.

"Please?" he pleads and there's this part of me, my heart maybe that seems taken by the way his voice sounds but my mind won't let me fall for it.

I shake my head again and he lowers his eyes away from mine, hurt by my response. It's confusing to me. I've read books about guys that act the way Kayden is. He's like Jekyll and Hyde and I wasn't a big fan when I read it. I'm definitely not liking the up and down of it in real life.

"Let me drive you home Isabelle," he states rather than asks, which just bothers me even more. "Please? I'll take you right there, no stops."

I want to ask him why he wants to drive me home. What he could possibly have to say to me that he hasn't already said. I want to ask why he sounds so sad every time he says please, but before I can even make an attempt at it, the bus pulls up and Eric is running up behind us.

Saying yes to Kayden is easy and I don't want it to be. I can't figure out why he gets to me when I know deep inside I'm upset with him. Why do I have to keep seeing him as the boy I used to play with instead of the mean guy he really is?

Eric makes his way around us and up onto the bus without even so much as a look back in my direction and that's when I make my decision. I'm pretty sure it's wrong, but since it's already like I've lost the only friend I ever had, I've got nothing left to lose.

I look between him and the door of the bus one final time before stepping back and motioning at Ronnie, my regular bus driver. I point toward Kayden. He nods his head and I turn, waiting for what comes next.

"You're going to come with me?"

I nod and the strangest thing happens. He smiles at me and it's even brighter than the ones he did the day before. It's like he's relieved, as his shoulders, which had been sagging only seconds before lift up again. There's a fluttering in my stomach noticing it and I have no idea what it means. Why does his happiness seem so important to me?

"Thank you." He says and waits for me to start walking before following closely behind. I stop as soon as we reach his car and before I know it, he's running into the back of me. I stumble and end up flat across the hood. He reaches out to catch me and again he's right behind me, but before either one of us can move, we hear the voices from the other side of the parking lot.

"Tap it hard, Kayden!"

"I knew she was easy!"

"Make her scream like earlier."

I didn't recognize the first two, but Dillon's came through loud and clear. My heart begins to race and I can feel my head getting fuzzy. I don't like the sound of his voice, especially when it's raised the way it is now. People think I'm stupid, but I know exactly what they're hinting at with their words and it makes me sick inside.

Kayden slides his arms around my stomach and lifts me back off the hood and before I can pull away from him, I feel his breath against the back of my neck.

"Ignore them."

That's easy for him to say. Tomorrow he'll have jokes thrown at him, but he won't have sick things said about the way we just were. That's all for me. I knew going with him was the wrong move but it's even worse now. I almost wish he'd never helped me out yesterday.

This time he unlocks the car from my side and makes sure I'm completely in and comfortable before shutting the door behind me. I can't help thinking its sweet, but the minute I think it, my stomach turns over and I feel sick. I don't want to think any of this is sweet. He's still the same guy he was earlier, even if he is taking pity on the special kid.

I'm so lost in my thoughts I don't even realize he's in the car with me until he slams his door shut and bangs his hands on the steering wheel.

I startle and realizing his mistake, he sighs.

"I'm sorry. I don't think." He leans over and I catch a glimpse of his bare skin as the shirt he's wearing rides up. Finding whatever it is he's looking for, he turns back around. "This time, I want to be prepared."

Looking at his hands as they're held out in front of me, I see what he's talking about. There's a notebook, complete with what looks like a gel pen attached and though I'm pretty sure he doesn't know this, it's my favorite color.

The thought that went into this small gesture gets to me. My hands are shaking under the force of it, as I reach out and accept the olive branch he's giving me. My fingers graze over his and I jump back from the sharp tingle that climbs up through my hand as I do it.

What is going on with me?

Pushing the reaction out of my head, I slide the pen off, open the book and start writing. When I'm finished I slide it across, careful to keep all contact to a minimum. I don't know what caused that sensation a minute ago, but it feels weird, so I don't want to repeat it.

Why did you want to drive me home?

He runs his hand over his hair and again he sighs. "I needed to talk to you—you know, about earlier?"

The way he phrases it as a question confuses me. There were a couple of things that happened earlier. He didn't show up to get me after class and he was bullying my friend. Which one of these could he possibly mean?

The stuff with Eric or earlier?

"Earlier?" he questions, but before I can write out a response, his eyes shine with recognition. "Oh, yeah I need to explain about that too. I mean, if you'll let me."

I don't want to let him. I want to just slide my hand over the door handle, push it open and get the hell out of here, but I can't do that. In accepting his ride home, I've given up the only other way I can get home, which means I'm stuck. Unless I want to walk and it's gonna take me at least an hour to do that.

You don't need to explain anything to me. I write out, this time lifting the notebook instead of sliding it to him. The back and forth motion is actually starting to bug me.

"Yeah, see that's what I thought too, except I do."

What does that mean?

He does the thing with his hands again and I'm actually surprised with how hard this seems to be for him. He's so confident and self assured at school every day, but here in the car, it's like he's a completely different person.

He's the boy that he used to be.

"I'm an asshole, Isabelle. I don't even know if asshole's the right word for me, but it's all I know. I hurt people for fun and most of the time I enjoy it. I haven't been able to enjoy anything since I saw what happened to you yesterday. I know what I did today, the things I said, the way I acted..."

He cuts off and my heart drops in my chest. He didn't finish what he wanted to say and despite how upset I am, not only with him, but me too, I really want him to finish. I'm conflicted because I want nothing to do with him, but at the same time, being here with him now is comfortable and I don't want it to end.

None of this makes any sense to me.

You are an asshole. What you did to Eric today was wrong. You say you don't like what happened to me so why do it to someone that's just like me?

"See that's just it. Fuck! I can't stand you thinking I'm an asshole. When I'm around you, I don't want to be the jerk. I want to be different."

So be different.

Things with me are pretty cut and dry. I don't understand when people state things like he just did. If he wants to be different then I don't see why he doesn't just do it. It's not like anyone can do it for him.

"It's not that easy. I wish it were, but this is all I've ever known."

I know all about his mom and dad leaving. I also know he got stuck with a brother that wasn't even mature enough to take care of himself, let alone a younger brother. I know how bad things are for Kayden, it's not hard to see when people show up at the house at all hours and Dean spends most of his time slurring his words and stumbling on his feet. Even though I told him to be different, I'm starting to see now that it really isn't black and white.

Not sure how to answer back, I change the subject.

Why didn't you meet me today?

His lips grow tight and there's something in his expression that tells me I'm not going to like his answer. At the very least he's struggling with it.

"I couldn't. People are talking and I just don't want it to get worse."

It hurts more than I want to admit. This Jekyll and Hyde thing he's doing should have prepared me for this kind of answer, but it doesn't. People have been talking about me, making fun of me for my problems forever, so it's nothing new to me. I never thought about how it would feel for someone considered normal when they're caught talking to me.

It doesn't just hurt for that reason though. It hurts because this guy I grew up knowing, the one I thought was never affected by what anyone said about him, is affected. In coming to my rescue the day before, he's having his life turned upside down, all because I'm different.

"Isabelle," he says with a sigh. "Please say something."

The way he speaks, asking me to say something, is not lost on me. I'm not sure if it was just a bad word choice, considering he knows how I am or he just means to write something, but either way, that hurt too. It seems like this entire moment is one big ball of hurt and I want it to be over.

Take me home please.

I lay the notebook back down between us and turn in my seat until I'm facing ahead. I feel his eyes on me for a few minutes and even knowing that he's doing it makes this even more uncomfortable. I'm not scared or uneasy really, it's just hard, not looking back over at him.

Before I can give in, he turns the key in the ignition and brings the car to life finally gunning the engine and peeling out of the parking lot. I breathe a sigh of relief that the conversation seems to be over and soon, I'll be home and safe where I belong.

It's only when he pulls into my driveway a few minutes later, putting the car in park and turning the key again that I realize the conversation is most definitely not over.

"I wanted to drive you home today because I wanted to say I'm sorry for everything. Not just what happened today, but for every single thing I've ever said or done to you. Isabelle, I know it doesn't fix anything, but I really do mean it. I'm sorry."

I want to believe his words, but I know that after I get out of the car and go inside, everything will go back to the way it was before this even happened. He'll go to school tomorrow, he'll torture Eric, or even me again. He'll laugh as he does it and we'll be right back where we were before.

I want him to be different but what he said earlier might be true. He really doesn't know how to be any other way.

Picking up the notebook, my hands shaking, I press the pen to the paper and I start writing.

Actions speak louder than words ever could, Kayden. If you're really sorry, prove it.

This time I don't wait for him to say something mean to kick me out of the car. There's nothing else he can do anyway. Not waiting for him to read my words, I push the door open and slide from the car, running across the lawn as quickly as I can.

I have to get away from him. I need to get away from the mixed emotions he brings out in me, things I can't even describe because they're all things I've never felt before. Mostly, I'm getting away from him because if I stay, I'm afraid I might do the one thing I swore I would never do.

Fall for him.

Chapter Six

Kayden

Shit.

That didn't go the way I pictured it in my head.

When I saw her waiting for the bus, something came over me. I was planning on just jumping in my car and going for a drive to clear my head, but something stopped me.

I couldn't leave without at least trying to explain to her why everything had taken such a shitty turn. I wanted to tell her about the deal I made with Dillon too, because I thought if I did, maybe she would understand things and realize I was doing it for her. I couldn't do it though.

Even if I am doing this for her, agreeing to this so Dillon will leave her alone; I'm still being a jerk in the process because I'm attacking her friends and other kids like her.

Now I'm sitting here in her driveway and I'm pretty sure her mom's gonna be home any minute, but I can't move. I'm stuck reading her words over and over. The last words she said to me, they're flashing at me so strong that it reminds me of those motel signs you see in the city, the ones that glow in the darkness of the night.

Actions speak louder than words ever could, Kayden. If you're really sorry, prove it.

What does she think I was trying to do in offering her the ride home?

I know I was an asshole to her and even to her friend, but I haven't been able to think of much else since. It's bad enough that I have to admit to myself that I might like this girl, but did I really have to grovel at her feet?

The short answer is, yeah, I do.

I'm haunted by the look I saw in her eyes in the hall today. I hate that she thinks of me that way. I get the feeling that because she can't talk; she sees more than the rest of us do, so she's seeing something in me that no one else can. Something that even I can't see in myself and there's the urge to be around her so that maybe she can show it to me.

I don't want to go home. I know what I'm going to find there when I do. Dean's going to be passed out on his ass again, angry because, as he says, I made him lose yet another job and we're probably gonna lose the house because of it. It's the same damn conversation every single day, especially when he's not working and I'm sick of it.

I can't stay here though. I don't want her mom to come home and see me. I'm not sure how much she tells her, especially the last couple of days, but if she's said anything about me or what happened to her then I know being caught isn't going to go well. I just don't know where else I'm supposed to go.

Times like this I wish my mom was still around. I'd be able to go home if she was here and I might be able to tell her everything that's going on. I could have her help me make sense of it. She was pretty flighty and at times I wondered what the hell she was even doing with kids, but there were good times when she was with us. She did try. It's those times now that I want so badly because I hate feeling this alone.

You don't feel alone when you're with her.

The nagging voice in my head, pointing out the obvious has been with me now for the last two days. It's right though. I don't feel alone when I'm around Isabelle. In fact I don't feel much of anything at all, at least the negative stuff. It's quiet, but it's comfortable. Even with her issues and the god awful way she smelled in my car yesterday, she still made me feel things that I haven't felt in forever.

She makes me want to be better.

I know what I have to do now. It's the only thing I can do. I have to take her advice because she's right. If she wants actions instead of just my words then I'll give it to her.

I just hope it works.

Belle

I'm not sure what I expected when I got off the bus this morning, but it wasn't this.

Standing at the curb, rolling back and forth on his feet is Kayden and instead of looking uncomfortable or like he would rather be anywhere else, he looks happy. The minute I step down off the bus and my feet hit the ground; he raises his gaze in my direction and smiles.

His smile seems to light up his entire face. I've seen him angry and stressed, but never quite like this. His cheekbones raised, his eye brows lifted and those eyes, the green that before had been deflated, are sparkling under the light of the sun.

When we were kids he used to have long shaggy hair and you were lucky if you ever saw his eyes, let alone this way. I hate admitting it, but I'm glad that he decided in our freshman year to cut it, because it gave me a full view of everything now. What had once been long and shaggy is now almost military cut, with only the barest bit of hair on top and completely shaven further down.

I don't normally give much thought to how people look, mainly because with everything I have to deal with, judging on appearance seems wrong, but I can't help myself this time because he looks beautiful.

"Good morning Belle."

No one calls me Belle. Well, other than my mom and sometimes Tristan. Adults seem to think that shortening my name makes it slang, so they go out of their way to make sure my entire name is said. I've gotten so used to hearing it that when he calls me Belle it takes me a minute to process it. I'm not sure how I feel about it, but with the way he says it so easily, I'll figure out how I really feel about it later.

I blink a few times and raise my hand in what I can only describe as my version of a wave. It's such a pathetic attempt even I regret it, but when the smile doesn't leave his face, I accept it and continue walking.

I enjoy the few minutes of silence as my moving forward takes him off guard, but in no time at all I see the shadow of his body beside mine and my heart almost beats out of my chest.

This is not good. I can't have this kind of reaction right now. I've been trying to live down what happened two days ago and now here he is, causing it all to come back around. I don't want to have an accident, but I don't have the first clue how to let him know that's exactly what's bound to happen if he keeps walking with me like this.

There's an electric surge through me as his hand brushes against mine while we're walking and it almost stops me in my tracks. If I didn't want to escape him and the way I'm feeling, I would stop, but my need to get away wins out. I can't let him, or anyone else, see me break down.

"Belle, stop." His voice commands softly and I'll be damned if my body doesn't instantly respond. It does nothing for the racing of my heart, but it does ground my thoughts, at least for the moment.

I raise my eyes in question and I catch his smile again. The fluttering I felt yesterday returns and I'm confused. What is it about Kayden that makes this happen?

"I want to walk with you, but it's like you can't get away from me fast enough."

"What do you want from me?!" I scream inside my head, wishing that the words would just come out of my now half open mouth. If I could just get the words out like a normal human being, maybe all of this could end and I could get back to normal, but no, that's never how my life works.

Sliding my backpack off my arm, I unzip it and drag out a notepad and pen. I begin scribbling and I push the pad at him, zipping up my bag and turning again to walk away.

Let him take what he wants from it, but I can't be a part of whatever it is he's attempting to do. I might not be like everyone else, but I did mean what I wrote him yesterday. I don't want to hear his apologies. I can't believe it.

"What do you think I'm trying to do?" he calls to me when I'm about three feet away. Stopping and waiting a few seconds to see if he's going to follow that question up with anything, I turn back on my heels and stomp back to him. Grabbing the pad from his hands, I again start writing. If nothing else comes from this, I need him to know that I can't be near him right now. It's doing more harm than good.

I think you're trying to do what you started with Eric yesterday. You told me you enjoy hurting people. So if this is your way of getting close to me so you can hurt me, just stop. I don't like you standing this close to me, touching me, because I don't know what it means. It makes me feel things I don't understand and it's scaring me. If you care at all, please, just let me go or everything's just gonna get worse.

I start to walk away again, but this time he doesn't give me a chance to get more than maybe two steps away. He grabs me by the wrist and spins me around until I'm facing him again.

"This isn't a trick. I know you don't believe that, so I'll let you go for now, but Isabelle Reagan, I'm not done with you."

True to his word he releases his hold and I just stare at the place where his fingers rested. My heart is still beating wild in my chest and the words I want to say are all garbled and stuck in my throat. Before I can start walking away, he does first and the minute he's out of earshot, I let out the breath I've been holding.

What does he mean by *'I'm not done with you'* and why did my heart still for a tiny second when he said my name that way?

Kayden

Whatever it is you're trying to do, just stop. Please leave me alone.

I actually expected to see those words, so when they came, it didn't even faze me. It was everything that came next that blew me away. It was hard to read at first, her having written it as fast as she did, but I got the gist pretty damn quick.

If I wasn't determined to do what she told me, seeing her back as she walked away from me would have seriously pissed me off. I've never had this much trouble getting close to a girl, let alone talking to one. Usually they climb all over themselves trying to get my attention and that's not me laying on an ego trip, it's the truth. When you're a football player, it's almost a god given right that every female within spitting distance will want you. At least that's how it is in Wexfield.

Isabelle has got to be the most difficult girl, no—person that I've ever dealt with and it's got nothing to do with what's wrong with her. She's just not like any other person I've met before and that's why I'm so damn determined to get close to her, even if it means blowing up the entire social order of the school to do it.

I know it's only a matter of time before word of me talking to her gets around. By lunch it's going to be front page news in the school paper for Christ sakes. It's just the way it works here, but I seriously don't care.

It makes me feel things I don't understand and it's scaring me.

She's not the only one that's confused by what they're feeling. She's also not the only one that's scared here. This girl, damn. I've been going out of my way to avoid her since the day I turned ten. What the hell I'm doing around her now is beyond me. I don't want to scare her, but I also don't think I'm quite ready to give up on her just yet. I need to know what it is about her that I can't seem to walk away from first.

When I brushed her hand, there was this second where it felt like I stuck my fingers in a wall socket. I was charged with a current so strong I can't even describe it right. I shook it off pretty quick, not wanting her to see me react, but it doesn't mean I didn't notice because I did and I liked it.

I'm fucking pathetic.

I walked away from her first because I wanted to make it easy on her, but I'm not entirely sure how much easier it's all going to be when my final words were that I wasn't done with her. If she wasn't completely scared and put off by me before, she most definitely will be now. It wasn't meant as a threat, but she doesn't exactly think the way everyone else does, so she probably believes I literally meant it.

It's another thing I'm going to have to go back and fix, that is if she lets me get near her at all. I'm determined as hell to see this through and prove to her that whatever it is she saw in me that first day isn't wrong, but I'm walking a fine line. I remember her serial killer comment well and if I push her too hard, I'm only going to make her think I'm no better and that's something I don't want.

Shit. Why does this girl get to me this way? She's got a list of issues so long it would take me forever to read through it. The right thing to do would be to leave her alone, but just like I've always been an asshole, I've also been known to be a stubborn one too.

"Did I really just see you walking with the retard?" I hear from behind me, not even needing to turn around to know who said it.

Yeah, it was definitely time for the rumor mill to start. By lunch I'd hear that I was screwing her on the hood of my car. It's something I definitely don't want Isabelle getting wind of. If she hears it, then she's going to think it started with me and I can't let that happen.

"Yeah, I was talking to her, so what?"

"I was right about the two of you, wasn't I? You do like her."

"It's called being nice, jackass. You should try it sometime." I answer back in response. There's no way he's goading me into saying something he'll use against me later. He can kiss my ass if that's what he's after.

"Maybe I should try it with her."

Even though I know he's joking, I can feel my blood boiling the minute he says it. There's no way in hell I'm letting him anywhere near her after all of the things he's done. I might have been a part of it before but that's done now. No one is going to hurt her again, not on my watch.

"You even so much as think of pulling something on her, I will end you. Fact."

I don't wait around for a response. As the final bell rings, I take off for the door. If I want to make things right then it has to start now. I need to talk to my first period teacher and get the okay to be let out early.

I have somewhere I need to be at 11:15 and this time; nothing or no one is going to stop me from making sure it happens.

Not even Isabelle herself.

Chapter Seven

Belle

There isn't a whole lot that I like about school. It's no real secret that the only reason I'm even here at all is because of my mom. If she didn't think it would be good for me, going through this the way I am, then I would be happier learning at home. She can't afford that and even if she could, she already has to deal with me enough, I can't imagine adding another six hours to it.

Even a mom needs a break from her kid every once in awhile.

For all of the things that I hate about school though, this is definitely not one of them.

As soon as I enter the class after my altercation with Kayden, I'm not in the mood to do much but pull out a book and get lost in it for awhile. Anything that will take my mind off the way he seems to make me go haywire every time I'm around him.

So it's like Christmas for me when Ms. Taylor tells us that today is free writing day. Considering how hard it is for me to talk, this is definitely something I enjoy. It makes those notebooks my mom bought me useful, which until now, other than in my afternoon classes they just haven't been.

The only problem is, the assignment she gives us isn't the type of thing I'm very good at. I have to talk to someone or at least talk to them in a letter. It should be easy considering I don't actually have to open my mouth to do it, but trust me, it's not. Writing to someone, whether you know their name or not, is not as easy as writing a story is. I don't like talking about myself at all, so I have a feeling that what she wants from us, I'm just not going to be able to do.

When she said free writing, I kind of hoped we could write stories. You know, ones where the girl, no matter how strange or different she is, always gets the guy in the end. The ones that no matter how similar some of the experiences might be to what you're going through, it's still obvious that its fiction so you don't feel bothered at all. Sadly though, I don't get my wish.

I do the assignment and of course I give it in the way I'm expected to, but I don't think I'll get a very good grade on it.

Free writing, even when I hate what I have to write, does make my day easier. It's this kind of happy go lucky thinking I'm filled with as I make my way from the class. It's only when I see whose leaning up against the lockers, with the same smile from earlier plastered across his face, that whatever happiness I was beginning to feel starts to fade.

What's he doing here? What does he want with me now?

It had taken almost the entire class to get his voice out of my head and just when I think that it's gone and I've escaped him, here he is, reminding me that no matter where I go, especially here in school, I will never truly escape him.

When is he going to learn that whatever it is he wants from me, he's just not going to get? With the amount of girls I've overheard talking about what they want to do to him, he's got no shortage of people to give him the attention he obviously craves, so why is he here trying to talk to me?

"You ready for lunch?"

Excuse me—what?

He can't be serious right? There had been a part of me yesterday that was excited at the idea of him standing outside of my class like this. It even made me stick around waiting until I almost missed my chance to eat, but today it's not at all the same. The excitement at seeing him here is gone and like earlier, all I want to do is get as far away from him as I could.

So that's exactly what I do.

I turn from the classroom, making sure to tear my eyes away from where he's leaning and I start making my way down the hall toward the stairs. I don't move fast enough to miss his reaction though.

"Son of a bitch!"

If I actually smiled for people to see, this would be one of the times I'd do it. Kayden Walker is an acknowledged asshole and he won't get any argument from me, no matter how cute his eyes look when he smiles. The time for him to be waiting for me would have been yesterday. Today he's too late.

Let him see that coming.

I start taking the stairs quickly, knowing that it can't be long before he's on my heels and making me face him, but by the time I get to my locker and take a look around me, I realize he's nowhere in sight. What I expected him to do based on the way he reacted this morning when I got off the bus, he hadn't done.

Crap. I thought I was being so smart. Turns out again, I'm the one being played.

Turning back to my locker, determined to get my lunch and make my way out to my normal spot, I don't realize that anyone has come up behind me until I see the shadow of an arm stretch out over my head.

Guess he found me after all. I think as I close the door and look up, expecting to see his very annoyed face looking back at me. It's not him I see though as my eyes come face to face with the person invading my personal space. It's someone even worse.

Noticing what I'm sure is a shocked expression, he smiles at me and the minute it happens, I'm taken back to two days before and the sick feeling in the pit of my stomach returns.

"Expecting someone else? Maybe, I don't know, Kayden?"

Keep it together Belle. Do not let him see how he's getting to you. I repeat over and over in my head as he stares at me. I want to say something to him, but like usual, the words won't come. I don't entirely understand sarcasm but right now, I wish I did.

"Oh that's right, you can't speak. I forgot you're retarded and mute."

I hate those words. I'm not any of those things, but with the amount of times I hear them, I'm sure it's only a matter of time before I start believing them. I let my eyes scan the hallway around us, looking for a teacher or even another student that might be able to stop what's about to happen, but when all I'm met with is other members of the football team, I know it's a waste of time.

They're going to recreate what they did with me in the parking lot and there's not a thing I can do to stop it. It only makes me wish I'd stayed with Kayden when he'd been waiting for me. If I did that, then maybe they wouldn't be doing this to me.

I'm scared and I'm pretty sure he knows it because as he bends in closer to me, he laughs as my body shivers. He has to know what being this close to me is going to do, yet he's making no move to get away from it. It's almost as if he wants it to happen.

"You know, I'm trying to figure out what he sees in you. What it is about you that he's willing to ditch all of his friends for. I can't figure it out. So, why don't you tell me?"

I'm not entirely sure what it is I'm supposed to be telling him, but before I can even get a chance to make sense of what he's asking, he speaks again and this time, it's even worse than all of the things he's said before.

"Is it true what they say about the quiet ones, Isabelle? Is that what you're doing when he drives you home? Giving it up in the backseat?"

Kayden

I was fully prepared to take off after her the second I saw her body turn, but before I can move, I feel the surprisingly tight grip from her teacher around my arm and I know I won't be going anywhere for awhile.

I watched Isabelle's form disappear down the stairs and there was this second before I turned to Ms. Taylor, that I felt a sick feeling in my stomach, something I couldn't place. It wasn't because she walked away from me though. No, this was something different and I didn't like it.

"Kayden, I need to speak with you."

Of course she does. She knew, just like Isabelle that I screwed her around by not showing up yesterday. I have no doubt I'm about to hear how disappointed she is.

I don't need this now. All I wanted to do was meet her and take her to lunch. Prove to her that I wasn't just gonna give up and walk away even though it's what she wants. I want to show her that the way she is doesn't scare me. I didn't sign up for a reprimand from a teacher.

"Do we really have to do this now, Ms. Taylor? I wanted to take Isabelle to lunch since I didn't make it yesterday."

It wasn't exactly a lie, but not the entire truth either. I actually want to get as far away from here as I can right now because no matter what I do, I can't shake the feeling that something is wrong. That I should have chased after her instead of leaving her alone. It's made even worse by the fact that I know Dillon saw us this morning. There's no telling what he'll do if I'm not there to stop it.

"This will only take a minute of your time and then you're free to catch up with her if you like."

Doing as she said, I make my way into the classroom and while she follows after me I take in my surroundings. I'd been in here yesterday but didn't really take the time to check out the class. Now that I'm getting the chance though, I can see that it's not all that different then my classes. There were a lot less seats, but other than that, everything looks the same.

"It's not all that different is it?" she asks as she takes a seat behind her desk, motioning at the same time for me to take one of the now empty seats across from her.

"No."

"Kayden, the reason I wanted to talk to you, it's about Isabelle." She says her face all business, matching the serious tone of her voice easily. "There's something I think you should see."

Well, this isn't the way I expected it to go at all. When she said she wanted to talk to me, I assumed she would drag me in here and let me know, in no uncertain terms, what she thought of the stunt I pulled yesterday. Not to mention what she assumed I was probably pulling now. The last thing I expected was that she would want to show me something.

"Show me what, Ms. Taylor?"

I watch as she opens her desk drawer and pulls out a piece of paper that I can see has writing on it, but I can't make out what. She passes it across the desk to me and as I reach out to take it, she speaks again.

"I gave the class an assignment today. I thought after everything that happened yesterday, she would enjoy it. I'm not entirely sure she was expecting it to be what it was, but with Isabelle, it's hard to honestly tell if she enjoys it or not."

"What was the assignment?" I ask, knowing that I have the answer to the question in my hands, but wanting to hear it from her.

"I wanted them to write a letter to someone in the future. Sort of like a time capsule assignment. I'm sure your teachers have done the same thing over the years in different ways. Anyway, writing is something Isabelle enjoys, so I thought this would be good for her."

I'm not sure how I feel about this. I have no doubt she's handing me Isabelle's paper. The one that she wrote to the person in the future and holding it now feels wrong. It's like in some way I'm invading her privacy even being this close to it, let alone actually reading it.

"Why do you want to show it to me?"

"To be honest, I'm not sure I know the answer to that myself. You just seem conflicted when it comes to Isabelle and I think that reading what she wrote, given that it is to someone in the future, might help."

Holy shit. Is it really that noticeable to everyone, the effect this girl is having on me? I thought it was bad with Dillon and the others catching on to it, but now I'm sitting here with a teacher, being told she can see it too. What the hell have I gotten myself into?

"I'm not sure I feel right reading this..." I answer hesitantly.

"Well we agree on that Kayden. I can tell you that what she wrote is more personal than what the other students did and I felt like I was invading something private, but I have a feeling that you need to read it, even if you don't feel right about it."

I have no idea what to say, so I just nod in response.

"Take it with you, but please be careful with it. I do not want it getting into the wrong hands. When you're finished you can bring it back to me. I'm here until four thirty tutoring."

Yeah, I don't want this getting into the wrong hands either and by wrong hands I think of Dillon and Tim. Even though I don't know what she wrote, I can only imagine the way the guys would use this against her if it ever got out. She's already a laughing stock; it doesn't need to be made worse.

Warning has been heard loud and clear. This is for my eyes only.

"Before you go, can I ask you for one more favor?"

"Yeah, of course, Ms. T. Anything."

"Whatever the reason is for you paying her this attention now, be sure of what you're doing before you do it, Kayden. That girl, despite being one of the strongest students I have, is also fragile and very trusting. The last thing I want to see happen is for her to get hurt."

I can hear in her words that my reputation precedes me. It's no secret the way I've been over the last few years and I'm sure all of the teachers are aware of just what an asshole I am. It's no surprise she's warning me off.

Blowing off this warning would have been my response before. In fact, it's not the first one I've had about certain people I've tortured over the last three years. I'm not going to do that this time though, because despite the teacher's concerns, this time, we're on the same page.

I don't want her hurt either. It's the last thing I want.

"Don't worry, Ms. T. I'm not entirely sure what I'm doing with her, but the last thing I want is Isabelle hurt."

"Well okay then. I'll take you at your word. Go on, enjoy the rest of your lunch." she says, motioning toward the door and as I turn and start heading out, I hear her speak again.

"You're a good guy, Kayden Walker. Remember that."

Chapter Eight

Kayden

The horrible feeling that's been in the pit of my stomach hasn't gone away, even with the time I spent talking with Ms. Taylor and after looking for her at her locker and her regular spot under the tree out front, no sign of her anywhere, I'm starting to realize just what the sick feeling is about.

Isabelle has always been a creature of habit. Well, I'm not even sure it's habit really, more like routine, but when she's not in classes or at home, there are only two places I've ever known her to be. I've passed her a bunch of times in the hall, usually walking by and catching her as she's got her head stuck in a book. When she's not there, she's outside watching the world go by underneath the ugliest looking tree on the entire campus.

Her not being in either spot worries me. I knew I should have chased after her when she took off and now the proof is being shoved in my face. It only makes me feel worse because if I just stayed away from her the way she wanted me to, maybe she wouldn't be missing now.

I pop my head into the library, knowing it's gonna be a waste of time and I'm greeted with the very shocked stares of some of the advanced placement students. I've never actually stepped foot in the library and it's obvious that everyone here knows it.

"Can I help you?" Ms. Reid, our librarian asks, as she comes to stand directly in front of my view of the room.

"No, I'm alright. I'm just looking for someone."

"Who would you look for in here, Mr. Walker?"

She doesn't come right out and say it, but trust me; I can hear it in her tone. She knows I don't hang out here and I wouldn't be caught dead around anyone who does. It's just another way the grapevine around here works. Everyone knows what I'm all about.

"Isabelle Reagan. I thought I'd find her at her locker, but she's not there so I thought maybe she came here."

"She hasn't been here today, but if she does make her way in, I can tell her that you're looking for her."

"That would be great. Thanks."

I've never been this polite before and I'm surprised by it. Normally, I try to run under the radar whenever I'm around teachers, figuring that if I can just blend in, they won't call on me or even notice my existence. Here I am now, actually having a conversation with one of them and acting pretty decent doing it.

When the hell did this happen?

"Well if there's nothing else I can help you with..." she says motioning toward the door.

"Actually, Ms. Taylor gave me something that I need to read over and get back to her. Do you think it's alright if I do that here?"

I can tell I've shocked her. It's not a secret that you don't have to ask to spend time here, but I figure with as weird as she's acting with me being here at all, the least I can do is ask for permission.

"Of course you can. Everyone is welcome here. "

She walks away from me after I slam her with one of the fakest smiles I've ever done and I make my way down into the stacks of books in the corner, hoping against hope there's a place at the end I can sit privately and read.

What Isabelle wrote is burning a hole in the back pocket of my jeans, so the sooner I pull it out and read it, the sooner the near obsession I have with keeping it close to me can end. I can do what the teacher asked of me, read it and return it to her, putting it out of my mind once and for all.

I soon realize the minute I sit down and unfold it in my hands, reading just the first two lines at the top, that the last thing I'm going to want to do is give this back when I'm done with it. No, this is definitely something I'm going to want to keep with me, just like I want to do with the actual girl herself.

To: The person in the future
From: Isabelle Reagan

There are people that will tell you that high school is the best time of your life. That when you're older and look back on it, there will be so many good memories and things you want to treasure and hold onto forever.

They lied.

High school is not the best time in your life or it isn't when you're like me.

When I was four, my mother was worried about me, so she took me to the doctor and even though it took awhile to figure out what was wrong with me, they finally did.

I'm autistic.

I know. You don't have any idea what that means and that's okay. No one does. I'm not even sure I do and I'm the one that's spent the last 13 years living with it.

Here's the thing. People think that because I don't talk much or I seem to always be lost in my own little world, that I'm stupid or deaf. Some even think I'm retarded. I'm none of those things and I don't like that word. It makes me cringe and want to cry every single time I hear it and trust me, I hear it a lot here in Wexfield.

Being autistic is different for everyone that experiences it. Some people have things that are similar, but for the most part, we're all different. That's why there's this whole list that doctors have about it because there's so many different forms, that you can't lump everyone in the same one.

For me it's like this.

When I was little, I didn't speak until I was six and even when I did, it was like I was two because I didn't speak the way the rest of the kids my age did. I would point, grunt and jump for what I wanted and when that didn't work, I would get frustrated and hit myself until my mom figured it out.

I didn't eat like anyone else. It had to be crushed and mushy so I could swallow it. It hasn't changed much since then either. I can eat a few things that I have to chew instead of just swallow, but for the most part, I still like the ease of just swallowing.

I wasn't completely potty trained until I was eight. I didn't understand the whole bathroom thing because I was so lost in my own thoughts that I didn't understand the feeling that happens when you have to go. Yeah, I know, it's gross, but that's just me.

I got better with it over the years, but I still have accidents now and I'm seventeen. For years, my mom would keep me home because of it, but eventually she figured I had to adapt to the real world so I started going to school. Trust me, that didn't help and I don't think it ever will. Sometimes I wish I was at home still because then if I have them, no one would be around to see it.

Just because I've got issues, doesn't mean it's all I am. There's a whole lot more to me, but no one really takes the time to get to know it. So I'm supposed to sit here now and write about it.

The one thing that still shocks people most about me is that I'm insane for numbers. I'm actually in advanced placement math because there's just something about it that's easy for me. As long as I have numbers around, I'm at my most comfortable. I guess that sort of takes away from everyone's belief that I'm dumb, so I don't go out of my way to call attention to it.

I also like stories. I guess when you're like me and spend most days being made fun of, called names or even worse, ignored, like you're part of the scenery, escaping into a make believe world where everything turns out right in the end isn't a bad thing. Usually though, when it happens, I end up talking to myself or to the characters I'm reading or writing about.

That's just another thing that makes me weird.

The whole point of this assignment is to explain yourself to someone in the future, so I hope that everything I've said explains me to you. I'm sorry if it doesn't.

I guess the one thing I hope for most is that whoever does end up reading this does the one thing that despite how badly I want to, I haven't been able to do. I want acceptance, but not for me. I want people like me to be accepted. Sure, you might not get it and that's okay, but do you really have to go out of your way to be mean when it's so much easier to be nice?

I don't want kids like me to be afraid of their own shadows anymore. I don't want different to be such a horrible thing. I won't ever be a cheerleader or go to Homecoming with the hottest guy in school (mainly because I'd just have an accident on the way there and ruin my dress), but I should be able to walk down the hall and not fear the names I hear every day. The way people sneer at me, or even plug their nose when I walk by.

The kids of the future, especially ones like me, deserve better than that. So if you're reading this, instead of that sneer I know you wanna make at the person you don't understand, why not try smiling instead?

I promise you, you'll make their day.

Most days I hate the way I am and wish so badly that I was normal like the other girls. Sometimes I even feel like the world would be better off, not to mention my mom and brother, if I just ceased to exist at all, but as much as I think it, I never do anything about it.

Don't make anyone feel that way. It's not worth it.

Make that statement from earlier that I said, true. Make these the best years of your life and become a person you're going to enjoy living with twenty years from now. Be the best person you can be.

I know you have it in you.

There's only one thing I'm thinking when I finish reading Isabelle's assignment. She doesn't realize it, but she wrote this for me and I'm going to do exactly what she wants me to.

I'm going to make this the best year of her life and I know just where to start.

Belle

I want to go home.

I thought everything was over when Dillon walked away from my locker, but I was wrong. Not only wasn't it over, but it was just getting started.

The entire time he was standing there, I'm pretty sure I didn't breathe, so when he walked away I let out the biggest sigh of relief I've ever done in my life. I was shaken by the way he acted and the things he said, but I was more than ready to get outside and underneath the safety of my spot. At least I was until Amy, Charlotte and Eve blocked me the minute I rounded the corner.

I should have known then that I wasn't going to make it outside, but maybe I'm as dumb as people say because I wasn't ready for what came next at all.

Without so much as a word to me, only their cold eyes and evil smirks to go by, they grabbed me, Amy the worst as she had my hair tangled around her hands. Before I knew it, I was dragged into the girl's washroom, and now I'm being slammed up against the wall.

Visions of what Eric must have endured the day before flash in my mind and before I know it, I feel the slap across my face and Amy directly in front of me as her friends hold my arms, pinning me in. I'm trapped. I can't get free and even if I could, there's no one in the school that I can run too. When I'm feeling alright, I can't talk to most people. With the way I feel now, I'm not even sure I'll ever talk again.

"Just what the fuck do you think you're doing, huh? I saw you talking to Dillon earlier. I don't know what you've done to Kayden, but you better keep your dirty hands off my man."

She slaps me again and this time the minute the girls let me go, my body slumps to the floor from the impact. Any break I thought might come doesn't materialize as I again feel her breath on my face, now down on her knees in front of me.

It's only when she reaches into the pocket of her jacket, pulling out the cigarette, that I realize what's about to happen. It's never happened to me before, but I've heard about it. The entire school has. It's the way that the girls do business. The guys on the football team haze kids using their fists, but the girls take it a step further. I just never thought I'd be on the receiving end of it.

The minute I hear the lighter flick, I flinch, which only causes the three of them to laugh and squeal in delight. I don't see what's so funny about any of this. Physically hurting someone is never funny. I might have a different sense of humor then most people, but I thought that would be universal. It's wrong.

The minute I feel the lit cigarette burn into the hairs on my arm, I cry out in pain and start rocking in place. No one knows this, but rocking is a coping mechanism for me. It can take me out of the most stressful place and calm me, but it isn't having the desired affect this time. Not even close.

That's when it happens, the pounding of my heart, the fear in my mind and heart all crashing into me at once. The laughter stops immediately and all three girls release me, letting me fall back against the wall.

"Gross, she just pissed herself." I hear Charlotte say, though it's muffled with how blocked my ears are with the sound of my own sobs.

"Eww, there's a puddle and everything!" Eve joins in. The only one completely silent is Amy, but it doesn't take much to find out why. Opening my eyes slightly and looking up, I see her face. The sneer is still in place and she looks pleased.

"Stay away from Dillon, you hear me, stupid? Or the next time this happens, it will be a lot worse than a burn on your arm."

I see her move out of the corner of my eye, going into one of the stalls and after a few seconds, she comes back out and throws what she's grabbed at me. Looking down, I see a long strip of toilet paper and I know what it's for.

"Now clean yourself up. You're pathetic. If I hear that you went and snitched about this to that retard teacher of yours, I'll come back again."

I feel the blast of air as they finally open the door to leave, but I don't dare make a move to get up until I'm sure they're gone. When I'm sure that I'm alone, I wipe at my eyes before looking down at the stinging spot on my arm. It's when I catch sight of the real damage they did, that I start to cry again.

Right above my wrist on my left arm is the red circular burn, so bright that it looks like it's flashing at me. Running my finger over it, I flinch in pain as it begins stinging even more. I know that I need to get up and deal with the other thing that happened, but I can't seem to move from my spot on the floor.

Not only is my hair completely pulled out of the ponytail holder, but my shirt is broken where the other two grabbed me so hard it popped the buttons. Add to that, the very large wet stain that's now covering my pants and I don't think I ever want to get up again.

I don't understand why they did this to me. They should know that Dillon didn't talk to me because he likes me. He did it for a completely different reason. Considering what they all did to me two days ago, it should be obvious what he's doing. I don't deserve any of this.

I just want this to end. There's only one way that it ever will though.

When I'm dead.

Kayden

"You should have been there D, it was hilarious. The minute we lit the smoke, she pissed herself. I mean it was pouring out all over the floor. We all had to jump back before we got hit with it."

"Did you do what I told you to?"

"Yeah, we did it, baby. Lit the smoke and put it right on her. She did a whole lot of squirming, but it's done. We might have been able to do more if she hadn't tried spraying us."

This is what I walk into when I leave the library after returning Isabelle's assignment to Ms. Taylor. This isn't the first time I've walked into this exact conversation, though this time I have no idea who the target was. Truthfully, I don't want to know. I always said that burning people would come back to bite us and with this newest one, I can't help feeling that way even more.

"Yo, where the hell you been man?" Dillon asks as he finally notices me walk up.

"I had a meeting with Coach." I answer, lying my ass off. As much as what I read earlier got to me, I'm not ready to be open about it, especially not with these guys.

"I was wondering if you were gonna show up. I missed you." Charlotte says as she scoots across the bench the minute I sit down, sliding her legs over mine, as if I wouldn't get the hint just from her words that she wants me.

Girl's man, I wish they'd get a clue.

"So what'd I miss?" I ask completely ignoring Charlotte, which I see the minute she realizes it, earns me a pout. "Who did you guys burn this time?"

The way everyone looks at each other puts me on edge. The sick feeling that I finally got rid of is back again and this time it's even worse than before. I put the pieces together at the exact second Tim speaks up.

"The retard. Dillon came up with the idea in study hall and man; you missed out on some fun shit. It went down perfect."

"Beyond perfect." Amy chimes in with a grin. "At least until she pissed on us."

I'm so angry listening to them laughing about what they did to her that I'm seeing spots in my eyes and they aren't the ones you get when you're dizzy. They're red, just like the rage that's threatening to boil over in me any second. If they don't shut the hell up, I'm not going to be responsible for what I do.

It's taking everything in me right now not to rip their throats out. I did everything Dillon wanted, so why the hell are they still going after her?

The minute I think it, I realize I already know the answer. They aren't doing this to scare her. It's all about me. Charlotte's reaction when I showed should have been the first clue. I've known for awhile she likes me and with Dillon catching me talking to Isabelle this morning, I'm sure he passed it along. It means they aren't doing any of this just to get to her, they're doing it to get to me. They're getting their wish too because all I want is them dead at my feet.

The bathroom.

I should have known to check there for her earlier. If I had gone there, instead of the library, maybe none of this would be happening now. Amy and the others always take their victims there. They put an out of order sign on the door and do their business, no one the wiser.

Shit. This is my fucking fault.

"Kayden, you alright man?" I hear Tim ask as I get to my feet again, this time clear on my destination.

"Yeah, I'm fine. I just realized I need to hand in a paper for History. He gave me two extensions already and if I don't hand the damn thing in, he's gonna flunk me. It's half the reason Coach wanted to see me so bad. I'll catch up with you later."

It's a lame excuse and I'm pretty sure one of them is gonna see through it, but it's the last thing on my mind. All of this is happening now because of me. There is no way I'm going to leave her in the bathroom with the way they're talking about everything. She deserves better than that.

As I go back into the school, Ms. Taylor's words play over in my head the more I propel myself forward.

"You're a good guy, Kayden Walker."

She's wrong. If I was such a good guy then none of this would be happening right now. No, I wasn't the good guy she believed me to be. I was the worst kind of guy. There's only one person alive that I don't want to be the worst for.

As I reach the bathroom, I take a quick look around, praying there aren't any teachers around to see me do what I'm about to. It's against the rules to be caught doing this and with as much shit as I've caused lately, I didn't need this being my last strike. Content that there's no one around that's gonna stop me from reaching her, I push on the door.

Where I expect it to push open easily, I slam into it, my face smacking off hard, my body stumbling back in response to the violation. Shaking off the sting my face takes as it hit, I push at it again, this time putting all of my body weight into it. When it doesn't budge, I realize what I'm going to have to do.

As much as I don't want to involve anyone, if the only way to get to her is to get one of the janitors to unlock the door, it's something I'm gonna have to do. There's no way I'm leaving her in that bathroom one second longer then she's already been. I'd deal with the fallout later.

It's only when I hear a sound from the inside that I place my head to the door. After a few seconds of silence, thinking that I'm just hearing things, I hear it again. It's faint, but it's a girl's voice and she's calling out for help.

Shit.

It's Isabelle.

Chapter Nine

Belle

Someone is banging on the door.

They've been doing it non-stop for the last few minutes and it's bothering me. I've covered my ears with my hands, tried rocking back and forth, nothing blocks it out. It gets louder and not even sticking my fingers in my ears gets rid of it. I just want it to stop and it won't.

Even though it took awhile, I tried my best to clean the floor underneath me. It's still stained and wet, but at least there isn't a puddle anymore. I really hate having accidents, but I hate the mess it leaves behind more. As much as I hate what they say to me when it happens, it isn't a lie. It does smell.

The problem with the smell is, I don't usually notice it as much, but this time, it's all I can smell so while I tried to clean it up, I got sick. Now not only am I burned and soaking wet, my brand new shirt is broken and damp. I want to get out of here so badly, but I don't have the strength to open the door and leave. The minute I open the door people are gonna see me like this and they just can't. I'm barely hanging on as it is.

I want my mom.

There's what sounds like yelling in the hall, but I can't make out the voices. All I know is that whoever is on the other side of the door is angry. So angry that I don't ever want them to get the door open because if they do, I'll be right back where I started before. Scared, alone and making a fool of myself.

Why did I agree to this when she asked me about it? I could have easily told her that I didn't want to go to school, that I was safer at home and she would have found a way around it. Why did

I have to do the right thing and say yes, so that she could finally have a break from me? All I want is to go home and never come back. I never should have said yes to this. Home school might be lonely, but at least I wouldn't be a crumpled mess on the floor.

The door opens and I crouch into myself, not wanting the people that are bound to walk in to see me this way. It's not as if I can hide all of it, but I really don't want to look anyone in the eye. I'm such a mess. A gross, disgusting mess and all I want is to be left alone in it, the way Amy and her friends wanted me to be when they left me here.

"Jesus Christ, Isabelle!"

Before I can even register the voice, I feel myself being lifted up from the floor. Keeping my eyes shut tight, I wait for what comes next. The voice sounds concerned, but with the way everything goes here and how much stuff goes unnoticed, I'm not sure of what I'm hearing.

"I'm here now. I've got you. You don't have to be afraid anymore."

I know the voice now, the more it speaks and it's the last voice I want to hear. It's the voice that no matter how hard I try, I can't seem to get out of my head even though he doesn't belong there. He hasn't earned it. He's a jerk, or as he says, an asshole. He's definitely the last person I want seeing me like this.

His arms wrap completely around me, my body being pulled into his and I fight against it. I don't want to be held by him. All I want is my mom. I want to go home, crawl into my bed and never come out again.

"Thanks, Jim. If you bring the bucket, I'll clean this up for ya."

"You sure you don't want me to get someone?" the voice I can only assume is Jim answers. I know Jim. He's the custodian for the school. He's actually been at more than one accident scene with me. Jim is nice. Jim isn't Kayden.

"No man, I got this. Just bring me the stuff and I'll handle it."

There's a gust of air as the bathroom door shuts and I feel his body shift beside mine. It's only when he breaks away from me and makes his way toward the door again that I realize he's leaving and the sob escapes my throat.

"I'm just locking the door, Belle. I'm not leaving."

It's as if he knows that even though I don't want him here, I also don't want him to leave. I can't even open my eyes. I'm just standing here, barely keeping myself balanced, shivering, shaking and waiting for him to come back. I'm not even sure I can move on my own anymore.

This is the worst it's ever been.

Before I know it, his hands are on me, except this time, they're placed on my shoulders and it's when I feel his hand under my chin that I realize what he's trying to do and I shake my head. No. I can't look at him. If I open my eyes and look into his, I'm going to crack even more and I won't do it.

"Belle, please look at me. I swear you're safe. I'm alone, there's no one here but me."

I keep shaking my head and I hear him sigh. I know I'm not making this easy on him, but I didn't exactly ask for him to open the door now did I? What did he expect me to do?

"Okay fine. You don't have to look at me, but I'm gonna ask you some yes or no questions okay? All you gotta do is nod or shake your head. Can you do that for me?" he asks, his voice so low, it's almost relaxing. Not at all the way I'm used to hearing it. There isn't a hint of anger or frustration at all.

I nod my head slowly, accepting what he needs from me, but still keeping my eyes firmly shut.

"Did they burn you?"

Again I nod my head and this time I feel his body tense. He didn't attempt to slam anything the way he did in his car, but it's obvious he's not happy with what I'm telling him. The minute I nod though, I realize that telling him, I've done what they told me not to and now they're going to come back again.

I start shaking my head no repeatedly and suddenly the hands that were on my shoulders are on my head preventing me from the continuous motion.

"Did they tell you not to tell anyone?"

I nod and he sighs.

"It's okay. They won't ever know you told me. I swear to you. Now, do you have spare clothes?"

I shake my head, embarrassed that I didn't take the emergency bag when I left this morning. Normally I'm so good about making sure I have it with me just in case, but today I rushed out the door and forgot. It figures the one day I forget is the day that everything happens.

Even more proof of how stupid I am.

"I've got some sweats in my locker. Would you wear them?" he asks, his voice still calm, but his body remaining as rigid as ever. He doesn't know he's doing it, but his voice is soothing me, something I didn't expect to happen, but I'm thankful for.

I nod my head, though I'm not sure I want to be wearing anything that belongs to him. He's best friends with the people that did this to me; the last thing I want to be doing is taking help from him. He's probably the reason this happened.

"One more question. Can you handle being here alone while I run and get them?"

I'm not sure about my answer to this one so I make no attempt to move my head in either direction. The last thing I wanted was for him to see me like this, but now that he has and the affect he seems to have on me since being here, I'm not sure I want to be left without him again. He's all I've got.

"Isabelle? Did you hear me?" he asks again and this time I nod my head. I had been alone for god knows how long already; a few more minutes wouldn't make a difference. I only hope that in agreeing to this, I don't live to regret it.

"Okay. I'm gonna go grab them, but I want you to lock the door behind me. When I come back, I'll knock like this," he says as he knocks twice on the wall. "That way you know it's me and you can let me back in."

I nod my head one more time and feel him break away from me, this time prepared for it and even though I still feel like I've lost something, it's not nearly as bad as it was the first time.

The gust of wind enters the bathroom again and focusing with every bit of strength I have, I open my mouth, needing to get the words out before they eat me alive. I only hope that this time it works.

"Thank—you."

Kayden

Dillon is a dead man.

The minute I see him, Tim or hell, any of the stupid girls that did this to her, I'm going to rip their hearts out and feed it back to them.

I thought I prepared myself for what I was gonna walk into when I finally got into the bathroom, but there is literally nothing that could have prepared me for the way Isabelle looked the minute I saw her.

The top portion of her body, despite her obvious attempt at getting it all in trash can, is covered in puke and her jeans are soaked through with what can only be her own piss. Her cheeks are stained with tears, her hair is half hanging out of a hair band and there are rips in her shirt.

These girls hadn't just picked on her, they destroyed her and it's my fault.

Jim came down the hallway right as I'd been about to kick the door down and after explaining to him that I had a friend of mine in there that I thought was hurt, he had no problem opening it for me. I know I was ready to deal with the fallout, but I'm glad I didn't have to. The last thing I want is to take ownership for this, no matter how guilty I am.

Not to mention if I get nailed for it, Isabelle will think I made them do it. I may have created these monsters when we started hanging together, but I was putting an end to it now.

It bothers me that she won't look at me, but my need to get her cleaned up and out of here outweighs it. I can handle her keeping her eyes shut, because honestly, she doesn't need to see any more of the mess that's left anyway.

Her agreeing to wear my clothes makes me feel good. I have a spare set of sweats for when I work out and right now, I can't bring her out of here without changing. Life here is already hard enough for her and the others, there's no reason to make it worse. That's not what gets to me most though. It's what happens when I'm leaving that does that.

It was quiet and for a second there I thought I imagined it, but it happened. She spoke to me. It wasn't anything major, at least not to anyone else that it might've happened to, but it was huge to me. A simple thank you was all I needed moving forward.

Letting the door shut again, I turn back to where she's standing, her eyes shut tight and her arms wrapped around her body, like she's hugging herself. Seeing her like this reminds me of the way she used to look when she was little. She's always been a timid person, but whenever I did get to see her upset, she did this exact thing. It's like nothing's changed since our time together and the reminder of the way things used to be only makes me want to protect her even more.

She can't go through anything like this again.

"Isabelle?"

She lifts her head at the sound of my voice and I take that as my chance to move closer. Wrapping my arms around her, pulling her back into my body, I let my hands rest on her head, stroking her hair gently. I have no idea where it came from, but with everything she's been through today, I figure it can't hurt. When no argument comes, either in being pushed away or a shaking of her head, I continue, the both of us completely still in the moment.

There is so much I want to say right now, but I know that none of it will come out right. I need to say something though. I can't just stand here like this, especially now that she's crying. The sound might be muffled, but I can still hear it clear as day and it breaks my heart.

"You're welcome."

Chapter Ten

Belle

I haven't been here since before his mom left.

That's what I'm thinking when he unlocks the door and motions for me to come in. The way I see it now, is definitely not the way it looked back then. It's completely different and it makes me sad.

There are broken bottles all over the place, old food wrappers and even all sorts of different cans thrown about. I really don't have any idea what to say or do seeing this. My mom doesn't even drink, so seeing how much of that goes on here is beyond anything I can even begin to understand. When we eat at my house, we always clean up after ourselves, no matter what it is we've made or bought, but here, it's like they don't even bother.

Is this really what he has to live with?

I can tell he's not sure what to say or do. I don't think he ever intended for anyone to see this. It's bad enough that he has to see it, but for anyone else, it's got to be even worse. I haven't seen him look so awkward before. For once, he's the one that's different and I can tell by the scowl that's creeping across his face that he doesn't like it one bit.

I can't say I blame him. I'm not sure how I would feel about this either.

"I'm sorry about how the place looks. Dean isn't much for cleaning." He offers up and I just nod my head. He was nice enough to bring me here; the least I can do is be understanding about it. He could have easily dumped me on my front lawn after getting me out of the school and not given it another thought. He didn't though and I appreciated it. Too bad I can't tell him that.

After standing with me in the bathroom for awhile, he broke away to get the change of clothes he talked about and within five minutes he was back and handing them over to me. I went into the stall to change and wipe myself up as much as possible, making sure that the minute the door shut behind me it was locked as tight as it could go.

He was doing something nice for me, but it didn't mean I trusted him. I don't think I've ever trusted anyone other than my mom when I get like this. She's the only one that's ever dealt with it and didn't look sad or pitiful. I needed that now, but since she isn't here, Kayden was going to have to be good enough.

True to his word to Jim earlier, he cleaned up the mess while I changed. I saw the outline of the mop across the floor and I couldn't help being impressed. That isn't the Kayden I know, at least not the one that he's been for almost eight years. The Kayden everyone sees wouldn't be caught dead doing something like that. He would the one off causing it.

*****

"Do they fit okay?" he calls through to me and the minute the question comes out, I hear him swear under his breath.

My mom taught me something a couple of years ago. If I wasn't comfortable enough to speak to her, especially when we were out in public, she told me to knock on the table or the door of a change room to answer her. One knock meant yes and two meant no. So that's what I did for him, even though I was pretty sure he wouldn't understand it. I knocked once on the door, attempting as best I could to let him know that they fit. It only took a minute or two before he seemed to piece it together.

"Does the knock mean yes?" he asks and I knock once again. I hear his laugh and despite how upset I am and how badly I want to get out of here, I'm happy. At least one of us can laugh in the situation we're in.

"It's all cleaned up out here Isabelle. I'm gonna put the bucket back out in the hall and when I come back, you can come out. I'll get you out of here as quickly as I can, but I can't promise that people won't see us."

I know he's trying to warn me, but right now, that's the last thing I want. For the last few minutes I've been able to focus on calming myself. Thinking about the looks I would get the minute I stepped out, in his clothes no less, just made it all come flooding back. I'm not entirely sure I can do this after all, even if he did his best to shield me from it.

When I finally come out, he takes me straight to the office. At first I thought he was bringing me here so he could tell the principal what happened, but the minute he flashes his smile, I know it isn't going to be that at all. In fact he's doing the one thing that I want more than anything.

"Isabelle needs to call her mom. I hope that's okay, Ms. Owens."

"Of course!" she answers easily. She's another one that is used to this. Needing to call home is definitely a repeated occurrence and no one usually stood in my way. Kayden didn't know that though. He lost the right to know anything like that when he ditched me to be cool.

"I'll be right outside when you're done. I'm gonna warm up the car and bring you home." He whispers to the top of my head before again flashing that award winning smile.

He's waiting out front just the way he said when the call is done and the minute I get into the car, I see the notebook with the gel pen waiting for me. I've never been so thankful to see paper in my life.

"What did your mom say? Is she gonna meet you at home?"

No. I told her I would be okay by myself. I can't have her missing work. She does that enough.

"That's not exactly the truth, is it?" he asks and I'm confused. Just what is he getting at?

What part?

"You being okay alone. The last time I drove you home and she wasn't there, you seemed pretty freaked."

He remembers that? All the talk about serial killers? I watched a horror movie the night before and like always, it bled over into my everyday life. I took it too far, too literal and now I was actually afraid of my own shadow. He's right though, I did lie to my mom. I really wouldn't be okay alone.

Yeah I lied to her. She needs to stay where she is.

"Well, you can always come over to my house. I mean, it's probably not as fun as yours, but you can hang there until your mom gets home."

$$*****$$

So here we are. We're standing silently in his living room, neither one of us looking at the other. If it's possible it's more awkward then it was at the school when he walked into the bathroom. I didn't know what to say, what to do and I didn't want to take one more step into his house until he gave me permission. I didn't feel at all okay here.

Maybe I should have gone home after all.

"Do you want something to drink?" Kayden asks, cutting into my thoughts. "Despite the way it looks, we actually have soda and juice."

He's trying to make light of the broken bottles and attempting to deflect off of the fact that there's a whole lot of drinking that goes on here. There's more that happens and I know all about it, but I don't even want to think about that. What happens in this house and with this guy is none of my business. I need to remember that during my time here.

Kayden might be helping me out more than I ever expected him to, but we're definitely not friends. I'm not even sure we ever could be considering who his friends are.

He moves away from me and goes to the fridge, pulling out two cans of soda and placing them on the bar. I didn't say that I wanted anything to drink, but apparently that didn't seem to matter to him. He was going to get it for me anyway. Just who is this guy and what did he do with the real Kayden?

He pats the empty chair at the bar and smiles, letting me know that it's alright to sit. It's looking at him the way he is now, the smile lighting up his face, I wish I could return it. I want to do something so simple for him because he deserves it.

"What the hell is she doing here?"

I flinch as I hear the groggy, yet angry voice behind me. I'm frozen in place, afraid to even turn around and see the face of Kayden's older brother Dean. It's only when I feel his hand squeeze mine that I allow my now hitched breath to release.

"She had an issue at school; her mom couldn't make it home, so I brought her here."

"So that's why the phone's been ringing off the hook for the last thirty minutes? You left the damn school!"

The way his voice raises scares me. I know that Kayden deals with this a lot so he won't be affected, but I don't like it. He left school for me because he wanted to do the right thing and yelling at him for it is wrong.

"So? I leave all the fucking time and you never say a word."

"It's different, Kayden."

"Why? Is it because for once, I left for the right reasons? Dean, get over it and stop yelling, it scares her."

"It's my god damned house! I'll do whatever I please, whenever I please, you hear me? I don't care what some stupid mute kid thinks."

He's still holding my hand and the way he squeezes isn't at all like it was a couple of minutes ago. He's tense and his eyes, they're scary now. He's getting angry. I really shouldn't be here, if all I'm going to do is cause them to fight.

"Well, I care alright. Just stop. You don't have to always be such a dick, Dean."

It's obvious looking at Dean now, that he's not sober. His eyes are glazed over and even as he lunges across the room toward

Kayden, I see he's unsteady on his feet. I don't have a whole lot of experience with people that drink because mom shelters me from them, but there's no doubt he was drinking a whole lot before we got here.

Kayden ducks out of the way at the last minute, allowing Dean to slam into the bar and before I know it, I'm being dragged across the room toward the door we just came in.

"I'm sorry Isabelle, but you need to get out of here. He's only going to keep doing this and I know it scares you." He sighs as he rubs his hand over his head and I feel bad for him. He's still trying to do the right thing by me even though he knows it's gonna make his brother worse. I don't exactly want to be alone, but if my being here is going to cause something worse for him, I know it's what I have to do.

"You're gonna pay for that, you stupid, son of a bitch!" Dean yells from his place hunched over the bar and I'm not the only one that flinches. Kayden does too.

"Do you have a phone?" he whispers pointing to my bag still wrapped around my back.

I nod and he unzips the back and starts searching around for it. When he finds it, he slides his finger across the screen and immediately begins typing quickly. He hands it back to me and smiles weakly before motioning toward the door.

"It's going to be okay, Isabelle. If you get scared, text me okay?"

I'm scared alright, but right now it isn't about me. I'm afraid for Kayden. As much as I want to run from this house and never come back, I don't want to leave him alone. He was there for me when no one else wanted to get within two feet of me and I want to do the same for him.

He can obviously see something in my eyes because he leans in and kisses the top of my head lightly before he whispers again.

"Go, Belle. I'll be okay."

Kayden

I knew it was a risk bringing her here. Dean hasn't been sober one second since he lost his job and I knew he wouldn't be out at the bar this early. No, he would be home and he would be the same as always. I just hoped that because she was with me, he would hold back on it.

I need to stop with this giving him the benefit of the doubt bullshit. It never gets me anywhere. You can't change someone who doesn't want to change. I know that better than anyone. It took having it slammed into me by Isabelle, for me to learn it. I still didn't want her to have to see him like this though.

She knows all about it, there's no way she couldn't. It doesn't mean I have to sit here and let her experience it for herself. It took everything in me to let her walk out the door. I know how she feels about being alone and I want nothing more than to keep her here with me, but if she stays here with him like this, she's going to be something a whole lot worse than scared.

I'm not sure what the hell I was thinking giving her my number, but it seemed like the right thing to do. I don't want her feeling like she did in the bathroom ever again, even if she's at home and it's not exactly the same. I want her to know she's got someone. She's got me.

Again, Ms. Taylor's words are ringing in my head when I type my number in her contacts. If the teacher that knows what I'm all about can believe I'm a good guy, then maybe, I can be what she believes me to be. At least I want to be, if only for the girl that seconds before had been afraid to even leave me alone here.

I could see it in her eyes. She was scared by the way Dean was carrying on, something that I'm beyond used to. She had a hard time turning her back on me and walking out the door. I don't have much of a heart, but her acting that way, it touched some part of me and I think I might have fallen a little more.

Admitting it isn't so hard anymore. I like Isabelle Reagan, even if I'm still not sure what I'm going to do about it. All I know is, I want to do right by her. She deserves that and it's been too damn long since anyone's tried.

"What the fuck is wrong with you, Kayden? Bringing the retard over here? Don't you know how stupid that is?"

I swear if I hear one more person call her a retard, I'm going to snap. I'm beginning to see why people hate that word so much. It makes me physically sick to hear it. Considering that up until I turned six, I couldn't even read and write and was called retarded myself, I should know how wrong it is. I know it now and I refuse to let it happen again, at least from the one person I can control. Dean won't ever say the damn word again. I don't care what it costs me.

"She's not a retard."

"Since when? You know the girl is a few bricks short of a full load bro, so when did you change your tune?"

"Since now, Dean. Don't call her a retard again."

He laughs and he reminds of another idiot that I have to deal with when I'm back at school again. Dillon. All I want to do is take every bit of rage I have inside of me for that guy and lay it on my brother. The two of them deserve each other.

"I can't believe what I'm hearing. You're the one that fucking called her that! I'm the one that used to tell you that she wasn't!"

"Right! I'm the one that did it and I was wrong."

"No you weren't. I've picked that kid up enough to know there's something wrong with her. I'm starting to think you were right the entire time."

Whenever Dean speaks, it's hard to understand him because he's so hopped up on prescriptions and booze that his words are slurred and now is no different. I know what he's trying to say though and that's why I'm not answering him anymore. I'm going to walk away.

Well, I'm going to if he lets me, which as he stumbles out from around the bar in an attempt to block me, is obviously not going to happen.

"Dean, don't fucking start with me. I'm not in the mood."

"What you gonna do boy? You gonna hit me because I called your girlfriend a retard?"

There's something in the way he draws out the word retard and laughs that completely breaks me. I shove him and I do it hard until he's falling backward, eventually finding his ass crashing into the table behind him. I'm not done though. I could easily walk away now that he's on his ass where he belongs, but I can't stop myself.

This isn't about me and the hatred I have for him or for all of the things he's said to me over the years to try and break me. No, this time I want to pound his face in for Isabelle. She deserves better then to be called a retard. Hell, the girl deserves better than to be called my girlfriend even though I actually like the way that sounds.

Just like he does with me when he gets in his drunken rages, I kick at him as he lays on the ground until he's hunched over holding his side, but I still don't stop. Bending down to his level and reaching my arm back, I punch him, in his face, his stomach, his legs, anywhere I can get an open spot and I keep wailing away until I'm completely worn out.

"Don't—you ever—call her—a retard—ever again." I say slowly as I try to catch my breath. Getting back up to my feet, I stomp into my room and slam the door behind me. I immediately throw myself down on the bed, disgusted with him and myself.

As hard as I'm trying to be different from the way I've always been, what I just did to Dean proves I'm no different. He's right. I'm the one that started calling her retard first and before he got so stupidly drunk all the time, he'd been the one to tell me that she wasn't. As different as I want to be, especially for that scared, yet special girl across the street, I really don't think I can be.

I'm always going to be exactly like Dean. I'm going to be an asshole and not even she can change it.

Until she does.

Are you okay?

That's the text I'm met with the minute I pull it from my pants. I know it's her because it's a number without a name on my screen.

I'm fine. Are u ok?

I text back, more concerned with how she's handling being alone than I am about myself and what I'm sure is going to come the minute Dean picks himself up off the floor.

I'm okay.

I'm really glad that she's not here because I think she's lying and there's no way if we were having this conversation face to face, I'd be able to hide my distrust in her answer. It's only when my phone goes off again, with the generic ringtone it affords new contacts that I realize I need to assign her one.

Not sure why it matters, but positive I want to do it, I start scanning through the music in my phone, searching for a song that's distinctly her. I want to always know when she needs me.

It's apparent after I've gone through every song I own, that I have no idea what she even likes, so I do the only thing I can. I text her back and ask her. I could have easily just assigned her a random tone, but I'm doing it for another reason. I don't want the conversation to end. Just in the few minutes since she sent the first text, I feel the rage inside me evaporating and like Dean and his addiction to booze, I need more of it.

What's ur fav song?

God let this work. I silently pray as I wait for her response.

After a few minutes of radio silence, I begin to give up on hearing from her at all. Just as I toss the phone down onto the bed and prepare to get up, it goes off again and it takes everything in me not to dive back on the bed and grab it.

Man, can I be more of a girl right now?

I smile when I see her response on the screen. It's not a song I have, but it's one that I can most definitely get if that's what it takes.

"A Beautiful Lie" by 30 Seconds To Mars

Before I can type her back a response, the generic ringtone goes off and I'm met with another message from her. It occurs to me as I read it over, that this might be the best thing I ever did. As okay as I am with the notebook, having her able to text me this way is even better. From now on this might be the way I need to go.

At least until I can get her to actually open up and speak to me.

Thank you for today Kayden.

I wish she had half a clue what seeing that happy face does for me. I can't quite explain it to myself, but I really wish she could know. It's like when she does it, it's all I can see and I want more of it, especially after the day we've had. I always want her making happy faces.

Even if wanting that makes me sound like a total pussy.

She doesn't have to thank me for what happened, but it's nice that she does. When she walked away from me this morning, I thought for sure I wouldn't get the chance to make things right with her. As horrible as what happened is, it did give me the chance to do the right thing, something I'm not the most familiar with, but I just have to do with her.

Isabelle deserves the right thing, even if the right thing isn't me.

Ur welcome.

I pause before sending the text, not sure I like it the way it is. I want to say more, but I don't have a clue what more there is to say. I just know I don't want this to end. I like the way I feel, the way I am when she's talking to me, whether it's in text or writing in her notebook the way she does. I don't feel like such a fuck up.

Knowing exactly what I want to text now that I've thought it through, I type it all out and hit send before I have the chance to regret it and erase it. This time though, I'm not going to stick around and wait for the response. No, I'm going to walk away and deal with the fallout with Dean. If I stay here waiting for a response and none comes, I'm not sure I'm going to want to step foot out of my room again, that's how much her and the silly emotes have gotten to me.

Holy shit.

I'm falling for Isabelle.

Chapter Eleven

Belle

Ur welcome. Can I drive u to school tomorrow?

It's been a week since he sent that text to me and I still haven't deleted it off my phone. I don't know why I kept it or even why seeing it a week later still makes me so happy, it just does. He's sent me the same text every single night for the last week, asking if he can take me to school, yet I don't save any of the other ones.

Only this one.

The day after Amy and her friends hurt me, I didn't go to school. I talked to my mom, told her everything, she bandaged the spot where they placed the cigarette to my arm and called the school board about it. Even after she took care of it, I still didn't feel strong enough to go back.

The day after, I thought he wouldn't want anything to do with me. Since my mom called the board, Amy, Charlotte and Eve had been suspended and even though he helped me, they were still his friends. It didn't help that I texted him the night before, telling him that he couldn't drive me because I wasn't going. I did it so he wouldn't feel burdened, but there he was the minute the bus pulled up, wearing the same smile he had the day at his house before everything went crazy.

Not only did he walk me to Ms. Taylor's class that day and every other one after, but he was also there waiting for me when it ended, taking me outside to the tree and sitting under it with me. I'm pretty sure he hated every second of it, with the looks and laughs we got, but he didn't ever make a move to leave.

It hasn't been easy for me coming back. I still hear the whispers in the hall even though Kayden does his best to shield me from it. I see the way people look at us, wondering what the hell he's doing with the school retard. By the end of the week I'm waiting for him to crack, give up on what he's been doing, but he never does.

The way he is only makes me want to talk to him more. Not texting the way we have been, but actual talking. I want to be able to open my mouth and have words come out, the way I did in the bathroom, but no matter how hard I try, I'm still not there yet. He seems to understand because he doesn't push me. He just points to the phone and smiles.

Despite everything that I see and hear going on around us, this is probably the happiest I've ever been in my life.

The only problem is, my mom doesn't know about any of it. I come home from school every day and we talk, so she can see that I'm doing alright, but I never bring up the reason for it. I just talk to her about what Ms. Taylor has us doing or what Tristan has been telling me when we've hung out and leave it at that until I go to bed. I'm not sure why I don't tell her. It's not like she hates him. She used to talk about him a lot, especially after his mom took off and then occasionally over the years. She feels a lot where he's concerned and would probably understand everything easily, but I just can't bring it up.

I want to keep it to myself for a little while longer.

There's something different about him today. He seems nervous about something. Whenever I catch myself staring at him, I take in the way he moves and acts and it's obvious something isn't right. I want to ask him about it, but with how good everything's been, I'm scared of making it worse. The last thing I want after the week I've had is for him to go running in the other direction.

Just as I finish packing up my stuff and get ready to meet him in the hall, keeping to the exact same routine we've been doing all week, my phone goes off. Stopping by the door and ignoring the look Ms. Taylor is giving me, her eyebrows raised and the hint of a smile on her lips, I pull out my phone and see his name at the top of my screen.

God, how badly I want to smile at this. It's been so long since I've done it that I'm not even sure my cheek muscles can handle it anymore. They might be stuck this way forever, the same way your tongue gets stuck to a frozen pole. That's what happened to the guy in A Christmas Story anyway.

Can you meet me in the parking lot? I want to show u something off campus.

He knows how I feel about routines. How much I need them in order to feel okay. He's actually been going out of his way this week to make sure we stick to it, so this change is unsettling to me.

As much as I don't want to focus on the past, it's hard not to remember the last time I went into the parking lot alone. Sure, it all brought me to now, with Kayden spending every spare minute he has with me, but it still doesn't change the fear I have inside about going out there again. When he's with me, I don't have to feel afraid, but to take the steps on my own, well, I'm not quite sure I can handle it.

I don't know…

His response is immediate.

Trust me Belle. I won't let anyone hurt u.

Okay…

I make my way to my locker, all the while checking around me, making sure that no one's around. Once I've grabbed my lunch, I slam my door shut and prepare to make my way out to meet him. It's only as I make my way past the office, a few steps away from the door that I see him.

Dillon.

The look on his face is as evil as always. Some book I read the other day says the devil can walk around among us and I swear if it's true, Dillon is the devil because the only thing I want to do when I'm within a foot of him, is run in the other direction.

Why did Kayden have to pick today to want to do something different?

As I do my best to ignore him, making my way past him to the doors that will take me to his friend, I hear my name and my heart freezes in my chest, the same way my feet do.

My phone chooses that second to go off and looking down at it, I see that again, it's Kayden.

I can see u. Hurry up.

Typing as quickly as I can manage, I press send and hope that he gets it quickly. Sometimes when we're texting, the messages we send don't go through and this is definitely not the time for that to happen. I need him.

Pls come inside. Help.

I don't breathe the entire time I stand there, at least not until I hear the familiar tone and look down and see his response.

Omw.

It's stupid, but with the way everything's been since that day, I've felt more confident moving through the halls, even with the looks. All of that can change though and as I turn and face the guy that called my name, I realize that if he keeps looking at me the way he is, it's most definitely going to change.

"I'm not gonna hurt you, Isabelle. I just wanted to say sorry."

He's kidding right?

I shake my head, not wanting to hear the lie and he takes a step toward me. My body, frozen in place, can't even move to step backward.

Where's Kayden?

"I know you don't believe me, but I swear to you. I am sorry. Amy and the others took it too far and I've lost my best friend because of it."

I don't want to believe a word he's saying, but there's this look in his eyes that makes me feel something other than fear. I feel bad for him. Kayden has been spending a lot of time with me, barely hanging out with the other guys anymore, so maybe there is some truth in what he's saying. Maybe he does want to do the right thing.

I can't respond to him, at least not in a way he'll understand. It's one thing for me to nod my head at Kayden or even the teachers and have them understand because they're used to it, but with Dillon, he won't get it.

"I know you called him since I see him running, but I really hope sometime we can sit down and talk. I want to make things right."

He turns his back to me and I'm finally able to breathe again. Sucking in as much air as I possibly can, I turn and run straight into the very guy I'd been waiting on seconds before.

"I got you. Are you okay?" he asks, his voice barely above a whisper, so only I can hear him, his eyes leveled in the opposite direction. They're full of the anger I've come to see is second nature in him and it's all directed at his best friend.

I nod my head and he tightens his hold on me.

"Let's go then. You can tell me about this in the car."

He turns his body, fully prepared to pull me along with him, but before we can take the few steps it would take to make it outside, Dillon speaks again.

"I'm gonna make this shit right, K, even if you don't want me to."

Kayden

Two weeks ago if you asked me if I would've run to the rescue of a girl when she texted me the word help, I would have laughed at you. Hell, it didn't even have to be Isabelle. I'm just not the guy that drops whatever he's doing and runs like a knight in shining armor, but the minute I got her text that's exactly what I did.

If I moved half as fast on the football field, I know for a fact that Dillon wouldn't be the QB. I would have kicked him out of the spot ages ago. It amazed me how fast I jumped out of my car, not giving a shit that the keys were still inside and booked it across the front lawn.

I knew there was something wrong the minute I saw her appear at the front of the school yet she made no move to come outside. Add that she texted me the short form of please, which she never does and there is nowhere else I needed to be. Screw the car; let someone steal it for all I cared. I just had to get to her.

Dillon being that close to her tore me apart. I've been doing everything in my power to keep them all away from her. The last thing she needs after being tortured and burned by these people is another go round. Sure, Amy and the others were suspended, but it all came back to Dillon. I have no doubt that they want another shot at her for getting caught and I wasn't willing to give it to them.

He needs to stay far away from her or what happened in the parking lot a little over a week ago would look tame. He already deserves so much more.

What he said before I got her out of there makes me sick. Him making things right is bullshit. I don't know what his game is, but I swear I'll find out before he gets to accomplish it. He will not get within a foot of Isabelle while I still have breath in my lungs. He never does anything without an ulterior motive and I'm damn sure this time is no different.

The problem is, I think she believes him. She hasn't said a whole lot since we got in the car, but I can tell something's off. She didn't look as afraid of him when I got there as I expected, which meant that whatever he said got through to her.

I want her to tell me. Hell, I want her to open her mouth and say anything right now, but I know that's impossible. I know she can talk, she told me that much one night when we were texting. There's just something that prevents her from doing it at school and especially around me. I want to find out what it is though because I want to fix it.

I've only heard her say three things but every single time, I liked the sound of it. When she yelled at us when we had Eric strung up, I didn't like the tone because it didn't seem right coming from her, but I did like the sound. My favorite might be when she said my name that first day though. I just can't tell her that. She's already under enough pressure to talk to me. I don't need to make it worse.

What did you want to show me?

The minute she puts the notebook down, I see her familiar scrawl and smile. Isabelle does a lot of different things I can't entirely figure out or understand, but this is one thing I did get. She didn't waste time with small talk when she wanted answers. She got right to the point.

"I wanted to take you off campus for lunch." I answer knowing it's not the answer she's looking for, but not wanting to give too much away. "I even cleared it with the office and everything."

Isabelle and some of the others in her class; they aren't allowed to go off campus for lunch. At least not without having it cleared through a million different channels first. I know about it because I've seen it happen before. My memory might not be the best, but I'm glad in this instance it didn't fail me because the minute I dropped her off this morning, I started the channel ball rolling.

So where are you taking me?

"Well if I tell ya that, it'll ruin the surprise. So just sit back, get comfortable and enjoy."

It's calculated and well thought out what I do next, but the minute I do it, I know it's the right move. Turning on the stereo and turning the volume up just enough for her to still be able to hear me reply if she writes, I scroll through my iPod until I find the right music. The minute the band starts playing; I look across and I'm met with the best reaction.

She closes her eyes instantly and leans back in the seat. I want to know exactly what she's thinking about as she's doing it, but saying anything now would ruin the moment. So turning back to the road, I pull out of the parking lot, my mind now focused on getting us to our destination.

107 | P a g e

I thought about this a lot last night while Dean was throwing another party. He did it twice a week like clockwork and with the music blaring loud outside my door, Isabelle texting me back and forth; the idea took form in my mind.

With the way she sits under the tree every day for lunch, I thought she would like it if we went to Wexfield Memorial Park. I haven't been there since I used to ride my bike on the trails, but the place is filled with trees, like the one she sits under and since it hasn't gotten too cold yet, it's the perfect time to go. Well, other than summer.

It's actually kind of selfish what I'm doing.

I used to do this kind of thing with my mom when I was little. She would take me out there and we'd sit under the trees and watch the leaves fall. She used to love being surrounded by all the colors. I don't have a lot of good memories with my mom, but this is one of them. Up until recently, there wasn't another human being alive I wanted to share it with.

It's stupid and probably a little gross, but she reminds me of my mom, at least in the way she seems to enjoy her time outside. That's why she's the only one I can do this with.

When we finally get there and I put the car in park, she opens her eyes and takes it all in. This is one of the times I wish she smiled, because I swear right now she wants to. I might be a total asshole when it comes to girls, well an asshole when it comes to everyone really, but I can tell right now I've done something right.

She starts fiddling with the paper and I watch as she scribbles fast across the page. With as fast as she's going, she's almost matching the beat of my heart with the eagerness I have to read what she's writing me.

You want to have lunch with me at the park?

"I do. I know it's not your usual spot, but just over the bend there," I say pointing out the windshield to what I'm talking about. "Are a whole lot of those same trees."

It takes her no time at all to write back this time and when I read the response as she unfastens her seatbelt and opens the door, I can't help but laugh. Yeah, I definitely did the right thing bringing her here.

Well what are you waiting for? Race you!

I give her a minute as I watch her race across the lot until she's on the grass, enjoying her happiness and excitement, something that even though I've known her my whole life, I haven't gotten to see. I want to lose this race if it means that I get to see her this way.

It's the way she should always be.

It's only as I finally get out of the car that I hear the now familiar ringtone go off and stop to check it.

You're slow.

Two words are all it takes and I'm doing it again. Smiling. I swear it's the only thing I'm capable of doing anymore with the way this girl brings it out of me. Typing back a quick message, I put my phone back in my jeans and take off running. It's time to make her pay for that and when I catch her, she's definitely gonna pay.

Chapter Twelve

Belle

This is probably the first time in a long time where I'm really happy.

The way the wind moves through the trees, the smell of the freshly cut grass crunching under my feet as I'm running as fast as I can away from Kayden, his laughter loud and clear as he chases after me. It all makes me happy. It's a breezy day for being early fall but not cold enough to bother me. It's pretty close to perfect.

Starting to feel the burn in my throat as it warns me I need to slow down, I ignore it and push even further ahead. I'm almost all the way to the very place Kayden pointed out from the car and for some reason I want to be the first one there. I might not get to come here as much as I used to, but I remember it well. Mom, Tristan and I came here a lot before, bringing the picnic basket and blankets along. It's some of the best memories I have, at least before everything seemed to get hard.

Right as I reach my destination, I turn around to celebrate and I'm swept up into a pair of strong yet familiar arms, being swung around in the air. I'm not sure what it is, but there's a squeak sound that comes out of my mouth as he swings me. He slows down so my feet touch ground and I immediately try and cover my mouth.

"Don't even think about it."

I'm confused. How does he know what I'm thinking and better yet, what part should I stop thinking about? It's crazy, but just when I start to feel okay around him something like this happens and I'm filled with uncertainty again.

"Isabelle, I just didn't want you covering your mouth."

I still don't get it and it's obvious from the look he's giving me that he knows it.

He moves closer to me and he reaches his hand out to my hair and catching a tendril in his hand, he tucks it behind my ear. His body so close in proximity to mine that I feel the breath escaping through his nose on my face, tickling me. It's only when I reach up to rub at my nose that he catches my fingers and brings them into his own.

I don't know if it's from the run or it's a reaction to him being this close to me, but I can feel the sweat rising not only on my face, but my hands and I'm embarrassed by it. He's holding my hand and is getting sweat on for it. I wait for him to notice and pull his hand away, but after a minute or so of being still with not even an attempt to pull away, I realize I'm over thinking it.

It's been so awkward being around Kayden, especially when we're like this. It's not the contact that spooks me so much. It's the way he is with me. Two weeks ago he didn't even blink in my direction and now it's the complete opposite. I'm not sure how to react to it. As much as I like it, I wonder when he's going to realize that I'm exactly what his friends think I am, get bored and leave me.

"You're frowning. You should know, that isn't allowed here. It's a pretty big rule and you're breaking it."

I'm not sure when the park started making rules, but I definitely don't want to break them. I pull the phone out from my jacket and I text him. If there are more rules I need to know about, he's the only one that can tell me. It's so beautiful here; the last thing I want is to be kicked out before I've gotten to enjoy it.

Are there any more rules I need to know? I don't want to get kicked out.

He laughs and it makes no sense to me. I read over my text and I don't see where I said something funny. It's only when my phone goes off, that it all makes sense.

I was kidding. There are no rules. Well other than making sure that the princess gets home before turning into a pumpkin.

My stomach does this weird flip as I see the emoticon on the screen. In the time we've been texting back and forth he's never once done one, happy, sad or otherwise. Seeing it now makes me feel all tingly. I really wish I understood what this means because it's strange.

"Come on princess, you need to eat. We don't have much time before we gotta head back." He says out loud this time before pulling me closer to the group of trees.

It's only when we're both seated across from each other, our hands no longer together, me already digging into my lunch that the questions start.

I'd been expecting them since he rescued me from school, but considering he went the entire car ride without saying a word; I thought maybe he didn't want to know what happened before he got there. I'm finding out now just how wrong I was.

"What did Dillon say to you before you texted me?"

Putting my canister of soup down carefully on the grass, I text back my response.

Nothing. I texted you before he actually said anything.

"Okay well, what happened after you texted me then?" he pushes and again I pick up the phone and answer him back as quickly as I can, hoping that my answer is good enough so I can finish what's left of the soup. If I don't eat all of it, my mom's going to worry and that's the last thing I want.

That he was sorry and he wanted the chance to talk to me about it.

"Son of a bitch!" he yells which immediately makes me flinch and back away from him. "I'm sorry, Isabelle. I'm not yelling at you. I just don't know what his game is and it's driving me nuts."

For two days after Amy and her friends hurt me, I didn't eat. I couldn't even look at food. The day I spent at home, my mom tried everything to get me to at least try and eat something, but I couldn't. It wasn't just because of what they did to me; it's also because of what I'd seen between Dean and Kayden. It was scary and it tied me up in knots. I hated that Kayden had to live with that, especially after doing something so nice for me.

I went back to school the day after and still wouldn't eat. She made me soup like she always does, but I didn't eat a bit of it. I just let it go lukewarm, then cold in the container. Eventually my appetite came back, but for a little while it looked like I might never eat again.

Talking about Dillon and what happened is bringing that feeling back again. I want the soup so bad I can taste it, but I feel my appetite fading fast. I just don't know if I have it in me to tell him that we need to stop talking.

"Here," he says as he lifts the spoon from the container, holding his other hand underneath it and moving toward me. "Someone needs to eat. I can see it all over her face."

As I accept the spoon into my mouth, I feel a familiar ache in my chest. I'm sure he wasn't intending for it to be anything other than sweet, but if he remembers anything about our time together when we were younger, he has to realize just how close to the way things used to be this is.

I feel like a baby.

"Talk to me, Belle. You went from being so damn happy, to looking like I ran over your cat or something. What's going on?"

Talk to me Belle.

If only it were that easy.

As I start typing to him, I stop because I feel the wetness on my cheeks before I even realize I've done it at all. I'm crying.

"Shit! I keep doing this to you. Belle, I'm sorry!" he says, his voice pleading as he reaches across to me and wraps his hand around my own. "I keep saying shit without thinking about it. Please forgive me?"

I want to text him and tell him he has nothing to be sorry for, that I have no idea why I'm crying and that it doesn't have anything to do with him, but I can't do any of that. The tears keep falling and my eyes are so clouded with them I can't even see my phone, let alone the letters to touch to get the words out.

He pulls me to him and I'm calmed by the beating of his heart through his shirt. It's strong and steady and at certain points it seems to speed up and then slow down again. It sounds like the beat of a drum, the steady rhythm that's happening now. It's only when I attempt to pull away that he stops me, placing both of his hands on my cheeks, his light green eyes locked on my now tear stained blue ones.

It's almost as if time stops in that moment and as much as I want to break the eye contact, unable to handle it, I'm frozen in place. I can't look away; it might actually hurt me to do it.

"Isabelle..." he says his tone calm, the sound of his voice low. "Say you forgive me..."

I know what he wants me to do, but I can't give it to him. Not without completely pulling away and reaching for the phone that somehow dropped when he pulled me to him.

"Screw it." He says, this time his voice crystal clear, but before I can process what he means by it, his lips press to mine and any thought I might have been able to come up with fades away.

At least it does until I remember that I've never done this before and I don't have the first clue what I'm even supposed to do. Our lips are pressed together, neither one of us moving. Just the way it was when we were looking at each other, we seem to be completely locked in place. My eyes are closed as I embrace the tingling sensation that came the minute his lips touched mine. The one I never want to end.

He breaks away, but instead of completely backing away the way I expect him to, he places two more kisses on the corners of my lips and the tingle, along with the scent of whatever cologne he's wearing, mix with the feel of his breath on my skin, making me lightheaded. It's only when he finally backs away that I open my eyes and I'm met again with the intense stare coming from his.

"I—forgive—you."

Kayden

I have no clue what I'm doing. I just know I can't stop.

I brought Isabelle back to school with five minutes to spare, proceeding to walk her to classes before driving her home. We fell back into the same routine, like we didn't just have this monumental shift happen a couple of hours before.

Not only did I do something completely out of character and kiss her, but right after it she spoke to me.

When I told her I was sorry, I meant it. Not thinking as usual, I lost my mind when she mentioned what Dillon said. I'm not sure how, but it seemed to get more messed up after that. All I did was attempt to be cute and feed her some of her food, but tears started falling. I screwed up again.

I could tell she'd never been kissed before. The minute I pressed my lips to hers, it's like she completely froze, but then again, so did I. It wasn't planned, me kissing her, but the way she looked at me, I knew I had to.

Her lips were so damn soft I didn't want to break away from them. I'm not sure what she puts on them, but they are the softest pair of lips I've ever felt before and it's not exactly a secret that I've kissed a lot of girls.

Things got even weirder after that because when I asked her to forgive me, it should have been for making her cry, but it wasn't, not entirely. I was asking her to forgive me for everything. I needed it like I need air to function, that's how important it was to me. I didn't expect her to ever say it out loud. All I wanted was her familiar text and I would have been fine, but I got so much more than that.

The minute the words came out, I went speechless. It's new to me because I normally have a response to everything, but this, no freaking way. She stunned me. It was a turning point for us or at least I think it is, but considering she went back to texting and writing after that, I can't be sure.

I need to go inside, but after dropping her off and driving over here; I can't seem to get out of the car. I don't want anything to ruin the way this day has been for me. I know the minute I get out and go inside, Dean and his stupidity is going to do it.

What I really want to do is drive back across the street, go to her door, knock and when she opens it, pull her to me again. It's so crazy, but it's the one thing that can make this day even better than it has been. She might not have a lot of experience with kissing, but it didn't mean she doesn't have someone dying to teach her.

When she told me that actions needed to speak louder than words, I really did take it to heart. The problem is, now that line is blurred. I still want to prove to her that I can be a better guy, but it's not innocent anymore. I want to do it because I like her. That guy that deep down I don't believe I can be, I want to be for her.

I can't be selfish with this though. I know how timid she is, how all of this must be for her and in order for me to be the person Ms. Taylor thinks I am, I have to do it right. I can't treat her like every other girl I've been with. She's not like other girls because she's different. I want her kind of different.

If I'm serious about being with her, I need to start at the beginning. I need to forget about how amazing her lips felt pressed to mine, the way hearing her speak stopped my heart and focus on what really matters. I need to understand her and change everything that for the last eight years I've believed about her. I need to make right all of the damage I've done.

It all starts with me. I need to learn everything I can. Moving forward with her depends on it.

Chapter Thirteen

Belle

It's strange. When Kayden dropped me off at class this morning, he actually stuck around longer than usual. He didn't do it to talk to me though. He was talking to Ms. Taylor instead.

It didn't last longer then maybe two minutes, but it's all I've been able to think about. I'm trying to focus on the math we're doing, but even my excitement over numbers can't distract me. I need to know what they were talking about. It's going to bother me until I do, I just know it.

I've been like this since Friday, when we kissed and I spoke to him. I can't concentrate on anything but what he thought about it. We haven't brought it up since it happened and I guess that's why I can't let it go. I'm thinking about it so much that it's becoming obsessive. I had to stop myself all weekend from spilling my guts to my mom, that's how much it got to me.

At some point we're gonna have to talk about it, but I don't want to be the one to bring it up. I'm already nervous as it is and I really don't want to know how he feels if it's going to hurt me. Things have been going so well and I just want to keep it that way for as long as I can.

There's something bothering me though. I told him that I forgive him, but haven't been able to say a word since. The way he's been should be enough to get me past this fear I have of speaking, but it doesn't. Maybe Mom's right and it's time to see the speech therapist again. I might not need help with words anymore, but I do need help to find out how to get over the fear I have of actually speaking.

I made the decision over the weekend and I haven't said anything to anyone. As much as I know my mom supports me, I want to do this on my own. She's been so good to me and this, well if I can fix it, is something I want to surprise her with. She deserves something good to happen after everything we've been through. I want to do it for Kayden too, but I'm trying my hardest not to make it about him because I still can't figure out exactly what it is that I feel for him.

Whenever we're together, I feel off kilter, like everything is always spinning. Sometimes he looks at me and I swear my heart flips in my chest or sometimes, even stops. The first couple of times it happened, I thought there was actually something wrong with it, but I'm starting to think it's not my heart and it's just me. Sometimes I sit and watch him while he's talking and just stare at his lips. It's not like I'm expecting them to have some hidden answer for me, but I can't look away.

I want him to kiss me again and every single time I think it, I immediately feel my cheeks get hot, even when we're not together. He sits so close sometimes that I get overwhelmed by the smell of him. It reminds me of the park and even though some scents overwhelm me and bring about bad responses, his doesn't. On top of being obsessive over things with him, I also seem to be addicted.

Is this what it feels like to like someone? Is this what other girls feel when they see a boy they like, spend time with him or even get kissed by him, or is this just another way I'm completely wrong and weird?

"Isabelle, is everything alright?"

It takes me a minute to register but when I do, I feel bad. I'm doing it again. I'm supposed to be focusing on one of the things I'm good at and I'm thinking about him again. My mom called me on it over the weekend too. I seem to start thinking about him and get this dreamy look on my face. If it looks anything like the girls I've seen in movies doing it, it's pathetic. I don't want to be caught looking like that.

"Yes, Ms. Taylor, I'm fine."

I want to say no, I'm not fine and that I won't be fine until she tells me exactly what Kayden talked to her about earlier, but I don't do it. It's really none of my business what they're talking about.

Maybe he finally realized he's better off without me and he's trying to get her help with it. He's been with me for almost two weeks straight now and even though it's the last thing I want to happen, I've been waiting for the day when it would. Maybe now's that time. He's finally figured out how useless I am.

If he wants that, then why did he kiss you three days ago?

Before I can answer myself, I hear Ms. Taylor speak again and the minute she does, my heart starts hammering in my chest. All of this thinking about Kayden has messed with something that before I would have had no problem with.

"Please bring your papers to the front."

My half empty paper stares back at me and I swear if papers could show emotion, this one would be laughing at me. I don't like the way this makes me feel. I'm not supposed to be like this.

It's all Kayden's fault. It's those green eyes and the smile he always seems to have for me. The way he looks after practice when he's still suited up and his hair's all sweaty.

Yeah, it's definitely his fault.

He's screwing everything up for me. As much as I don't understand it, I think I might be falling for him.

Falling for Kayden can't happen. Not when he's the very person that taught me eight years ago exactly what a broken heart feels like.

Kayden

Something's wrong.

She's barely texted anything since I picked her up from class and she won't even look at me. She's not looking at me when I'm looking at her anyway, which I'm doing a lot. I can't seem to take my eyes off her.

I know she's probably wondering what happened earlier when I stopped to talk to her teacher and I really want to tell her, but I can't. I don't have a whole lot of experience with this and even less with asking for help, so the fact that I did it at all says a whole lot about how serious I am about this.

When I said I wanted to start at the beginning, I wasn't lying. I've kept true to my word too. I'm a guy, so of course when I do catch her looking at me, like she did this morning, I can't help the way my body reacts and the urge to kiss her that follows. I'm dealing with it though and so far, I think I've done really well.

We're doing the same routine as always and it's just as easy as it was the first day, but I can tell, for her, it's not going to be that easy. She seems lost and I want to know why. I don't want her thinking that because I can't tell her what I'm doing with Ms. Taylor that I'm keeping things from her or doing something that will hurt her.

"You okay?" I ask, keeping my voice light.

The text comes through instantly as it begins vibrating across the grass in front of me.

Yeah. Why does everyone keep asking me that today?

"Who else asked you?" I question, wondering who else has noticed the strange way she's acting. With Eric not coming within a foot of her since the two of us started hanging out, I have no idea who it could be.

Ms. Taylor. She asked me in class.

Well that makes sense.

"Amy and Charlotte got back today. I guess she's worried, like I am that you're going to have a hard time with it."

I'm not made of glass Kayden.

Yeah, there it is.

I'm not the smartest guy in the world, but even I can tell something's wrong. She never answers me like that, even when I've upset her. I just don't have the first clue how to make her open up about it. I want her to give me a happy face again just so I know that somewhere in her mind, she's okay.

"I know that, but it's a big deal. They hurt you, Belle."

I've been calling her Belle a lot more lately. I like the way it sounds better than her full name. The first few times I did it, there was this weird look in her eye, like maybe I shouldn't have done it. After awhile she stopped giving the look though and I figured everything was alright.

"I know that. Can you please tell me what's wrong? You're acting weird."

The minute the word comes out I know I've chosen the wrong one. I do that a lot with her, but the way her body seems to freeze, I know I've picked the worst possible one this time, well other then calling her a retard, something I won't ever do.

Isabelle doesn't exactly go out of her way to talk about it, but I get the feeling she wants nothing more than to be like everyone else. In fact, the way she looks at some of the other girls in the hall speaks to it. She tries to hide it, but she frowns sometimes when she sees groups of girls talking and laughing, some even talking about guys. She wants to be like them and can't be.

If I'm so weird, why are you still here?

I'm about to tell her exactly why I'm there, words I've never spoken to another human being in my life, let alone another girl, but I stop myself. Now is not the right time for that and besides, we still haven't talked about the kiss we shared the other day, so I have no idea if she even thinks about me that way.

God, this is so frustrating. Every time I think I take steps forward with her, I seem to be pushed right back. I just want her to let me in. If she did that, then maybe we could work together and fix everything she thinks is wrong with her, even though I don't see anything wrong with her at all.

"You really wanna know why I'm here, Isabelle?" I ask using her full name this time, making sure she's aware of how serious I am. She needs to know this isn't a joke to me.

Yes.

"Because you're the only real friend I have."

It's the truth. Maybe it's not exactly what I want to say, but it doesn't make it any less true. She really has become a friend to me. I've got a lot of friends, but with her, it's not because of a position I play on a team or because of the way I look. It's because she actually sees me.

I need to go. I'm sorry Kayden.

I start to get up the minute the text comes through and she holds out her hand to stop me as she gets to her feet. It's only when the next message comes through that I realize why she's stopping me.

Alone. I need to be alone.

For the first time since the day my mom walked out and never came back, I feel it. As I watch her turn and walk away from me, I'm twisted inside and I hate every second of it.

I feel my heart breaking.

Chapter Fourteen

Kayden

"Kayden, I didn't think I was going to see you until later."

When Isabelle took off, I wasn't entirely sure what to do. With as much time as I've been spending with her, I knew I couldn't just get up and find Dillon and the others and honestly, I didn't want to do that anyway. I couldn't stay there under that tree though. The longer I did it, the worse I felt because of just what that stupid tree meant.

It's only right to sit there when she's with me. It never had meaning before I started spending time with her and if she's going to walk away and leave me alone; it was going to go back to being that way. Nothing about staying there felt right without her.

When I dropped Isabelle off and talked to Ms. Taylor, I was actually setting up a time to come see her and talk to her about things. My idea to go back to the start meant that first I had to learn everything I could about Autism. If I want to spend time with Isabelle, I couldn't do it without understanding exactly what it is she goes through. Once I understand, maybe I can change the way it's looked at. Who better to change a bunch of kid's minds then one of the most popular guys in school? Even if lately that social standing is falling apart by the second.

I want to know her, every single thing about her. A lot of that is what she deals with every single day, both the good and the bad. I need to learn all I can about autism and what it really means, so I can move forward with the promise I made myself that day in my car.

"You were, but I've got practice after school today. I should've remembered that before."

"Well, we can do this now." She answers and I smile weakly, thankful she's willing to fit me in. "I hope you don't mind me asking, but where is Isabelle?"

I know I'm here to learn about her, but do I really have to talk about her? I don't want to admit that I upset her again, for what feels like the hundredth time this week and she took off on me. If I do that, Ms. Taylor will see me for the screw up that I am and won't help me.

I can't risk that. I need her help.

"She wanted some time alone. I guess I've been smothering her lately."

"Don't think like that, dear. I've never seen her happy like this before. I think what you're doing is good for her."

What Isabelle has she been seeing, because with the way the one I've been hanging out with has been acting lately, it doesn't seem like I'm making her happy at all. In fact, I think I might be doing the opposite. Ever since the kiss, even though we go through the motions, I can tell things are different.

I screwed up—again.

"Not sure about that Ms. T, but I'm hoping that maybe doing this might help."

"Well, why don't you tell me what you need my help with and I'll see what I can do?" she asks with a smile.

"How much do you actually know about Autism?" I realize it's a stupid question the minute the words come out, but I can't take them back. She's a special needs teacher for crying out loud, she has to know a hell of a lot about it. "Sorry, I mean, what can you tell me about it?"

"It's okay, Kayden. Sometimes teachers get moved around and a lot of times we get placed with students that we don't entirely understand or haven't been informed about. It's okay that you asked it like that. Can I ask why you want to know about autism?"

Well shit, I thought that was pretty obvious lady. I think to myself but don't dare say.

If it wasn't for Isabelle and the way she's been making me see things differently, questioning everything I've ever known or believed, I don't think I would be here at all. I would still be hanging with the same bunch of assholes, doing the same horrible things without a second thought to how she felt.

"I want to understand Isabelle better. I know that there's more to her than just her problems because I've seen it, but in order to know her the way I want to, I think I need to know more about what she actually deals with."

I swear to god, this is the most I've ever said to a teacher in one sitting before. Sure, I talk to Coach a lot, but definitely not like this. It's mostly back and forth and always about sports. I'm doing something new right now and I'm not entirely sure how I feel about it. It's strange.

"Honestly, I figured it had to do with her. I just wanted to see if you would tell me."

She laughs and I smile weakly back at her. Who knew teachers had sense of humors?

"Isabelle has what the medical professionals call High Functioning Autism. As I'm sure you've seen, there are some weaknesses, but for every weakness she has, she has double it in strengths."

"Is her inability to speak one of those weaknesses?" I ask, needing to know the answer. It's not the most important thing to me, but it does rank pretty high.

"Yes, in a way it does have to do with it, but Isabelle is a bit of an anomaly in that regard it seems."

"What does that mean exactly?"

"Isabelle struggled with speech for a very large part of her childhood. She eventually came into her own with the help of speech therapy, but it doesn't mean that she doesn't struggle to this day. What I was getting at is, with Isabelle, there's also a fear that seems to trigger her silence. So I do not believe her inability to speak in a social setting is autism related, at least not entirely."

"What can cause her to be like this? Is it because of everything people have said and done to her?"

"It could be, but from what I've seen, she's been struggling with this for some time. Her mother and I have spoken about it and it appears as though there is more to it then bullying, though I can't say that what's been done to her has helped in the slightest."

She levels me with this look and I know it's a dig at me. I used to be one of the worst offenders where she's concerned and the teachers know it. I'm the reason everything's gotten this bad with her. I don't need to be reminded. It's just fact.

"What else can you tell me about her?"

"Well, I can sit here and tell you everything that I'm sure you already know, but I don't believe that will help you. So I'll tell you things that you probably don't know. She loves anything to do with math. Well, I can't say that she loves math, but she loves the numbers. She's got an amazing visual memory and just seeing a problem on the board, she can work it out easily in her head."

"You're aware of her penchant for writing as I have already shown you. She also likes to draw, but it was like pulling teeth to learn that one."

Doing this was definitely the right thing. I'm learning so much about her just in the little bit that Ms. Taylor is telling me that I feel closer to her then I did before. I hate to admit it, but with as long as I spent believing that because she didn't talk, she was actually stupid, I'm shocked to learn how smart she really is.

"If someone needed help in math, could they get help from her?" I ask stupidly, but selfishly at the same time. I've hated math since the second grade and it's only gotten harder for me as the years went on. If she could help, it would be awesome.

"She has the knowledge to help college students, Kayden, so of course one could go to her for help. It's a sad reality that because of her issues in speech that most won't."

She's right about that. We all believe her to be defective and considering her other issues, we're afraid to get up close and personal with her or that's how it used to be, at least for me.

"What are some of her struggles? I mean I know some, like her accidents and the speech thing, even her aversion to loud noises and yelling, but what else is there?"

"She has sensory issues as it relates to certain surroundings and struggles as it pertains to food textures. I'm not sure if you've ever come across this since the two of you have gotten close, but when she enters a room where there are a lot of things and/or people that she isn't used to, she tends to meltdown."

I've seen that. My mind flashes to the way she was in the bathroom the day I found her and my stomach turns. There wasn't all that much in there to be stimulated by, but I have no doubt that she was broken then. It's all I have to go on.

"When she has what they call a meltdown, she reacts, but it's not in the way you or I would. She will hit herself, she will cry and as you are aware, she will lose control of her bodily functions. It is like her entire body just shuts down, or breaks. She has learned quite a few coping strategies over the years, but sometimes, depending how far into one of the episodes she is, they may not work in time."

I remember a little of the way she used to be when we were kids and I remember her hitting herself. I just assumed it was because she was frustrated. It's something about her I never found weird because I did the same thing when I used to get really pissed off.

"What you need to remember most, Kayden, is that she isn't what people believe her to be. I know I used the word break earlier, but she is not broken. She is not defective and she most definitely isn't retarded, slow or stupid. She is just different. She is uniquely Isabelle."

"I know that, Ms. T. I think I'm the only one besides you that gets it. I just think that maybe I learned a little too late. I can't seem to do anything right with her."

"Would you like to know a secret?"

"Sure, I guess."

"Today when she should have been doing her math, I caught her doing something out of character. It was actually the first time I have ever seen her do it."

"What was she doing?" I ask, more curious to know now then when she first brought it up. When I leave her here every day, I have no idea how she acts, but it looks like I'm about to get a bird's eye view and I can't wait.

"She had her head leaning on her hand and this glazed over look in her eye and no matter how old you get, you always know what that look means. Add that to her being angled toward the door and it was pretty easy to see what was going on."

"I still don't get it."

"Boys, I swear." She laughs. "Kayden dear, she was completely lost in thought and I'm willing to bet my salary I know the very reason for it. He's standing in front of me now."

Me.

If what Ms. Taylor says is true then Isabelle was blowing off something she loves because she was thinking about me. It's all the information I need. I got what I came for. Whether she realizes it or not, the teacher just made everything clear for me.

I know what I have to do now.

It's time to make Isabelle mine.

Belle

This is what life with me is like.

If I could speak, I would've warned him about the way I am, but because I can barely get my own thoughts straight when I'm with him, of course it's impossible to talk to him. He didn't even do anything wrong this time, not really. All he did is ask why I was acting weird and that's all it took.

I felt the panic rising in me just with the sound of the word. I know I'm acting irrationally, but I've spent the last ten years being called weird and names that are even worse, so even the most basic use of the word gets to me. He wasn't literally calling me weird and deep down I know that, but I couldn't stick around and explain it to him.

The truth is, I don't want him to see me this way. He's already seen me at my worst, but this, after the almost two weeks we've had hanging out with each other, well it's embarrassing and I don't want him to have to deal with it. I've gotten better lately. I thought I was stronger, but this just goes to show that I'm not strong at all.

I'm still a weak, waste of space.

It's not only the fact that he called me weird that's bothering me. It's what he says before I have to bolt that cuts even deeper. With everything I've been realizing about the way I react to him, I wanted him to say something more than he did. It's stupid of course, but I like him and it's the first time I can remember really liking anyone, so I just wanted it to mean something to him.

That's my fault though. He kissed me and I just went back to the way things always are with us. I didn't bother trying to tell him how much it means to me. How much he means to me. If I could just open my mouth and speak to him like every other girl in the school maybe none of this would be happening now.

I wouldn't have run from him.

Kayden has no idea, but I really liked him when we were younger. I don't mean that I liked him in the boyfriend way, but he was my best friend. I loved it when he would come to visit, even after his mom took off. He would still come over and play with me despite knowing how different I am. I always wondered if he would still visit if his mom didn't make him and he'd proven himself. At least he had until he turned ten and everything changed.

He stopped coming around and even went out of his way to avoid me altogether. It was like our time together as kids completely vanished and he didn't even know me anymore. He broke my heart when he did that, but he has no idea because I've never told anyone. The same thing happened again when he said I was his friend, even though that's exactly what I've wanted so badly for years.

Kayden, as my best friend.

Now it seems I want more though, so I'm sitting in the bathroom stall again. The only thing missing is the girls, cigarettes and a whole lot of yelling.

I want to cry and I can't. It's like all the tears I've spent the last ten years letting spill have finally dried up and there's nothing left. I'm not sure if I'm happy about that or not. All I know is, I'm more alone then I've ever been and all I want is to cry it out until it's gone.

The door opens and I tense. He was right earlier when he said that Amy and the others were back and the last thing I need is to run into them. Until now, Kayden has done a great job keeping me protected, but I ruined that when I walked away from him. He didn't follow me which means that anything that happens now, I'm on my own for.

Bringing my feet up off the floor, I pull them into me and I hold my breath, praying that it's not the mean girls on the other side of the stall. I'll wait them out and hopefully they'll think no one is here and leave when they're done. I want it that way so badly because I don't think I'm completely over what happened two weeks ago, though I've tried my best to act like I am.

"Isabelle?"

It's not the girls, but it's not much better. I know that voice. He's the reason I'm like this at all. Well, part of it. Doesn't he know I just want to be left alone? Hasn't he done enough already?

"I know you're in there. I saw you run in a few minutes ago and I waited for you to come out."

Searching my pockets for my phone, I sigh when I can't find it. I know I took it with me when I left Kayden, so where is it? He might not like me much right now, but I know he would come if I needed him. He's proven that to me over the last two weeks.

"Isabelle, I'm not gonna hurt you. I just want to talk."

Dillon Murphy. From what Kayden told me he's the one that got Amy and the others to come after me that day. He wasn't happy with everything he said to me, so he sent the girls to finish me off. That's another thing that Kayden doesn't know about. Exactly what Dillon said to me. He doesn't even know he talked to me at all.

His tone of voice though, it's the same as it was Friday before Kayden came to my rescue. As much as I don't want to open the door, prepared to stay in here forever if I have to, I know that I'm going to do it because until I get it over with, this is just going to keep happening.

It's only when I take a few tentative steps out that I see him leaning up against the wall. I expected him to be smiling, acting like his normal self, but he's anything but. He looks sad, which only makes the struggle I had even opening the door to come out even worse.

"I saw you in Science the other day, you were writing to your lab partner with a pad. I hope it's okay that I brought this."

Sure enough, in his hands is a tiny notebook, smaller than the one that Kayden had in his car. Attached is a pen, again different than Kayden's.

Why do I have to keep comparing everything to Kayden? This isn't him, it's Dillon.

He extends the pad to me and moving around me he goes to the door. My heart begins to speed up as I realize that if he does what I think he's going to do, I'm gonna be locked in here with no way out.

He'll have me caged in.

"I'm just gonna lock it for privacy, I swear. If you want to leave at any point, just tell me and I'll unlock it."

Before he even finishes his explanation, I've already written out what I want to ask him first. I can't handle the way he's acting and I need answers.

What are you being so nice to me?

"Because what happened to you was wrong and I want to make it up to you."

Why now?

"I told you the other day. I miss my best friend."

That's all?

"No it's not all. Isabelle, I practically run this school. People expect me to act a certain way so I do it. Amy was actually the one that chose you that day in the parking lot. I went along with it because I have a rep I need to maintain. I feel like shit about it. All of it."

That's great for you. Are you done now?

"I guess I am. I just wanted to tell you that I'm sorry and I won't do it anymore. I'll make sure the others leave you alone too."

Right now I'm seeing Dillon in a way that he's never been. He does seem to be sorry and wants to make up for it. His face looks pained and as much as I want to believe he's just playing me again, I don't. I think he means every word of what he's saying.

Thank you.

"Don't thank me. I don't deserve it."

You're going to tell your friends to leave me alone, so you should be thanked.

"If you say so. Look, I know I don't have the right to ask you for anything, but do you think you can talk to Kayden for me? I really do miss hanging with him."

This is where he loses me. He's on the football team with Kayden and they have practice tonight, Kayden warned me about it last night before we stopped texting. If he really misses his friend that much, why can't he talk to him at practice? Why does he want me to do it?

Why don't you just do it at practice later?

"Because you're probably going to see him first and it might sound better coming from you considering everything I did."

Well I can't come up with anything to say back to that, so I let my eyes stray off him and over to the door. A move he catches because he steps toward the door and unlocks it.

"I told you I would let you go when you wanted to leave. I meant what I said, Isabelle. I really am sorry."

I write one final message before making my way past him and through the door. Turning around once I'm back in the security of the hallway, I press the notebook to his chest and hope he gets the message.

I'm going to talk to Kayden.

Kayden

The last thing I expect to see when I round the corner is Isabelle standing directly in front of public enemy number one.

What the hell she's doing with Dillon is beyond me, but unlike the other day when she had to text me to help; she wouldn't have to wait this time. I was more than ready for him this time. Him and whatever sick game he's playing.

"There you are!" I call, coming up and wrapping my arms around her, hopefully making my position known to the asshole standing across from her. He might be trying to make Isabelle believe he's sorry, but I knew better. This kind of leopard never changes his spots.

Dillon would always be running a scam; it's what made him and Dean so alike. They were both snakes.

Taking my feelings completely out of it, what we did to these kids for the last four years was wrong on every level imaginable. We tortured them thinking it was fun. Sure, I don't want that happening to Isabelle because of the way I feel about her, but it doesn't mean I'm gonna stand by and let it happen to anyone else.

At some point we all have to grow up. Sure, high school might be the best years of our lives the way people say, but once that's over what are we gonna have? An old football career if we don't play college ball and a whole lot of broken people on our conscience. I don't want that.

Maybe there's hope for me after all.

"Are you okay?" I whisper and she nods her head. I look up to see Dillon watching us and I'm just waiting for him to make some crack or even smile. I'm more than a little ready to pound on him again. It's only because of the petite blonde in front of me that it hasn't happened yet. I refuse to let her see me like that.

"See you around, Isabelle and thanks." He says before turning and jogging the opposite way from where I'd come. It takes everything in me not to run after him considering even being in the same space makes me want to hit him, but Isabelle shifts under the weight of my arms and again, I'm focused solely on her.

Whatever's gonna happen between me and Dillon is gonna have to wait until I see him later. Until then, I have a girl in front of me that again, I need to apologize to. I don't think she was expecting me to show up and go all caveman the way I did.

"I was looking for you." I say as I remove my arms from around her. When she doesn't make any attempt to pull out her phone to answer me, it worries me. Is she still upset with me for what happened at lunch or is there something more going on?

"Isabelle, about earlier...I'm sorry. I'm not sure what I said, but I know I said something. I'm sorry for whatever it is."

She doesn't answer me or even move, though her eyes are frantic. There's something she's trying to tell me or that I should just know and I don't. It's times like this I really wish she spoke. Not being able to connect with her was going to drive both of us insane fast.

"Where's your phone?"

She shrugs and now I know why she's not answering. Needing to talk to her, I take her hand in mine and head for the nearest classroom. We've got maybe five minutes before we both need to be in our afternoon classes, so I've got to get her to talk quick.

Grabbing a piece of paper off the teacher's desk and a pen from the holder, I hand it to her and pray she'll talk. I'm not sure what happened earlier is healed and I don't want to imagine how it's going to feel if she doesn't answer me right now.

"What did Dillon want?"

She leans over the desk to write and even though I feel bad for doing it, I watch her body as she does. Her shirt lifts just a little as she's bending over and whether she's aware of it or not, her lower back is exposed. I've spent the last eight years ignoring this girl, but one small view of her back and it's putting my body into overdrive.

I've never wanted to kiss someone there so much in my life.

She lifts herself up and hands me the paper and before she can catch me ogling her, I shift my eyes back up, though with the heat on my face, I'm pretty sure she can tell I did something I shouldn't have.

What is it about this girl that makes me act this stupid?

He wanted to talk and say sorry. He misses you and wishes that you two could be friends again. I told him that I would talk to you. I believe him Kayden. I think you two should talk.

As much as I care about her, I hate that she's this gullible. Doesn't she realize that Dillon will say and act any damn way he needs to in order to get close to her again?

I would have done the exact same thing. Hell, I would have cried if it meant getting the girl to believe me.

"He's full of shit. He's just doing this to get to me."

If I didn't see it happen I wouldn't have believed it, but she rolled her eyes at me. If it wasn't such a serious conversation I would've laughed. She's not all that different from the other girls. The difference is, when others girl do it, it's annoying. With Isabelle, it's kind of awesome.

"I know that you want to believe him, babe. I do. Dillon is like that. He will say and do whatever he needs to in order to get what he wants. I won't tell you what to do, but please, if you're ever alone with him again, promise me you'll be careful?"

She nods and I exhale the breath I've been holding. That wasn't even what I intended to say, but now that it's out there; it was the smartest thing to say. Isabelle has been treated differently her entire life, having people making decisions for her and telling her what she needs to do. I'm not even sure she knows how to make a choice for herself. I want to be the one to do that for her.

"You ready to go to class?" I ask and before I know it, she's lacing her fingers through mine and nodding her answer.

The only thought I'm left with as I finally come to terms with exactly what she's done and we make our way to our classes is so simple, yet hard at the same time.

I am so in love with this girl.

Chapter Fifteen

Belle

This makes no sense at all.

I'm standing outside the office, after being handed my phone and even though I'm happy I've got it back, I don't even know how it could have gotten lost to begin with. I had it with me when I walked away from Kayden at lunch and I know I didn't put it down anywhere. I might be different from everyone else, but when it comes to my phone, I'm the same. I don't let it out of my sight.

How did it end up in the office and who found it?

I should just be thankful it's been found, but it worries me. Up until last year I didn't even have a phone. I don't know a whole lot about it yet, so everything I've ever said or done is still on it. I don't delete anything. Even though our conversations are innocent, someone finding out that I've been talking to Kayden and exactly what we're saying to each other scares me.

I don't want anyone knowing that. It's only for me.

"Here you are!"

I spin around at the sound, not even realizing that I'm not alone anymore. I'm met with a concerned pair of green eyes, ones that considering what time it is, I didn't expect to see again until tomorrow. He's supposed to be on the field for practice soon, so what's he doing standing in the hallway with me?

"What are you doing here?"

I pull my phone from my pocket and hold it up to him in explanation. Now it's his turn to share, because not only do I need to be outside in five minutes to catch my bus, but he has to be on the field.

This is something I do a lot. I'm good with details. No one can beat my ability to memorize and remember.

"I gotta get to practice, but I wanted to make sure you got to the bus."

My phone still in my hand, I unlock the screen and start typing. A nod or a shake of my head won't do.

You don't have to do that.

"I know I don't, but I wanted to. I also have something I want to ask you."

Okay.

"Can you meet me after practice? I usually get done here around six or so."

I don't know to answer this. In the last two weeks, the only time we've actually hung out together has been at school. Well, other than the one time we went to his house, but I don't count that. We didn't spend any time alone. It's always just been texting back and forth at night.

I'm not sure I want that to change, especially since I haven't even told my mom about any of it.

I don't know if that's a good idea.

"Please? It doesn't have to be for long, but I really want to see you after practice."

Why did he have to go and say it like that? The way he says please softens me and I know I'm going to say yes, even though I don't know how I'm going to make it all work yet. I want to see him too. At least if the way my stomach is reacting is any indication.

Okay. Not for long though.

"I swear it won't be long."

Before I can think of a response he's closed the gap of space between us and his lips are pressed to my forehead. Anything I might have come up with to say goes out the window. All I can feel is the warmth of his lips on my skin. Why is it that every time he gets close to me I can't seem to think straight?

It's like there are a bunch of mice running around inside of my tummy and no matter what I do, I can't seem to get them to stop.

"See ya in a few hours, princess." He says as he backs away. It's only when he turns away from me and makes his way back down the hall that the scurrying feeling in my stomach stops and I feel okay again.

Now I just need to figure out how I'm gonna make all this work. After what just happened, there's no way I'm missing out on seeing him tonight. In fact it's pretty much all I want to do now that he's brought it up. There's one way I can do it, but it means doing something I'm not exactly looking forward to.

Telling my mom everything.

Kayden

As I make my way into the locker room to suit up for practice, I feel like I'm on cloud nine. There isn't anything that can get to me now, not even the eyes I'm getting from Dillon the minute I open the locker door. I'm so damn happy that I'm pretty sure I'm wearing the world's goofiest damn smile, but I honestly couldn't care less.

She said yes.

With everything I learned today and what I already knew, but wasn't ready to admit to, I knew what I had to do next. I care about her and now I know she feels the same way. Sure, Ms. T warned me that she might not understand what she's feeling because it's another one of her weaknesses, but she still felt it and that's all I need to know.

I can get there with everything else. I've got all the time in the world, especially with her.

It's kind of crazy because with anyone else I would have never acted like this. Understanding is just not something I do. Of course with everyone else, they lay their shit out easily so there's no confusion about how they feel about me. With Isabelle though, I want to take everything slow and do it right because she deserves that.

"Someone's happy."

"Yeah, I am." I shoot back. As much as I can't stand the sound of his voice, I'm not going to sit here and pretend I don't hear him. "What's it to you?"

"Chill man, I didn't mean it in a bad way. It's nice."

Is he serious? Since when is me being happy nice for him?

"Yeah, it's pretty damn nice."

"Is it 'cause of Belle?"

He has no right to ask me that, or even say her name, especially the way he is. I'm trying to stay chill about everything, but the way he says it gets under my skin. It took me weeks to say her name that way and for her to be okay with it, there is no way he should get to so easily.

"Actually, it's Isabelle and yeah, it's because of her. Not that it's any of your business."

"So that means she didn't talk to you then?"

"She talked to me."

It's true. She told me earlier what she thinks, but I'm not buying into it and a few words in the locker room isn't gonna change it. He might make you believe that he's different and can be a good person, but he will never change. He's too damn good at being who he is.

I should know. I trained him to be that way.

"Then she told you that I'm sorry right? That I miss hanging out with you?"

"Yeah, something like that."

"So can we get past this? It really is bullshit, K."

It might be bullshit for him, but it would never be that way to me. The way things used to be doesn't work for me now, which means I don't think I can ever be friends with him again.

"What you did is bullshit. The way you put Amy and the other bitches on her is bullshit, but the way I'm reacting isn't."

"What else can I say to you? I went to her, told her I was sorry and exactly why I was sorry. What else do you want?"

"This conversation to end."

I know I'm being a total douche to him, but he more than earned it. I'm here to play ball, that's it. I don't want to sit here with Dillon and hash out everything that's happened or why I'm not cool with it anymore. I just want him to shut the hell up so I can finish getting ready and get the hell out on the field.

"If the girl I hurt can forgive me for what happened, why can't you?"

He doesn't say another word after that and with the sound of the door banging shut; I know he's not even sticking around to hear the answer. As much as I don't want him getting to me, I can't help it. I know the answer to the question, but I'm not exactly in the mood to admit it out loud.

I can't forgive Dillon the way he claims Isabelle has for a couple of reasons. One, I know who he really is and I know he's not trying to be a better guy. He's just trying to play a part. He's one of the best actors I know. The second reason though, that's the one that's hard to live with.

The real reason I can't forgive Dillon, is if I forgive him then I have to at some point forgive myself for putting all of this in motion to begin with. I might not have been the one to pick her out in the beginning, but I didn't do a damn thing to stop it once it started.

Isabelle might have forgiven us both for the horrible things we've done and that's really great, but he doesn't deserve it and deep down, I don't think I do either.

Chapter Sixteen

Belle

"Belle honey, you've barely touched your dinner. Does the girl's being back at school have something to do with it?"

I've been doing this since she got home and I should've known that she was going to notice eventually. I've been trying to work up the courage to talk to her about everything I've been going through, but every single time I feel like I'm getting close to doing it, I find a reason to stop.

As much as I say that I'm gonna be okay with however she reacts to everything I tell her, I'm not. If she tells me that I need to stay away from Kayden, especially with everything he's done for me the past couple of weeks, I think I might die inside. She knows Kayden, so she probably won't say that, but it's been a really long time since he spent any time with our family.

"No, Mom."

"Well then what's on your mind, and don't tell me it's nothing."

Now's my chance to open up, but with Tristan sitting across the table from me, his eyes darting back and forth between us, it's not like I'm dying to open up.

"I can't talk about it right now."

I raise my eyes in my brother's direction and she seems to take the hint easily.

"Tristan honey, you've been done your dinner for fifteen minutes now. Why aren't you asking to be excused?"

"Because I got something I wanna show Isabelle."

"If I promise to send her up to your room the minute we're done, will you give your sister and me some privacy?"

My mom's real big on giving us choices. At any point he can tell her no and she'll just postpone our conversation until he's out of ear shot. It's the way it's always been here. Even with everything she's been through with me, she still gives me a choice, even when it's something small and basic like the one she's giving Tristan now.

"I guess, but you better make sure she comes up because it's super important."

He excuses himself from the table as she laughs and again it feels like there's a spotlight being flashed on me. We're alone, so there's nothing stopping me. I still don't know how I feel about it though.

"The last couple of weeks, there's something different about you. I know you think I'm too busy to notice it, but I'm not. Is that what this is about?"

I nod slowly and she smiles, but it's weak because it doesn't even reach her eyes. She's not sure if the difference in me is a good or bad thing.

"Well you know I'm here to listen, even if you think it's something I won't like hearing."

Crap. She's making it even harder now. I think I want her to be one of those moms that are too busy to hear what their kids have to say just so I don't have to say the words. She's not though and if I want to meet Kayden in an hour, I need to do this now.

"How do you know when you like someone?"

She leans back in the chair and I start wondering if this was the right question to start with. It's what I want to know most, but now she's gonna know I like someone and it will change the entire way this conversation goes.

"Well baby, I don't know how it feels for you, but I remember what it was like for me. Is that what you want me to explain?"

I nod again and wasting no time she picks right up where she left off.

"Well it might sound a little cliché, but when you first notice someone you like, you get butterflies swimming around in your stomach, you sweat a whole lot and sometimes, it might even be hard to breathe."

The way she's describing it is like she's pulling everything I've been feeling right from my head. I've had all of that and more with Kayden, so it's pretty obvious I have my answer.

"The more you're around them, you might notice your heart racing, but considering yours does that in other instances as well, you might not catch on to it right away. When you're not with them, it will feel like a part of you is missing. Does any of this sound familiar to you?"

I nod. I want to admit to it all out loud, but everything she's saying is so familiar that it's making me speechless.

"Oh Isabelle," she sighs though she's smiling again and this time it's actually reaching her eyes. "Who is the lucky boy?"

This is where things are about to get awkward, well more awkward anyway. It's the point where the fear from earlier comes back and I'm not sure I want to tell her. I don't want her to think it's wrong or tell me that I shouldn't feel that way for Kayden, considering the way he was before.

"It's Eric, isn't it? I always did think that boy liked you a little more then he let on."

I want to laugh so bad right now.

"No it's not Eric. Mom…"

I'm gonna tell her. I have to tell her and hope it turns out alright.

"Isabelle, this is such a big moment for you. I know that I seem a little over eager, but it's only because I wasn't sure this moment would ever happen. I want to hear everything."

"It's Kayden."

There. It's out now and while I sit there in complete silence, waiting for her expression to change, holding my breath, the strangest thing happens.

She laughs.

"I always figured it would be."

What does that mean? How could she know that I would fall for Kayden Walker when I wasn't even sure myself until about five minutes ago?

"You were expecting me to react differently?" she asks and I nod in response. I expected her to do anything but what she actually did. She's never been much of a yeller, but that was more expected then her laughter.

"Yeah, I guess I was."

"Well, let me explain. From the time that boy was about three, I noticed something different about him. When he would spend time here, I would watch the way he was with you. This was before everything happened of course. Anytime you got upset, he was always jumping to his feet to help you. He always had a smile for you and when he looked at you—"

She cuts off and there's this second where I want to scream at her, dying for her to finish what she was gonna say, but I don't do it. I don't remember Kayden ever being like that, so what she's saying now is like music to my ears. It's like the Kayden she remembers and the one that I know now are the same.

"How did he look at me, Mom?"

"His eyes were always so—tender. I think that's the word. That boy lived for your smile. He even went out of his way quite a lot to make it happen. I guess that's why I'm not surprised. With the way he was with you then, even if he has changed over the years, it makes sense that it's him now."

I have no idea what to say. I don't remember any of it and I have the best memory of anyone I've ever met. For the first time since I got home today, I'm happy. Bringing this to my mom had been the right thing after all.

"But what if he doesn't feel the same or I'm too weird for him?"

"We're all a little weird, Isabelle. It's our differences that make us unique and you shouldn't let anyone, even a boy you might like, tell you anything different."

This isn't the first time she's said something like this to me. In fact, this is one of her go to speeches when I get bullied. I'm not entirely sure I believe in it, but I do know she wouldn't say it to me if she didn't believe it.

"I'm not sure what to tell you about him feeling the same because I can't speak for him, but from someone that gets the pleasure of living with you each and every day, I can tell you that he would be stupid not to."

"You're required to say that."

"That may be so, but I mean every word of it. You have come such a long way, especially these last few years. You're at an age now where everything you're experiencing is normal and whoever is lucky enough to earn your trust and affection better know what a gem they have."

"You know the only thing missing from that is a shotgun and shovel right?" I ask and she laughs.

"Someone's been spending too much time watching movies."

I just shrug in response and again, she laughs. It reminds me how lucky I am to have her. Not everyone can have a mom like her. It also reminds me of Kayden. He doesn't have this kind of thing at home. It makes me sad thinking about it because that's the one thing I want for him. I want him to know what it feels like to be loved unconditionally, just the way I am.

"I get the feeling that there's more that you still need to tell me. Am I wrong?"

"No, you're not wrong."

"Well then what are you waiting for? Spill it young lady!"

"Is it alright if I go out later?" I ask knowing it's a long shot, but hoping that her response to Kayden might change her mind.

"Define going out."

"Kayden said he wants to stop by and talk to me after practice. I said it was okay, but I wasn't sure if you would be okay with him being here. I just wanna meet him out front."

"So you just want to sit out front with him?"

I nod and again she's flashing her mega-watt smile at me. Maybe she's not going to freak out after all.

Going out is a topic that hasn't really come up before, but with how protective she can be over me, I know it's one she's concerned about. The closer I stay to home, the easier it is to protect me and up until Kayden asked to meet me earlier today, I agreed with her.

"That's fine, Isabelle, but promise me something?"

"Okay."

"If it gets too cold out there, promise me you will come inside. Kayden was welcome here years ago and he's welcome now."

I've lived with this woman for almost eighteen years and somehow she still has the ability to surprise me. If I can turn out to be half the person that my mom is, I'll be the luckiest person alive. I think I already am.

There's still one more thing we need to talk about, but this time, it's nothing I need to be worried about. This is something that's been a long time coming.

"Mom, there's actually one more thing I need to talk to you about."

"What is it honey?"

"When you get the chance do you think you can make an appointment with Dr. Stevens?"

"Of course I can. Any particular reason why?"

The way she asks this, her tone drenched in concern makes me want to explain everything in detail, so she knows she has nothing to worry about, but I don't do that. Instead I go with the vaguest answer I can think of, but one I know she won't question, at least not right away.

"I need his help fixing something."

Kayden

My body is killing me and I definitely need a shower, but instead of sticking around once practice is over, I do the complete opposite and book it out of there as fast as I can.

The one rule Coach has, both for practice and games, is that we always keep our head in the game, but tonight, out there on the field, that's the last place my mind was. I did everything I was told and I think I played my ass off, but my head and heart were definitely not in it.

I left both of them with the girl that I'm now about to go see. The girl that the minute I see her, I'm going to pull as close as possible to me and ask to be my girlfriend.

As I throw my stuff into the backseat, I pull my phone out of my back pocket and slide behind the wheel. There are two missed notifications and without even looking, I hope they're from her.

Scrolling through my phone until I get to the messages screen, I see that both are from Dean. Against my better judgment I read them and just like every other time I have any contact with him, I feel sick.

Where the hell are you?

Kayden, answer the damn phone. I need you to go to the liquor store. We're all out.

It's times like this that remind me of who I really am and why I'm not the guy for her. That despite all the changes I've been trying to make for me and for her, I'm still a stupid idiot underneath.

Dean asking me to drive and get him booze happens a lot more then I want to admit. He's always too drunk to go himself and honestly, I'm happy he's at least that smart. It's so often that I do this that the guy at the liquor store doesn't even card me anymore. I had that covered pretty well with my fake ID though. It never used to bother me because I used to drink with him half the time. It was a win-win situation for both of us.

At least it was until her.

Now, seeing these messages makes me sick. He damn well knows I have practice after school though with the haze he's always in, I shouldn't be too surprised that he didn't remember. I just know that if I don't make an appearance soon, at least in text, he's going to lose it even worse when I do walk through the door.

I haven't gotten drunk in over two weeks. It doesn't hold any appeal. Life with Dean makes me want to drink sometimes, but I don't do it. I want to be better than that. If I keep doing what I've been doing, I'm only going to turn out exactly like the very guy texting me now and I want better than that. I always have. It's just recently that I'm seeing it.

It's because of her.

Calm urself man. I just got out of practice.

That's going to have to be a good enough answer because I have somewhere I need to be and it's definitely not filling a cart with liquor. This outweighs all of that and not even my brother is going to take me away from it. I bailed on her once. I won't do it again.

I wait a few minutes for him to respond, but when nothing comes, I pull up Isabelle's messages from earlier and type one out quickly. I could just show up at her door, but I get the feeling she might not appreciate that too much. She doesn't seem the type and I want to do this right.

Just got out. Omw. <3

Why the hell I put the heart at the end of the message is a mystery, but I can't take it back and even if I could, I don't think I want to. It's strange staring at it because it's actually the first time I can remember doing it. I'm pretty sure half the girls I dated would have killed for something like this from me, but I've never had it in me.

I'm definitely not that guy. At least I wasn't, until now.

It's only when I get her response back a few seconds later that I'm even happier then I was when she agreed to see me at all.

See you soon. <3

I'm not sure what's gotten into me, but I can't stop staring at the message and the emoticons at the end. I've seen her do the happy face before, it's actually one of the things I really enjoy when we're texting, but the heart, something new stirs inside of me. I can't let her message sit there like that, I have to say more. I know for a fact that I'll put the key in the ignition, start the car and drive to her, but not until I do one more thing first.

Not soon enough. I miss you.

Going through the motions, I toss my phone on the seat and focus on the road ahead of me. The road that will take me to the one place in the world, in this exact second, I want to be more than anything.

With her.

Belle

I hear his car before I see it, but before I can head for the door, I hear my mom call from behind me.

"Take this out to him. If he's been at practice all night then it's a sure bet the boy didn't eat."

I'm pretty sure there's more that she wants to say, but she doesn't. I know she's aware of the way Kayden lives. She just hasn't gotten to see it firsthand like I have. I know she's passing me the slices of pizza because she knows that otherwise he won't eat at all.

"Thanks Mom." I answer as I take the plate from her, pressing my body to hers in a weak hug. I mean it though, I'm so thankful that she just gets it and she's okay with it.

"Remember what I said!" She calls as I turn and start walking toward the front door. "If it gets chilly, come in."

"I will!"

As the door shuts behind me, I start making my way across the lawn. Even in the dark I can see him behind the wheel; at least I can until he turns the car off and the entire area is blanketed in darkness. I'm not sure, but I swear I saw him smiling before everything went dark and just like my mom explained; it makes my heart do the butterfly thing.

"Hey." He says when he reaches me. "Is that for me?"

He's pointing to the plate in my hands and I push it toward him. Once he takes it and my hands are free, I pull out my phone and text him.

My mom figured you'd be hungry after practice.

"She was right." He says in between bites, my eyes locked on his mouth as he seems to inhale the first slice. The way he's eating reminds me of Tristan on pizza nights. It's identical. It must be a guy thing.

When the first slice is completely done, he wipes at the corners of his mouth with his hands and I can't help staring at him. I've never done anything like this before, but there's something about what he's doing that draws me in and I can't look away.

"Tell your mom I said thank you for the pizza." He says and I focus again.

Okay.

We're silent for a few minutes after he gets the text and I'm not sure what to do. He's the one that said he wanted to talk to me and now that he's here, I expected him to get right to it, but he's doing the complete opposite.

You said you wanted to talk to me?

"Yeah I did. I'm just nervous about it."

I've known Kayden a long time and I don't think I've ever seen him nervous about anything. He's actually one of the only people I know that never shows it. He's always so confident. If he's nervous about something now, maybe I need to be worried. It's not like he said what he wanted to talk to me about was good. I just assumed.

Did you talk to Dillon? Is that what this is about?

I don't ask what I really wanna know because I choke up just thinking about it. If he talked to Dillon and everything is good between them again, is he here now to tell me that he doesn't want to hang out anymore? I don't want to think like that, especially after he said he missed me and sent me a heart, but I don't exactly know how guys act when they do things like this.

"Trust me Belle. This has *nothing* to do with Dillon."

Okay then. Well, what's up?

I'm actually trying my hardest to act like none of this is bothering me, but it is. I'm not used to him like this. If this has nothing to do with Dillon, I have no clue what it could be.

"Shit. Okay. I'm just gonna come right out and say it."

I start to type, but stop the minute I feel his hand rest on top of mine. Looking up and catching the intense look in his eyes, I hold my breath and wait for whatever's about to come next.

"I like you, Isabelle."

Why is he telling me this? I already know that he likes me, considering he told me earlier that we were friends. All of this is just becoming more confusing by the second.

"Shit, that didn't come out right did it? Of course it didn't, because I never say anything right and damnit, I really wanna get this right!"

He takes his hand off mine and covers his face with it and I wonder what's so hard about what he's trying to say that's making him act this way.

Just say what you feel.

I wait for him to get the message, thinking that when he sees it, things will be easier for him. It's not though, as the only sound around us now is the breeze passing by. We're stuck again.

"What do you feel, Isabelle?"

That's a hard question for me. For a long time, I didn't feel much at all. At least I don't think I ever felt anything before. I always just felt numb. It's only in the last year or so where I've actually started feelings things, but usually it's for other people and has nothing to do with me.

If it will help him open up and tell me what he wants to talk about though, I'm willing to do anything. I have to stop being so afraid some time and there's no better time than now. So, that's exactly what I do. I open up the text message and start typing, not stopping until it's all out there. I hit send before I can think it through and wait for him to get it.

It's scary waiting for the familiar tone because I've just spilled everything out. I haven't even admitted it to myself, but this isn't just some random person I'm telling it to. This is Kayden. He's the first boy I ever cared about.

The first boy I ever loved.

For a long time I hated you, but not because of the names you called me. I hated you because when you left that day almost eight years ago and never came back, you broke my heart. You were my only friend and I wasn't enough for you. I don't remember feeling anything after that, not until two weeks ago. Since then I've been feeling a lot of different things and they scare me, but I know what it all means now.

"What d—does it mean?" he stammers as he takes in everything I've written.

It means I like you, Kayden. I like you a lot.

Kayden

I'm one of the most confident SOB's alive.

When I'm on the field, I own it. I make it my own and nothing can stop me. I'm in a zone like no other and I am the best at what I do. When I'm with Dillon and the others, he might think he runs the show, but everyone knows that I do, or at least I did before Isabelle came back into my life. I can talk myself easily out of any situation I find myself in, especially with adults.

I have never had a moment of self doubt. At least I didn't until that day in my car when she told me that if I wanted to be different then to be different. Everything changed that day. I doubt myself a lot more and right now, the way I'm acting proves it.

Telling her I like her isn't enough because I don't just like her. I'm in love with this girl, but I know I can't tell her that. It's too soon and I don't want to scare her away. I've only loved one person before, so it's all I have to base this on and that person lost the right to have my love a long time ago. Isabelle is different. She doesn't have to earn it; I freely want to give it to her.

I want to give her all of me even if she deserves so much better.

What she texted me, I don't know how to respond. I had no idea that she felt that way when we stopped hanging out back then, but considering everything that's happened since, I'm pretty sure it's a safe bet that even if I did know, I wouldn't have cared. I really wasn't lying when I said I was a first class asshole.

Things are different now. I don't want to be that guy anymore. I want to be the one that I always ripped on other people for being. I want to be the one that loves, protects, adores and cherishes. I want to be a Valentine's Day card brought to life, even if I suck at it. I want to do that and more, but not for just anyone.

Only for Isabelle.

It means that I like you, Kayden. I like you a lot.

It was supposed to be me making the night perfect and with a couple of words, she's taken it from me. When I asked her what she felt, she didn't hesitate telling me and it's about damn time I do the same for her. Whatever nervousness I feel about the way this might go is gone now. She's taken that away too.

"I like you too, Isabelle and it's more than just a lot."

What does that mean?

"It means that I lied to you at lunch. You're more than just a friend to me. I think you always have been, if that makes sense. I just know that what I feel for you, it's something I've never felt before and I'm so damn scared I'm gonna screw it up. I really, really, really don't wanna screw it up."

You like me?

This girl I swear. Normally if someone acted like this around me, I would just get up and walk away, but with her I'm completely frozen in place. Even if I wanted to get up, I can't. She consumes me so completely. It's her lack of understanding and her childlike innocence that I love most about her. She's unlike anyone I've ever known.

I more than like you.

Before she can respond I type out another one and hit send, knowing how cheesy it's going to sound, but no longer caring. I'm willing to be the king of cheese, whipped or whatever else, as long as it's with her.

Will you be my girlfriend?

Two things happen the minute she sees the text and I'm not sure which one affects me more. First I see the tear as it slides down from her eye, followed up by another one, but before I can reach out and wipe them away what she does next stops me in my tracks.

Her lips curve up and for the first time since I've known her, or at least of what I can remember of my time with her, she does it.

She smiles.

Chapter Seventeen

Belle

Contrary to what people think, I can remember smiling before. It's not like I've never done it or something. It's just been a really long time since it's happened. The only time I've ever really smiled in the last couple of years has been because of Tristan. It's true what they tell you about little kids. It's hard not to smile around them and my little brother is no different. He can get to me in a way that the rest of the world can't, at least until the exact second I read the text from Kayden.

Something shifted when he asked me to be his girlfriend. For the first time in so long, I'm happier than I've ever been and I didn't need a little kid to get me there. This time it's all on him.

I'm not sure the best thing to say to a guy you like is how much you hated him, but this is the way I am. I tell the truth always, even when it might hurt and with Kayden especially, he deserves it. I guess in a way, my mom was right, because when I told him everything a few minutes ago, I knew my worth. No matter how he took it, at least I know I was completely honest and left nothing a secret.

I wasn't intending to cry. Normally when that happens, there's this buildup and I can feel it happening before the tears actually fall. This time, they escaped before I even realized what was happening and I didn't want to stop them. These weren't because of someone intentionally trying to hurt me. They were because of the overwhelming happiness I feel inside.

"Isabelle…"

That's something different too or at least something I never paid much attention to before. The way it feels when he says my name. My mind is always running. There is always something going on inside and most of the time, whatever it is, it's so strong that I can barely register much else. When he says my name though, especially this time, everything seems to just go still and for once, it's quiet and he's the only sound I hear.

The reaction I'm having is part of the reason I asked my mom to make the appointment for me earlier. If it feels this way for me, I wonder if it will feel the same way for him when I finally do speak. I know I've done it a few times over the last couple of weeks, but it's never been because of something this good. I forced out his name the day he saved me from Dillon and I yelled at him the day he picked on Eric. When I want to speak most though, in moments like this, it won't come and it just makes me want to fix this even more.

He should know how he makes me feel and it shouldn't come in a text. I want to be able to tell him aloud how just one simple question made me lose my breath, brought butterflies floating up until I can almost feel the fluttering head to toe. He should know that my brain feels fuzzy and my entire body is warm, because he's the one that caused it.

"I dreamt about this."

He what?

"Yeah, I know. It's weird."

The last thing that comes to mind when I think about Kayden is that anything about him is weird. I might not understand what he means by what he's saying, but it's definitely not weird. I know what weird is because I live it every single day.

It's not weird. I just don't understand what you mean.

"You know how shit is with Dean—well, there was this one night, I don't remember when, but he was going off on me like usual and all I could think about was you smiling at me."

Usually when people think of me, it's a pity thing or in a bad way. Hearing Kayden now, his reaction completely different than any I've ever experienced, I don't know what to say. It's made worse by what happened to make him think of me.

He's right. I do know what his life is like with Dean. I know a lot about it. I just wish I didn't. Even when we weren't speaking to each other, I hated the way his life was and hearing about it now makes me hate it even more. No matter what kind of person he is, he doesn't deserve what Dean puts him through.

"I said something wrong didn't I?"

No. You said everything right.

"Then why do you look so sad?"

Dean.

It's silent for a few seconds after he gets the text and I wonder if we're about to go back to the way we were before. It's only when he turns his body toward me, pulling me to him that I know I've got nothing to be scared of.

"I don't want you to worry about him okay? I know what happened the other day scared you, but I swear to you, I can handle it and I'm fine."

I try my hardest to focus on his words and believe in them, but with the way his hand is running up and down my back it's hard to think of anything but the way he moves. His hands aren't even on my skin, but with every movement, he's making me feel like I'm on fire, like he's burning me.

Yes.

It's the only thing left to say now, at least for me. He asked me a question and I got so caught up in the feelings that I didn't answer it. I just hope he knows what I'm trying to say as he reads it.

"Yes? Are you saying—is this about us or what I said about Dean?"

It happens again and this time it doesn't just affect my lips, but my entire face. I can feel my cheekbones rise and my eyes crunch in. This smile is definitely different than before, but because of the way I'm positioned in his chest, he can't see it.

Ask me again and find out.

He laughs, not as loud as times before, but he does exactly what my text says just the way I hoped he would.

"Isabelle, will you be my girlfriend?"

I already have the 'yes' text from before copied and pasted back into the texting box so before he gets the words out, I send it and as the ringtone goes off, I smile again. Before I can stop though, he catches it.

"How many times have you done it now?"

I feel the heat rise in my cheeks and I try to bury my face in his chest. Not letting me hide from him, he leans down and uses his hand to bring my face up until I'm looking only look at him.

"Tell me."

Holding up my hand, I lift three fingers, bringing the other two down and smile again. Taking his hand and pressing it to mine he pulls the fourth finger up and meets my smile with one of his own.

"I'm just gonna pull the last finger up too, okay? Because you're totally gonna do it again."

He brings my pinky finger up until our hands are completely open and pressed together. Blushing and lowering my head, it slips past my lips and I'm not sure which one of us is more shocked by it.

It was one thing when I smiled at him, my first real smile for someone other than my family, but this is something else entirely. Laughing is something I really don't remember doing at all and here I am doing it and all it took was him.

"Holy shit! You just laughed."

The minute I smile again, he grins at me and nods toward our hands.

"I told you."

With everything that's happened I haven't paid much attention to how close we really are to each other. When he lifted my chin so that he could see me, it put our faces in perfect proportion to each other. Noticing it now reminded me of the time in the park when we had been this close and exactly what happened because of it.

The way his eyes are looking down at me, tender, just like my mom told me earlier, I know what's about to happen next. I'm just not sure I'm ready for it.

"Belle, I am so..."

He stops himself and his eyes go wide, like he can't believe what he was about to say and it annoys me because I really want him to finish his thought. Pulling my hand away from his, I start typing. At the exact moment I hit send, he slides the phone out of my hand and lays it down on the other side of him. It's only when he does the same with his phone that I start to worry what he's about to do next.

He knows that's the only way we can communicate, at least it is until I can talk to my doctor, so taking it away is only going to make things uncomfortable and right now that's the last thing I want.

"No more phones, Belle. I don't want to talk anymore."

Kayden

Sitting here with her like this, I'm starting to remember things that for whatever reason I pushed out of my mind. Well, I know why I pushed it all down, because it came from my mom before she split, but why I'm thinking about it now really doesn't make any sense.

I wasn't always a total ass. I used to be a pretty good kid or at least that's how I remember it anyway. I made friends easily with everyone in the neighborhood, helped people when I saw they needed it and generally had a pretty good time. It's only when she bailed that everything seemed to change and I became the person that's sitting with Isabelle now.

Well, maybe not the person sitting with her because I'm not sure what version of me is sitting here right now. I like to think it's a middle ground between the good kid I used to be and the monster I became when she split. I'm not stupid enough to think

I've been cured of the asshole gene, but I know I'm not as big a one as I was before.

It's the way Isabelle smiled at me and when she laughed that's bringing all of these old memories back to the surface. For whatever reason, she's here and she's giving me this chance to be someone that's worthy of her. I never want to lose that or let her down. I'm afraid though. With everything she's bringing to the surface inside of me that letting her down is exactly what I'm going to do.

Deep down, I'm exactly like my brother and my father before him. It's my own mother's words that slam it home to me and it makes me want to bail, even though doing that would break everything I worked so hard to build with the beautiful girl in my arms right now.

"I had one wish before you were born and it was that you wouldn't turn out like me and your daddy. I wanted you to be better than that, better than us."

I don't really remember much about my dad. I know he was a pretty mean drunk and more than once beat on my mom and maybe even Dean. The thing is, her wish never came true because neither one of us turned out any better than them. Maybe that's part of the reason she took off. She didn't want to see me and Dean turn into what we are now.

We really are our father's sons. We're both filled with a rage that even beating on each other never seems to cure. We're angry and lonely at the same time. We're lost and every single day it feels like we're drowning with no way to be saved.

That's what is so damn hard to handle with Isabelle. She's like a life preserver that can save me from drowning. She probably always has been, but because I chose the anger over anything else that might have been available, I didn't know until now. It makes me want to grab on to her and never let go. I can see what my mom wished for every single time I look in her eyes because she brings me to the place where I know I'm better than the way I've been raised.

It's more than just that old stuff I'm remembering though. I also remember her talking to me about Isabelle.

"Isabelle isn't like the other girls, Kayden. I can't put my finger on it, but that little girl is better. She's gonna need a good boy like you when she's older."

Isabelle really isn't like other girls. She is different, somehow better. Looking at the way she looks now, under the dimness of the street light, I've never seen another person that looks more beautiful. I've spent so long looking at her issues and not at her that somewhere along the way I forgot everything my mom said to me. I hadn't been there when she needed me. I was the one she needed to be protected from.

That's all over now. I'm never going to be someone she has to fear again. If I have to spend the rest of my life proving that to her then that's what I'll do, because what I didn't see then, I see now. She really is better, but my mom was wrong about one part. She doesn't need me.

I'm the one that needs her.

Almost telling her how I feel about her, letting those three words slip because I felt them so strongly, was a stupid move. After hearing her laughter and seeing her face brighten as she finally smiled for me, the only thing I could think about was how much I love her. I didn't stop myself because I don't want her to know, I did it because when I finally do say the words to her, I won't be taking them back and I want it to be perfect.

As great as this moment is, having her close to me, able to breathe in her scent, experience what it feels like to have my hands on her body, it's not perfect. I don't know when it will be, but I'm willing to wait.

I can tell that I've freaked her out not wanting the phones anymore. I'm tired of talking and it isn't because I'm the only one speaking. If anything, I think communicating the way she has been makes me see and experience what normally I just don't when people talk to me. I'm able to hear her loud and clear and she doesn't have to say a word.

Not wanting to talk, it's selfish. I want to kiss her again. I've been thinking of nothing but kissing her since the day in the park. It's just gotten worse since I saw her before practice today. I had to stop myself from kissing her the moment she came outside to meet me. That's how powerful the urge is and I'm losing the fight.

"Can I kiss you?"

I've never had to ask a girl to kiss me before. Me taking away her phone, I know it's going to bother her that she can't answer me, but this isn't a question I'm looking for an actual answer to, at least not one that's verbal. The answer will be in her eyes and looking at me now, I see that she doesn't disappoint.

She's giving me all the answer I need.

I trace my finger across her lips and like magic they part for me, her breath releasing, warming me. Keeping my eyes locked on hers, determined not to look away and miss the way she looks in the moment, I lean myself in closer until my own lips are resting dangerously close to hers.

"I'm going to kiss you now…"

The second the words fall, I press my lips to hers and it's as if everything in me is finally set right. The softness I felt before greets me again and with every move our lips make from that moment on, she's with me every step of the way. I feel my eyes closing, no longer focused on seeing her, only experiencing her and it's in that moment that I'm completely lost.

She owns me.

Chapter Eighteen

Belle

I've never noticed before, but when something really big happens to you, it's pretty amazing how quickly everything changes.

It's been exactly a week since Kayden sat outside my house and asked me to be his girlfriend. It means there's been a week of us being together and a week at school where everyone seems to know about it.

He warned me that because of his reputation and the past he had with a lot of the girls, going back wouldn't be easy. With the way I'm used to being treated, I didn't see how it could be much worse. I know how popular he is and what him being with me means. As sweet as he is worrying about me, I expect everything that happens.

There are girls that give me dirty looks, but because they used to do that anyway, it's almost like things are the same as always. The name calling is still there and even some new names are added, ones I don't understand, but I don't think I'm supposed to. Something does happen though that even with all of his warnings, I didn't see coming.

Dillon has been spending more time around us lately. Kayden is still staying as far away from the others as he can, but Dillon doesn't let him do it all the way. It's so strange. For the last two days now, he's been sitting with us under the tree and though he gets looks for it, he doesn't seem bothered.

I guess I was right about him after all. He misses Kayden and he's trying to do whatever he has to in order to prove it to his old friend, even though Kayden still doesn't trust it. He's tolerating it though and I know why. He's doing it for me because he thinks it's what I want. What he doesn't realize is that I want what he's comfortable with. If Dillon being here isn't what he wants, it's okay.

It's like my mom taught me. We all have a choice. I believe that Dillon means what he says, but Kayden doesn't and it's alright for us to handle it differently.

I'm just glad that things haven't changed with us. When I showed up at school the next day, I wasn't sure how I was supposed to act, but Kayden made it pretty clear that just because we were together, it didn't mean things had to be different.

He holds my hand as he walks me to classes now and makes sure to kiss my forehead or brush his lips against mine before leaving me to make it to his own. That's the only difference. It makes me feel better knowing that just because our relationship changed, we don't have to change with it.

At least that's how I felt until I start seeing the cheerleaders decorating the school for Homecoming.

I might not have any experience with being a part of one before, but I do know what a big deal it is, at least for the people that go here. It's the chance for everyone to let loose and have fun even though it takes a ton of work to get to that point. It's the one time where people that normally walk the halls alone, become part of a couple and talks of dresses, football games and after parties are common.

Watching the cheerleaders selling tickets as we pass in the hall just reminds me of what's coming and how different things really are. Is he going to want to go with me and if he does, why hasn't he asked me yet? Would going with me embarrass him too much? Is that why he's so silent about it, even though everywhere we go it seems to be staring us in the face?

I'm not bringing it up. I'm not sure if I want to put myself through it, much less questioning why he hasn't asked me. There's a small part of me though, that does hope he asks because it's always just been me standing on the outside looking in and this time, with Kayden by my side, it doesn't have to be.

His practice schedule is increased because of the Homecoming game in a few days. I've never actually been to a football game, not understanding sports at all, but I would go for him. Plus, I know Tristan would love it, but it's just another thing that hasn't come up. Another way we've changed.

Kayden isn't the only one who is being quiet about things. My mom came through and I'm going to see my doctor. I want to tell him about it, but with how busy things are around here, especially with him and football, I can't do it. He's been so good to me this past week and I know he would drop it all to be there. I can't let him do that.

"Hey. You're doing it again."

This isn't the first time he's caught me lost in thought. I'm pretty sure he's caught me every time I've done it. Looking up at him and smiling though, seems to do the trick. He stops in the middle of the hall, just like always and he touches my face where my lips are raised, almost as if, just like the first time, he's blown away that it's even happening at all.

Like he thinks this is a dream.

"Is your mom still okay with me coming over after practice?"

I nod and that's when I'm rewarded. He grins at me and just like every other time he's done it this week, it makes his eyes crinkle. That's probably the coolest thing about Kayden. I can see myself reflected like a mirror in his eyes and my smile is as big as his. I wonder if because my eyes are lighter, the same thing happens to him.

"Awesome." He answers, before pulling me into his arms and stroking my hair, another thing he's been doing a whole lot more of lately. "Have I told you lately how great it is that your mom is okay with this?"

This means us. The first time he came over after practice, he'd been afraid to come in, but the minute she held the door open and flashed her smile, he was taken in just like everyone else.

Kayden isn't used to being openly accepted, especially considering the way things used to be. I know he expected it to be much worse. He just doesn't know my mom the way I do. He doesn't realize that like me, she can see what's underneath and not just what's sprinkled on the top for the rest of the world.

I nod and my nose tickles from the fabric of his shirt. I laugh and I feel his lips brush the top of my head and it's in that moment that it hits me. I'm not really so different from everyone after all. I understand now why girls go so crazy over boys, especially when they do things like this. It's something that has the risk of becoming addictive.

Or I'm just biased because it's Kayden.

"Wanna hear something strange?"

I lean back from him a little as I look up, nodding.

"I kind of wanna tape you laughing so I can have it with me whenever I need it."

This is one of the times I wish I could tell him that he has no idea what strange really is. All I hear is something nice. It's a first for me, hearing him say things like this. I know that he knows it, but the way he doesn't call attention to it, is what makes me like him even more.

Feeling brave, I wrap my hand around his back, sliding his phone out of his back pocket. Once it's safe in my hands I look up and see his eyes have gone wide, but he's still wearing the grin.

"I didn't know you had it in you. That's a very naughty move, Belle."

I laugh, but this time I hit record at the exact moment it happens. It's not a fake laugh or even one that was planned and that's exactly what makes it so perfect. He never asks for anything or even gives me a clue what he really wants when we're together. This time he did and I really want to give it to him.

It's only when I hand the phone back and point to the screen, that his cheeks flush and his eyes go soft. He opens his mouth to say something and pauses, which only confuses me. It's happened a few times before and each time I wonder what it is that he's holding himself back from saying.

"I'm the luckiest SOB alive."

I shrug and he laughs again which just makes me smile. When you spend as much time alone as I have, you observe a lot of what happens around you when you're in public situations. In the last three years I've only seen him laugh three times total and it was never like this. It's the same way when he smiles. In the last week, it seems like he's making up for lost time.

He should always be this way. It suits him.

"I gotta go, baby. Coach wants to talk before practice." He says and his lips instantly begin to drop, as if he's realizing what him leaving means. "You want me to walk you to the bus?"

I shake my head, more than capable of getting to the bus the same way I've been doing for years. I know he walks me because he's protective, but to tell you the truth, I'm actually looking forward to the time alone. I've still got a lot to think about and having him near me means I won't do much thinking at all.

"Text me the minute you're on the bus. I wanna make sure you're okay."

Some things never change. Accepting that this is something I don't want him to change, I nod and smile.

"I'll see you in three hours, princess." He says as he places a small kiss on my lips. As he turns and heads down the hall, he calls back to me. "I can't wait."

Kayden

I don't know if you can screw up a voice file, but with the amount of times I've played it since she recorded it almost an hour ago, I'm definitely testing it.

I have never been this happy in my entire life.

Well I guess that's not exactly true. I was happy before, but it was because of stupid little things that now don't mean a whole lot. When I would get a new Hot Wheels car, I'd wear the world's biggest grin, until I played with it so much the tires ended up falling off. When Mom would take us out for tacos or pizza, I'd eat until I couldn't move and spend the entire night blissfully happy.

It's never felt like this before though. This experience is new. Even with all the girls I've dated in the last five years or so, nothing compares to the way it is with Isabelle. I don't want it too. I still have a hard time believing that she's my Belle now. Somehow, I was lucky enough to have this amazing girl fall for me, the way I did for her.

Sometimes it feels like we're kids again, but this time, I'm not a total jerk and well she's just exactly the same. We have moments when we're walking down the hall and she'll squeeze my hand and I'll answer back with squeeze of my own. It's like we have our own secret language that no one but us knows.

When she feels herself getting overwhelmed by sensory stuff, she lets me know without saying a word and I hold her until it passes. It's crazy, but for the longest time all I thought I was good for, was playing football and causing shit and now, I'm seeing that everything I thought is wrong. I was made for this and I can't even explain how much that means.

The more I'm there for her, the less my mom's words haunt me, almost like I'm doing what she knew I would all along. I'm actually feeling the changes too; they aren't just inside me. I don't hate as deeply as before, which is proven with the way I am with Dillon now.

He came up to us about two days after I asked her to be mine, trying to talk to me. When he didn't get his way, he went through Isabelle the way I expected him to, except her being her, she did answer him back. Eventually he started coming around more and he didn't try to talk to me. He only talked to her. It's easier to not want to kill him and see what she's seen for the last two weeks when I see the way he is with her.

We won't ever be what we were, but if this is real and he means what he says, I can't hate him anymore.

Does it mean that I trust him completely or that I think he's not playing a game that somehow involves my girlfriend? No. I still think there's more going on, but until I can find some kind of proof, I've got to go with the flow.

"You asked her to the dance yet?"

After talking with Coach, I've just been chilling in the locker room, already suited up for practice and waiting for the others to show up. I'd been so caught up listening to her voice file and my own thoughts; I didn't realize I wasn't alone.

"You mean the 'everyone gets drunk, makes asses of themselves and screws like rabbits' thing that happens in a couple days?"

"Yeah, that's the one. You ask her yet?"

Truth is, I haven't asked her and it's because I'm afraid to. I bought the tickets at the beginning of the week, wanting nothing more than to take my girlfriend to the dance after I play one of the most important games of my life. Having the tickets means nothing though, not when I'm not sure how to bring it up with her.

She's never been to a football game before and I know for a fact that she's never been to a school dance either. I'm not sure if it's because it's not her thing or because of everything she's been through, but it makes me wary to ask. I'm not a school dance guy, but this year, it's all different.

I did these things before because it was a way to get the people around me to shut up about it. I actually want to go to this game, win it with her cheering in the crowd, get dressed, pick her up and spend the night with her wrapped tightly in my arms while we dance together. I want to experience everything instead of just gliding through it after being forced.

I'm just not sure she feels the same. So I've kept my damn mouth shut even though we walk by the decorations every single day.

"No, not yet. I'm not really sure it's her thing."

"It's every girl's thing, K."

"What did I tell you about that?"

"Jeez man. Sorry. Look, I know she's different, but I'll bet my position on the team that she wants to go to the dance. You need to ask her before someone else does."

I finally get on a level where I don't want to punch him in the face every time I see him and he has to go and say something like that. I'm not against most of what he said, but the way he sounds when he talks about someone else asking her, makes me insane.

"No one is going to ask her to the dance but me."

He can think he's changed all he wants, but he definitely won't be taking her. That will happen over my dead body.

"Chill man, I just mean that since you two hooked up, people are noticing her more. She's not quite the freak she used to be."

"She's mine. I don't care whose noticing her, they aren't getting her. Ever."

"You really like her don't you?"

This is the strangest conversation. I can't believe it. Us sitting around talking about my feelings for Isabelle, since a week ago I wanted to run him down with my car.

"Screw off. I'm not talking about that shit with you."

"So that's a yes."

I throw the balled up towel at him and laugh as it hits its mark. It's only when he tosses it back that I realize what's happening. It's like old times with Dillon again. The stupid way we used to be before the team, girls and competition got in the way. He's obviously not the only one that missed it because the way I feel now, I did too.

"Ask the girl to the damn dance, Kayden."

Before I can come up with a response, I hear my phone vibrating against the inside of the locker. Reaching up and grabbing it down, I slide open my messages and I'm met with another reason why I love this girl so damn much. She knows how I worry about her, especially after everything that's happened and she's giving me what I needed to chill out.

I'm on the bus. Miss you <3

With Dillon's words playing in my head, I start typing out the question I need to ask her. It hits me pretty quick that this is definitely not the way to ask a girl to the dance. Erasing the message and starting again, I keep myself on track.

I would see her in a few hours anyway and that's when I'd ask her and as I hit send, I know exactly how I wanna do it.

Not as much as I miss you, princess. See you soon <3

As I put my headphones back over my head, I scroll my way into the voice files and put the sound of her laughter on repeat, closing my eyes and enjoying the sound. It's this that's gonna get me through the next three hours and probably the most grueling practice of my life. So until the guys drag me away, the only thing I want to hear is her in my head.

Exactly the way she already is in my heart.

Chapter Nineteen

Belle

I'm going to the Homecoming Dance.

Not only that, but when he came over the night before, he asked me to be there to watch him play too. In fact, he said that he wouldn't go out on the field unless I showed up.

It's strange how it all happened. He came over after practice, just like he's been doing for the last week, but this time instead of coming right for me, he went to my mom first. After waiting on the other side of the kitchen wall, trying to hear some of what they were talking about and failing, they finally made their way out and everything came out.

*****

"I need to talk to you about something Belle. It's kind of important."

I nod my head slowly and he motions toward the sofa, wanting me to sit. He stands waiting until I do it and then sits down beside me. I'm scared to find out what he wants to talk to me about, but with him looking at me that way, his eyes so bright and the tiny smirk on his face, I'm comforted enough that whatever it is, it's not bad.

"I wanted to talk to your mom about it first because what happens actually depends on her more than it does you. Well, sort of."

My mom, standing in the doorway of the living room, smiles at me and it's because of that smile that I stop worrying. If he feels comfortable enough going to her with it, then it really isn't anything bad. She might have her hands full with me, but she wouldn't let him hurt me.

"Isabelle, even though I waited way too long to ask you, I need to know. Will you be my date to Homecoming?"

It's no surprise when the tears start spilling.

I nod my head, still not sure how I feel about going to the dance. What I do know though is that he's the only one I want to do something like this with.

"There's actually something else too." He pauses; his face scrunches up like he's trying to figure out how to say it and I can't help but smile. He has no idea, but his face right now reminds me of a squirrel. I blush the minute I think it and he notices, because his eyebrows raise and he laughs.

"Why are you blushing?"

Pulling my phone out of my sweater, I start texting and when I finally finish and send it, I sigh. He's going to think I'm silly.

When you're thinking about stuff, you look like a squirrel.

He laughs loud, but unlike times before, I don't jump or flinch. Things have been happening that way lately. Its proof that the more time we spend together, the more comfortable I feel.

"Okay, well this squirrel needs you to come to the football game on Friday and he's not taking no for an answer. If you don't say yes, I won't play at all."

I can't let him do that. Football is something he enjoys and the team needs him. I don't want to be the reason that the team loses the game.

I nod hesitantly. Going to the game is the last thing I want. I don't understand sports and knowing me, I'll just make a fool of myself by cheering at the wrong time. I already have to adapt to being the girlfriend of a football player, the last thing I want to do is embarrass both of us publicly.

The alternative is him not playing and well, that can't happen. I won't let it. So as nervous as I am about all of this, I have to see it through.

"Does that nod mean you'll do it?"

I nod again, more sure this time and he grins, his eyes shining.

"Just so you know, I still would have played. I just wanted you there because I don't think I can play to win without you. You're my charm."

*****

So here I am, on the city bus after texting Kayden and telling him I was safe. I'm about to make my way on my own to the doctor. It might not be the school bus the way he thinks, but since he isn't supposed to see me until later anyway, it's not like I have to worry about it.

The last time I was here, the doctor called my issues social anxiety, something that if my mother was willing, could be treated with medication or even different forms of therapy. I don't doubt that it had something to do with anxiety or in my case, absolute fear, but now that I'm surrounded by people that I no longer have to fear, I'm ready to find out what the new explanation will be.

I only hope that it's something that can be fixed. If it's related to the autism, I'll learn to be okay with it, but something tells me that it's not that kind of problem. This is something more and with the way I can write to Kayden when doing it usually overwhelms me with most people, I need to get answers once and for all. I'm not going to run from it anymore the way I did before.

I owe it myself to figure it out.

Kayden

She's hiding something.

I've had my head in the game so much the last couple of days that even when I'm with her, I know I'm not entirely with her, at least not the way I wanna be. Maybe the only thing that's off is, she's sensing my disconnection, so she's pulling away. I can't shake the feeling though, that there's something she's hiding from me.

Asking her about it, there's just never a good time. If we aren't being shadowed by my annoying best friend, we're in and out of classes or she's off with her mother in an attempt to find the world's most beautiful dress. We're spending less and less time with each other and when we are together, we're so lost in our own thoughts and shit that we don't actually do much talking.

She's been helping me with math lately and I do need the help, but truthfully, it's an excuse I came up with so I didn't have to go home. Dean's been getting worse by the minute and anytime I am back there, all we do is argue, call each other names, fight or threaten to end each other. It's toxic and it's because of all the time I'm spending at her house, seeing the way a normal family can be that I see it clearly. Something has got to give between my brother and me and it has to soon, because if it doesn't, I'm almost afraid one of us is gonna end up dead.

Aside from the math help, we haven't talked much at all. There's been stuff about the dance and she asks me what she can expect at the game, but it falls apart after that. I just wish she trusted me enough to tell me what's actually going on in her mind. I can tell there's something there, but I can't help her fight until I know what I'm helping her fight against.

Part of me thinks that Amy's up to no good again, but the one time I bring it up to Dillon all he does is shake his head at me. Nothing happens in the school without me or Dillon knowing about it, so if he's saying no then it's gotta be true. If it's not trouble with Amy, or even Charlotte or Eve, then just what the hell is it?

I wonder sometimes if being with me is more than she signed up for. Like, maybe it's too much and she just doesn't know how to end it. I want to believe she isn't like that, but the only real thing I've got to base it on is the way my mom up and left. If she could do it so easily and I'm her son, it's gotta be simple for a girl, even if she's more than just a girl to me.

I don't want to fail her, let her down or be who I was before, but all this stressing out and worrying that I'm doing is really starting to drive me insane. It's making me wish for the times when everything was easier. Walking the halls without a girl on my arm and creating havoc every chance I got is preferable to the unease I feel at not knowing just what the hell is going on.

She wasn't all that different with me earlier, but then again, she never is. She smiled at me like always, held my hand, kissed me back at all the right times. Everything is as amazing as it always is, but no matter how perfect it all looks on the surface, shaking the feeling that something is waiting to boil over is hard.

It's all I can think about as Coach has us running drills. I can hear him yelling at me and I'm doing what he says, my body being worn down in the process, but it's robotic because I'm flooded with thoughts of her.

Where she is right now, what she's doing, if she's thinking of me like I am with her. It's all repeating in a constant loop and no matter how much I try to drown the questions out, focusing on the action on the field, I can't do it.

It's only when practice is over that I finally get a reprieve because Dillon's voice instantly fills my head.

"Amy and I are getting a limo. You want in?"

"Nah man, it's all good. I'm gonna pick Isabelle up and head over in my car."

He laughs and I resist the urge to hit him. "I'm giving you the chance to get in on impressing the hell out of your girl with a limo ride, one of the most romantic things around, and you're turning me down for a ride in your beater?"

My car is not a beater. It's old, sure, but it's most definitely not a beater. Mom left it behind when she bailed and after a few years of working on it after practice in junior high, I finally got her running. It's a second generation Dodge Charger, from '68. It was red when mom owned it, but I got it detailed and now she's black, inside and out.

"You don't get it. If it's too much, it's gonna screw with her and I don't want that."

"Screw with her how?"

"Sometimes things are too much for her to handle and she sort of breaks down. If there's too much happening at once or too many people, it overwhelms her. I want this night to be perfect, so we're just gonna go in my car. She's comfortable there."

"Your loss."

"Honestly, it's my gain. I get my girl to myself, away from you and the girlfriend from hell."

"Ames isn't that bad. She's cool now."

"Not with me, and not with Isabelle either."

"Whatever. If you change your mind, let me know. It's cool with Amy if Isabelle comes along and I swear she won't screw with her."

There was a time when saying something like that would have made me laugh, but now I get the feeling he means every word of it. I hate to admit it, but ever since he said sorry to Isabelle, he's been a totally different guy. He's proving me wrong and I know him better than anyone.

"Thanks, but no thanks."

"Okay man; don't say I didn't offer."

He splits off and instead of following him in; I veer off to where I threw my duffel before heading out onto the field for practice. I know it's gross and I should stay behind and shower, but with as much as she's been on my mind for the last three hours, I know I won't be able to completely settle until I see her again.

Until I make her tell me just what the hell she's hiding from me.

Belle

When I got here, I expected to hear more of the same stuff I've heard since I got the diagnosis years ago, but instead, I'm hearing things I never dreamed possible.

There's actually a name for what I'm going through and even more than that, it's treatable.

"So you don't think it's a social anxiety anymore?"

"As I explained to your mother the last time you were here, I believe that it is social anxiety, but what I didn't speak to you about then, is that I also believe you suffer from something else. I'm actually surprised that it wasn't diagnosed in you sooner."

Dr. Stevens hasn't always been my doctor. In fact, for the first ten years after I was diagnosed, he wasn't even in my life at all. So what he's saying about this being caught sooner makes sense. The reason Mom changed to begin with was because she didn't think she was getting the answers she needed from my old doctor. Turns out, she was right.

"So you think I have Selective Mutism and Social Anxiety?"

"Yes I do. You are unable to speak aloud in the academic setting because of the mutism, but you are able to write and even text with certain people because in that regard you are comfortable enough to do so. That is a step in the right direction. What's important to remember is, this is treatable and it doesn't always have to be with medications."

That was a big thing with my mom the last time. She didn't want to feel like she was drugging me to solve my issues, so when she was told that I should be put on anxiety meds; she ran from the office and never looked back.

If there's a way to treat this like he's saying and it doesn't have to be just medication then I'm even more determined to do it.

"Is it just the speech that it affects?"

"I'm actually glad you asked me that. It manifests itself in other ways as well. The other ways may go unnoticed in most situations because of your autism diagnosis. There are a lot of similarities that can sometimes be confusing."

"Like what?"

"Speaking from a purely physical standpoint, it can cause extreme bouts of nausea, stomach aches, headaches, vomiting and joint pain. It also explains the accidents you continue to have. All of which, I know from your previous visits that you continue to experience."

Gee thanks Doc, I totally needed that reminder.

"You must remember that just because you have this, it doesn't mean that you aren't a social being. It just means that you are dealing with severe anxieties in those particular settings. There are various techniques and therapies we can try in order to help you manage it. There is also the road of medication, but that is not a road I want to put you on right at the beginning. I want to start small."

"Can I ask you something personal?"

"You can ask me anything, Isabelle. I am here to help you as much as I can."

"Not that long ago, I started dating someone and I can text him, even write to him, but I still can't talk to him, no matter how hard I try to do it. I don't want to talk to anyone else, but with him, it's all I want to do. Will I ever be able to do that?"

"With time, that is what I hope to accomplish. I won't sit here and tell you that it's going to happen overnight, because it won't, but if we work at it, I hope to get you to a point where you'll be able to open up."

"Is it happening because I'm not comfortable with him?"

I know how the question sounds, but I need to ask it. With everything that Kayden and I have been through, the switch in gears from being nonexistent, to his girlfriend, is huge for me. As much as I care about him, I still remember the way he was toward me before and I'm wondering if because of that, I'm stopping myself from opening up completely.

"It very well could be. When you are at home, you feel safe. There is nothing to fear. It is the perfect environment for you.

When you're not there, things become that much harder. If I may ask you, is your boyfriend understanding of the way things are?"

He's not asking the right person this question, but since I didn't even tell Kayden I had this appointment, it's not like he can ask him. The way he's been with me, it stands to reason that he understands, but I can't be sure. Not without coming right out and asking him myself.

"I think he is, but I don't really know."

"Do you feel safe when you're with him?"

"Yes."

"Well that's good to hear. That is what you need to surround yourself with. I do believe that in order to move forward in treating this, you feeling comfortable and safe needs to be our top priority."

I have no idea if he realizes it or not, but he's giving me hope. I felt lost before, stuck even and now that I know what I'm going through, I feel stronger than I did before I walked in.

If Dr. Stevens believes that we can treat this and that one day I'll be able to speak again, then it means all is not lost. I'm not a lost cause and I might even be able to do things the way normal people my age do, even if I'm still different.

As he makes his way from the office with the promise of a phone call about next steps, there's only one thought running through my head and it's so strong it makes me move faster than I've ever done before in an effort to get home.

I can't wait to tell Kayden.

Kayden

Pulling onto my street and slowing down to a crawl, I feel torn.

In a couple of seconds I'm going to have to make a choice. Go to my girlfriend's house and get answers so I can slow my mind down or turn into my own driveway, go home and face another night with the brother from hell. It should be an easy decision, but nothing about this is easy.

I want the comfort that being around Isabelle brings, especially when it's time spent with her entire family, but being unable to shake the uneasy feeling inside of me, I'm not sure it's where I should be right now. If this was any other person, I would have said screw it and gone home, sat down with Dean and gotten drunk, but she's not some other person.

As I make the decision, my phone starts buzzing off in the passenger seat. Reaching over and grabbing it, I see the flashing notification on my screen and I know that I made the right choice after all.

It's a text from Isabelle and even though I have no idea what it says, just the fact that she's messaging me at all gives me everything I need. I have a feeling that no matter what choice or decision I'm faced with in my life, it's always going to end with her.

Pulling into her driveway and putting the car in park, I swipe until I'm back in my messages and I finally read her words.

How much longer until I get to see you?

Smiling, I lay on the horn. It lets out three short blasts and I turn it off. I see the front door open and she's running out the door and across the lawn toward me. Pulling the seatbelt off as quickly as possible, I slide myself from the car, slamming the door behind me, opening my arms just in time to catch her as she dives toward me.

Well this isn't at all what I expected when I got here.

"Well, hello to you too." I choke out through my laughter. "Looks like I wasn't the only one missing someone."

She pulls back and shakes her head which I hope means she missed me too.

The way I feel about Isabelle has never had anything to do with the way she looks. It's just impossible to be that shallow and one track minded when I'm with her. There's no denying that she's beautiful. The way she looks now, I see that she shares a lot of the same features as her mother. From the blonde hair and blue eyes, to the shortened height and tiny hands, it's almost like the two of them could be twins.

It's her eyes that I focus on the most, even though her peach colored lips hold their own separate kind of appeal. They're a light blue, like the sky on a spring day before the clouds get in the way. They're reflective and every second that I stand here staring at them, I can see reflection and the way I look when I'm completely absorbed in her. If it's possible for a person's heart to shine through their eyes, then that's Isabelle right now.

Pressing my lips to hers, I allow myself to take in not only the softness that I've been missing for hours, but also the scent. It's peaches and cream this time. Every day is a new experience when I get to smell her, but this one might be my favorite. She really is good enough to eat and just admitting that makes me sound like such a chump.

"So," I ask breaking away from the kiss, watching as she laces her fingers through mine. "You gonna tell me what that welcome was about?"

She squeezes my hand once, telling me yes and then lifting our hands she points to the house. Well, if she wants to tell me something and she wants to do it inside, I'm more than willing to go along with it. Not only have I been dying to see her again, but I'm also curious to know why she seems so damn happy all of a sudden.

It's only when we're both locked inside and sitting around the kitchen bar that she passes the paper across to me and I see the words she's written there. The minute I do, my heart drops in my chest.

So, I went to the doctor today.

I knew she was hiding something from me, but I had no idea it was something medical. I thought that maybe she was starting to regret agreeing to come to the game or that she really didn't want to go to the dance after all, definitely not this. Is something wrong with her? I didn't even know she was sick. The questions flood my mind and I close my eyes in an effort to force them to stop.

She's happy right now; I need to focus on that. Nothing else matters.

"When?"

Her answer as usual is quick, something I've come to expect from her. She is definitely a writer.

After school. I know that you're gonna figure out I lied to you and I'm sorry for that, but I had to do it.

Isabelle, my Belle, lied to me. I can't seem to see anything else on the page but those words. It's not a big lie and judging from the way she's been acting since I showed up, I know I shouldn't focus on it, but I can't stop myself. It's just something that I never thought her capable of doing.

Maybe she's not so different from me after all.

"Why did you go there? Are you sick?"

Well duh Kay, I'm autistic, of course I'm sick.

There's not a damn thing funny about that, but the happy face steadies me. She's attempting to make a joke and I need to see it for what it is and not overreact. She's the one that's actually dealing with this and I'm the one losing my shit. How wrong is that?

"You didn't answer my question."

I went to talk to my doctor about what's wrong with me.

"There's nothing wrong with you."

She blushes and it turns me inside out. Even when her cheeks are completely red, she's gorgeous. I wasn't trying to say anything sweet, but her reaction shows me that it's just something I do easily when it comes to her. I hope it's something I get to do forever.

Kay, it's about my speech problems.

"What about them?"

I wanted to know what's wrong with me. I wanted to see if there's a way that I can talk again.

"Did he tell you something good? Is that why you're so happy?" I ask, even though it's not the question I really want an answer to. I want to know why she felt she had to keep it from me.

She nods and then starts scribbling on the paper, but this time she's taking her time, almost as if she's making sure she gets everything out.

"Can you also tell me why you felt like you needed to hide it from me?" I ask as she's pouring her heart out on the page. She looked like she was about to stop once the words came out, but just as quickly as she paused, she started again. It's only when she slides the paper over and I see she answered both that it makes sense.

He told me what's going on with me. It actually has a name and there are treatments for it, ones that have nothing to do with medication. He's going to call me in a day or so with a plan moving ahead, but Kay, I'm happy because it means there's hope. I'm going to be able to talk to you.

I didn't tell you because it was something that I needed to do on my own. I didn't even tell my mom. You have so much to worry about with the game; I didn't want to take your focus away.

I'm sorry.

As much as it touches me, her thinking about me and what I need to do, she doesn't have a sweet clue what actually matters to me these days. Football might have been my life before, but that was before she walked back into it. She isn't my entire world, but she's damn close.

If she's facing something as big as what she just told me, the last thing I want is for her to go through it alone. I'm glad that it's good news and trust me, seeing how hopeful and happy she is makes me happier than a pig in shit, but if it hadn't been, she would have been completely alone, something I swore she would never be as long as I'm here.

"Belle...you really don't get it do you?"

Get what? She writes quickly, her eyes locked on mine, searching for some sort of understanding of what I mean.

"I don't give a shit about practice or focusing on what I need to do on the field. What I do care about is you and making sure that you're okay. That's all that matters to me. If you just told me about this, I would have been there for you."

I know which is why I couldn't do that. You would have dropped everything and this game is super important, Kay. It's your future. I know scouts are gonna be there. I heard Coach talking about it before I left.

"Eight years, Isabelle. Eight years I spent trying to forget you exist. I called you names, made other people treat you like shit and honestly, I didn't care about you at all. Eight years is what I've got to make up for now. So yeah, I would have dropped all of it, if it meant being there for you the way I should have been from the start."

I'm so sorry, Kayden.

"You still don't get it. I'll try and explain again." I say, desperate for her to understand. "You have nothing to be sorry for. I do. You were thinking of me and I love you for that, but next time, just tell me, even if you don't want me there."

I always want you there.

It doesn't slip my mind that I just said I love her, but that's the last thing I'm focusing on now with what she just wrote on the page.

"Then there is where I'll always be."

Chapter Twenty

Belle

I'm the one that was asked to the game, but it's obvious from the way Tristan can't sit still that he believes it's him. My mom isn't much better either, humming and smiling all over the house, making sure that we've got everything laid out for later.

I know going to the dance is a pretty big deal for her since it's my first one and all, but does she really need to act like she's the one that's been asked? At least with Tristan I expect it, he's six. With her though, it's Freaky Friday and we've swapped spots.

"You sure you don't want me to hang around until after the game? You're gonna need a ride back to get ready, so it seems like I should."

That's the third time she's asked that, but this time, Tristan answers her before I do. It looks like he doesn't want her there either.

I love my mom, I do and I know that it's been a really rough road getting to this point for all of us, but this is something I need to do on my own.

It's hard to explain but I'm tired of living the way I have been. For years I liked having her there with me when I had to do new things, but that's starting to change. I guess I'm growing up now, even though for most people it happened years before.

It's not that I want to do this alone because I don't, but I need to.

Yesterday, seeing Doctor Stevens is when I realized it. I've never been to a doctor's appointment on my own before. She was always with me and with the way she fights for me so strongly, I always just let her. I'm seventeen now though. I don't want to always need my mom. I have to stand on my own two feet. I have to finally give her a chance to live the life she's been putting off for so long.

"Belle doesn't need you, Mommy. She's got me."

Tristan may only be six, but he's an old six. Just like he was the only one until Kayden that could really make me smile, he's also that way when it comes to being protective. The first time he ever stood up for me it was against our Mom and since then, it's never stopped.

He's right; I don't need her because I do have him, even if it should be the other way around and be me protecting him.

"So, I'll just drop the two of you off and head out for coffee then. You can text me when you're ready to come back."

There's sadness in her tone, almost as if she feels left out. Maybe it's not that at all and she's just worried about me taking the steps away from her constant supervision. Whatever it is, I don't like it and the last thing I want to hear from her, especially tonight, is sadness. This is a big moment for all of us, even if she did just spend the last half hour dancing around our house like a crazy person.

"I'll text you the minute it's done." I say smiling brightly at her. "It's all going to be fine."

That's not exactly the truth, but for now it's going to have to do. I'm going to the school to see Kayden play football for the first time. Kayden, my boyfriend, the one person in the world besides the two people in this room that wouldn't let anything happen to me. Of course everything would be alright.

He won't allow it to be any other way.

"When did you get that?" she asks motioning to the arm of the sofa where Kayden's jacket sits. "Did he give that to you when he was here last night?"

Before I can answer her, Tristan grabs her attention, pointing to the jersey he's wearing and I can't help but laugh at his excitement.

"Yeah, he gave it to me last night. He wanted me to wear it tonight. Once he heard how excited Tristan was to go though, he made sure he also got something to wear tonight, as you can see."

"Are you sure your brother's not the one dating him?"

"Not sure. With the way he's jumping all over himself, I'm thinking he might be."

"Well alright then. Since Tristan has his boyfriend's jersey and you've got his letterman jacket, it looks like we've got everything we need. You ready to go?"

I nod and stand up from the sofa, making sure to pull Kayden's jacket with me. I definitely can't forget this tonight, especially not after what he said to me before he let me have it.

"Most guys on the team, they give these to their girls to get them off their back. That's not the way I look at it. I want you to wear this because everyone needs to know who the real star of the team is, and it's not me."

He doesn't realize it, but when he said those words, I knew for sure.

I'm in love with him.

Kayden

Tonight is one of the biggest nights of my life and I'm scared shitless.

It's not the first time that college scouts have shown up at games, I mean they've been doing that since my freshman year, but tonight it's not only about the scouts. It's also the first time I'm going to have my girlfriend watching me play.

People can say that my future depends on how I play tonight because in the end it will determine if I get a scholarship to play ball, but that's not true at all. My future depends on tonight, sure, but it's not because of the scouts. It's because of her.

Every single vision I have of the way I am in the future, she's a part of. I'm not sure exactly when that happened but I like it. I want her there. I'll play my ass off tonight, talk to some of the scouts and make a road map to my future, but none of it matters at all if she's not there. I see meeting her after classes next year, going on dates with her, playing football and having her there cheering me on. It's crystal clear in my mind.

It's damn near perfect.

I'm not scared of any of that though. I'm scared because this is the first real event I've taken her to. Sure, I've hung out with her every single day, but we've always been alone. I've never taken her on a real date and this, tonight, is as real as it gets. The whole damn school already knows how I feel about her, what she means to me, but tonight the entire world or at least the entirety of Wexfield, is gonna know it.

How she's going to handle that is what scares me. She seems different lately, stronger even and I want to take credit for that, but I can't. Her keeping the doctor's appointment from me just proves it. She did all of that on her own and even seemed happy after it, which is a way that I've never seen her. Isabelle is different now and it's got nothing at all to do with me, it's all her.

A high school football game though, even the strongest person in the world, one that doesn't struggle with anything the way she does, can break at one of these things. I only hope that it goes off the way I want it to and she enjoys herself. I want her to look back on everything one day and realize that these really were great times, just the way she said in her letter.

I've been trying my best to keep my head in the game, focusing on exactly what I'm going to need to do on the field, but I can't. It always seems to come back to her and how eager I am to see her when she finally gets here. How it's going to feel, looking up in the stands and seeing her there, along with her little brother, smiling down at me.

She doesn't realize it, but a couple days ago I took a video of her. She thought I was taking a picture and I just let her believe it, but I taped her as she did the most mundane things. That's what I'm looking at now. That's my pre-game ritual. Watching her run her fingers through her hair, the wind blowing it in a million different directions and her laughing as it does. The way those eyes of hers lock straight on me for a split second and she smiles so bright that I'm sure she's giving the sun a run for its money.

Yeah, I've got it pretty damn bad.

I've been playing her voice file a lot, but not because of the laugh anymore. I have her laughing in the video and that suits me just fine. I listen to this file because she made it for me. She stepped out of her comfort zone that day, doing something I'm pretty damn sure she's never done and in doing it, changed the course of everything.

She changed the course of me.

I wish I taped her last night before I left. Giving her my jacket, knowing what it means, at least what it means to everyone at school was a huge thing for me, but no one deserves to wear it more than her. I meant what I said. She really is the star and I need everyone to see that, just the way I do.

It was so huge on her that I debated taking it back, but by the end of the night she wouldn't let me. You couldn't see her hands, unless she rolled the sleeves up a dozen times but she didn't seem to care. She just laughed every single time she did it as if it was the most normal thing in the world.

I'm still blown away by the way everything's happened with us. How one day, I went from not even registering her existence, to being completely consumed by it. The way she said my name that one day changed the course of forever for me. When I'm with her, everything feels like it's the way it's supposed to be.

If Isabelle Reagan can take a guy like me, turn him into someone worthy of respect, then it's mind blowing to think about what she can do for the rest of the world. Or even what we could do for it together.

We might be able to change it.

Belle

We've been here for ten minutes and I can already feel eyes on me, no matter what way I turn.

This is actually what I expected when I got here. I hoped that because I had Tristan with me, it might have been a little bit different, but I knew it would still happen. People can't figure out what the retard is doing here, wearing one of the players jackets no less. It's wrong to them because it's not normal.

Wearing Kayden's jacket is sort of like putting a big old bull's-eye on my back, but there's no way I'm taking it off. It might only be a jacket to some people, but I can tell with the way he gave it to me, it's something more so I'm going to wear it proudly. Even if doing it earns me death glares from practically every person here.

The sad reality is, it's not just the people I go to school with that are doing it. It's their parents too. Their noses are all turned up at me, like because of my diagnosis; I'm an alien to them. I'm not like their sons or daughters so that means I'm not worthy of respect. It's been like this forever and no matter how hard my mom fights, it never changes.

"Stupid people, their faces are gonna get stuck that way."

I hear what Tristan's saying, but I don't register exactly what he means until I turn and see what he's looking at. Amy's parents are about three rows up behind us and just like their daughter does when she's at school, they're sneering in our direction.

I hate that he has to see this. With him being in the elementary school, he's separated from me for the whole day, so he's safely kept away from what I deal with. I want it to stay that way. He deserves better then to be judged because of who his sister is.

"Come on, I see Kayden." I say, ignoring what I've just seen and pointing to where I see Kayden making his way toward us.

"Yes!" he yells and I can't help but laugh. It seems like Mom was right earlier. Kayden might be dating the both of us after all. It's actually the first person I've seen Tristan get close to besides me. It's nice.

"You're here." Kayden says the minute he reaches us, immediately wrapping me up into his arms, before reaching down and shaking his hand through Tristan's hair. "And you brought the midget too."

"Pfft," Tristan scoffs. "I'm so gonna grow up and be bigger then you, just watch."

"Sure you are buddy. I can't wait to see that."

He turns his attention back to me and places a soft kiss on my nose.

"I'm so glad you're here and that you're wearing this." he whispers as he fingers the sleeve of the jacket that's securely wrapped around me. "I know how weird this is for you."

There was a time not that long ago when he would say words like 'weird' or 'stupid' and it would bother me, but now it's like I know he doesn't mean them the way everyone else does. I don't flinch at them anymore and he doesn't react the way he used to. We've both come such a long way with each other.

"I need to get back down there, but Isabelle, thank you for doing this. You being here, it's everything."

He kisses my lips gently before again patting Tristan on the head, beaming his smile down at him and before I know it, he's gone and we're left alone again.

"Kayden is awesome!"

"Yeah, but don't tell him that. He'll never let us forget it." I whisper before we take our seats in the stands. As uncomfortable as it is having all of these eyes on me, I'm actually glad I did come because the look that Kayden had before he went back down to the field is one I want to see him wearing always. It's one that he hasn't worn much at all in the eight years since we stopped talking.

I'm not naïve enough to believe I'm the whole reason for it, but if my being here, especially wearing his extremely oversized jacket, contributes at all to what he's feeling right now, I'm happy to do it. He's given me so much since he rescued me that first day. Any chance I have to pay it back, I'll take.

"Oh look Char, the freak is here."

"Gross, they're gonna have to disinfect that area when she leaves."

"Impossible, they don't make a cleaner strong enough to mask that."

I can tell with how close they sound that they're behind us but I refuse to turn around in order to confirm it. Their words get to me though. I've managed to avoid seeing them this week, so having them here now brings everything to the surface. It's like I'm back in that bathroom all over again.

My heart starts racing and I breathe in and out, timing myself, in an effort to calm down before Tristan figures out something's going on. He's used to things happening with me, but usually Mom is with us. We're on our own now.

"How about you shut up?"

"Tristan, don't. You know Mom hates you saying that word." I whisper the minute I realize that it was him answering them back.

"Oh look, the retard can talk after all."

Well I could before you had to call attention to it. I think the minute Charlotte says the words.

"She sounds like a mouse, doesn't she, Ames?"

"Yeah, she does. A stupid mouse though."

I can't let them see that they're getting to me. If I do, I know what's going to happen and tonight I'm determined to not let it get that far. I knew this might happen, so now I just have to suck it up and deal with it. I can't let my fear win.

"Stop talking about yourself." Tristan snaps again, his eyes never shifting from their vantage point on the field. Whatever the reason is for why he's doing this, he's not giving them the satisfaction of looking at them. He's six and he's stronger then I am.

"I feel bad for Kayden, I mean he gave his jacket to her and all she's gonna do is piss all over it."

Charlotte's comment gets to me despite all of my attempts not to let it. Anytime someone brings up my accidents, I always react, even though I don't want to. I can feel the tears building up in the corner of my eyes and the pounding of my heart in my head, loud as ever. If I don't get out of here or get control of it soon, I'm going to make her words a reality.

I stand, grab hold of Tristan's hand, whispering to him that I need to get out of there and he instantly starts walking, pulling me with him. He might not entirely get what autism is or why it makes me the way I am, but he does get that it's causing me pain and just like he said at home, he's protecting me.

"Hey, Isabelle!" I hear Amy call out before we're able to get away. "You think Kayden really likes you, but he doesn't. You were his choice. He's been playing you the entire time."

There's a crushing weight on my chest as she speaks, but before I can get out of there I feel Tristan's hand slide out of my own. Before I know it, he's walking toward both girls. Raising his leg, I watch as he stomps down hard on Amy's foot before turning to Charlotte and kicking her in the knee. It might not be the right way to deal with things, but as they both react, I can't help feeling a little proud of him.

"Stupid girls." He says before coming back and sliding his hand in mine again. "Let's call Mommy. I wanna go home now."

Kayden

There is something seriously wrong with this picture.

We won the game, I've talked to a total of three different scouts for various schools, I'm riding the biggest high of my life and she's nowhere to be found. Not only that, but she hasn't been here the entire time and I should know. I checked every single time I was brought in off the field.

No Isabelle. No Tristan.

I knew asking her to do this for me was huge and I sort of figured she might not make it the entire time considering that a football game can be overwhelming, but she didn't even make it through half of it. It's like I talked to her and she disappeared.

I saw the looks I got when I pulled her close to me earlier. I also saw the reaction when I placed my lips to hers. None of these idiots understand it, so they're sitting there judging it. It's like we're some weird kind of reality show to these people and I can't stand it. If I wasn't trying to stay calm for her, I would have said something to every single one of them for the shit they were whispering and the looks they were throwing our way.

You never really think about what people go through until you're thrown into it. I did a lot of things believing that the impact would be worth it when I picked on people, but I never gave much thought to how the actual person being picked on feels. I get it now. Hell, I see it because I'm getting it too.

People are way too ignorant and I should know because I was the same way. If I can learn to be different though, can't they? Is change really that scary?

I have no idea what this means, her not being here, but I'm not gonna spend the night walking all over the field looking for her or waiting for her to come back and find me. No, I'm going to her and I'm gonna find out once and for all what made her run. If it's because it was too much, I can handle that, but if something else happened then I need to know so I can deal with it.

If no one else is gonna stick up for this girl then I'm going to do it and I honestly don't care what it means for me in the long term. I would rather be a total nobody at school, kicked completely off the team if it means I can change the way things have been here from day one. Something has to give and if they aren't gonna do anything on their own, I'm gonna change it myself.

It's only when I pull up in front of her house twenty minutes later that the doubt starts creeping in.

Am I the reason she left? Is being with me too hard for her and she's finally realizing she can't handle it?

I make my way to her door, watching my feet as I place one foot in front of the other, each one leading me one step closer to what's waiting behind that door. Will she be the one to answer or will it be her mom? Will they be happy to see me or just want me to get as far away from her as possible?

Before I can even raise my hand to knock, the door slides open and the light from inside spills out into the darkness, bringing a shadow across me from the person inside.

As my eyes adjust to the lights, I see it's Isabelle and the look on her face tells me everything I need to know. There are dried tear marks on her cheeks and the brightness I'd seen only a few hours before is completely wiped out. Her lips that for the past week have been frozen in a permanent raised position are mirroring her eyes as they're completely straight and displaying no real emotion at all.

Seeing her this way makes my worst fears a reality.

"Belle..."

She shakes her head at me, something she hasn't done in weeks and I swallow the lump in my throat. She's shaking her head because she doesn't want to talk to me. It hurts.

I watch as she moves away from the door and I wonder if I should follow her, but before I can move my foot in the direction she just disappeared into, she's back and this time she's got her phone with her. The problem with this is that I left my phone in the car, which means anything she says, I won't get.

"My phone's in the car. So whatever you wanna say, I won't see."

She slides her phone across to me and the minute our hands connect as I take it from her, she flinches and backs up. Whatever happened tonight while I was playing has done a lot more damage then I realized. It's almost as if we're right back where we were weeks ago. I don't like it.

I need to find a way to fix it.

You need to go.

"I'm not going anywhere, Isabelle. Not until you tell me what's going on."

I hand the phone back out to her and she grabs it, but this time she positions her hands differently somehow because we don't touch. She doesn't have a clue of course, but not touching her is ripping me apart inside. I want to be able to touch her. I have never felt so lost in my life.

I know everything now. Amy told me. I know it was all a game to you, Kayden. You don't have to act anymore.

"Wait, what?" I question as I read her words over a couple of times. "Amy told you what?"

Before she can type a response, another shadow enters the doorway and looking up; I see it's her mom. As much as I don't want to deal with an adult right now, only wanting Isabelle to tell me what happened, I realize that she might be the only person that can get me the answers.

"Isabelle, go inside, Tristan wants you."

She nods her head and just like that, she's gone and I'm completely alone. It's something I haven't felt since the day my mom left. I hate that there's anything with Isabelle that I can compare to that woman. They're nothing alike, but there's no denying that the minute she vanished, I felt empty, just the way I did then.

"What happened?" I manage to choke out. "Everything was fine before the game."

"I think deep down you know what happened tonight, Kayden. People happened."

"What does she mean by *'I know it was all a game'*?"

"Tristan told me that a couple of the girls said some things to her about you."

She doesn't need to say anything else. I know exactly what girls said things and the minute I get back to the school I'd handle it. Amy and Charlotte have pissed me off for the last time. First though, I need to make sure that everyone here knows the truth. I can't stand them believing that I was lying or playing them. It wasn't like that at all.

"It's not true."

"Well honey, I know that and deep down I think Isabelle might know it too, but you have to realize how hearing those kinds of things is for her. She might not be able to say the words, Kayden, but my daughter cares very deeply for you."

Shit. Now I feel even worse. I could easily tell that she liked me, her smile told me that, but the way her mom sounds now, it's something more. Something that I thought I was the only one feeling.

"Tell me how to fix this."

"I'm not sure that you can right now. Isabelle needs time. I believe that you're sincere, but when the majority of the people she comes across are not that way, it's hard for her to see it the same way I do. I can talk with her and do my best to get her to go to the dance, but for now, I think you need to do as she asked of you."

"You want me to leave?" I ask, already knowing it's the last thing I want to do.

"For now, I think it would be best if you did. Go to the dance, Kayden."

"I'm not sure I want to leave her when she's like this, especially since it's about me."

"I know, but it's something that she needs. Like I said, I'll talk to her and do my best to get her there. You can handle it from there, but if you continue standing here now, I'm afraid that nothing I say will get through."

I have to do what she's asking because the last thing I want is to make anything harder for Isabelle, but I don't like it. Leaving her seems so wrong and I'm tired of doing everything wrong. I should never have let her go when we were kids. I should have kept her close to me so that this pain didn't exist now.

It really is my fault. Amy and Charlotte did this because of me.

"Okay...I'll go, but, Mrs. R?"

"Yes?"

I know what I'm about to say, but before I can form the words, I stop myself. No, I can't say this as a message passed along. It needs to come from me.

"Just tell her I'll see her there."

As she says goodnight and shuts the door behind me, I don't make a move to turn and go. I know that I need to do what I've been told, but I still can't shake the feeling that me leaving right now is only going to make it worse. I need to talk to her and explain that those girls are full of shit. I need to tell her that they couldn't be more wrong.

Most of all, I need to tell her what I should have told her days ago.

I love her.

Chapter Twenty-One

Belle

I can't believe I'm doing this.

The last thing I wanted to do after what happened at the game is come to this stupid dance, but as always, my mom said all the right things and well, here I am.

There was this moment when I saw Kayden walking up the driveway that I wanted to open the door, run to him, have him hold me and never let go. I thought that being in his arms could erase everything that Amy and Charlotte said. That everything could just go back to the way it was before I agreed to go.

It can't though.

When I opened the door before he had the chance to knock, I told him to leave. It's better this way, not only for me, but for him too. There's a part of me that knows Amy was lying to me about him, but it doesn't change how wrong we are for each other. We might make each other happy, but that's bound to wear off sometime and its better we stop now instead of waiting until both of us are in too deep.

He deserves to be with a girl that he doesn't have to constantly worry about. He should be with one that doesn't have accidents when she's under pressure and one that doesn't cry every second. Most of all, he deserves a girl that can really give him everything he needs with no fear. She will be able to talk to him, laugh at his stupid jokes and constantly challenge him to be better.

He deserves someone I can never be.

I know I'm not defective the way people believe. This isn't about me thinking I'm less than other people. It's about me wanting to do the right thing by this boy that I love so much. I need to let him go now, even if it breaks me in the process.

When I told my mom all of this, she didn't agree with me, but because she always lets me make my own decisions, she backed down easily. The only thing she didn't back down on, was me coming to the dance.

She feels that I owe it to myself to go through with this, considering how much work we put into making sure I could. The dress and shoes bought, her prepared to do my makeup and hair for me. We had it all planned out for days and she felt that turning my back on it now, would become a regret later on.

I couldn't disagree with it, so that's why I'm here. It's the reason I've got makeup on for the first time and why I'm wearing a smile that even I can't believe in.

I'm determined for this to be a night to remember, but more than that, I'm determined to see it through for her. She took pictures before she drove me here and I really want this to be something she can look back on and be pleased with. It really is because of her and her never say die attitude with me that I'm even standing here now. She deserves this moment even more than I do.

As I make my way into the school and down the hall toward the gym, I can feel the eyes on me but this time, I don't hear the name calling that usually comes along with it. I don't hear anything actually. Usually, there's always a whisper, along with the traditional name calling, but this time, it's just silence.

When I get there, I see the doors are open and the dance has already started. There are couples clinging to each other in the middle of the room, as well as groups of friends standing in clusters on the sidelines. There are lights hanging from the ceiling and they seem to be casting blue stars below. There are banners and streamers hanging in all four corners and I'm struck by just how beautiful it looks.

It's like this room was made for someone like me. The lighting isn't bright, which calms me. While there are a lot of different things happening at one time, I'm okay with it because nothing is moving fast. It's all far away from me. The sensory overload that I normally feel just isn't there.

This really is a dream come true. For the first time, I feel like a normal girl.

A movement catches my eye on the right side of the room and as I turn and look out, I see him. Standing alone, looking like he wants to be anywhere but here, is Kayden. He's scowling and it makes me sad. This is supposed to be his night. He won his game. He should be in the middle of the room, dancing and having a good time. Not like this.

His hair is completely slicked back, the normal dirty blonde shade, looking almost black under the starry lights. He's rocking back and forth on his feet, his standard black boots sticking out from the tuxedo he's wearing. I don't think I've ever seen him dressed like this before, but it's another reason I'm glad I came. If anything, I want to remember Kayden like this, even if after tonight we no longer see each other.

He looks beautiful.

As I try and will myself forward, I feel an arm brush across my back and I freeze. With Kayden all the way on the other side of the room, it's not his familiar touch that's with me now, but I do know that whoever it is, I don't want it.

"You came."

Dillon.

I nod and as I look up, I see him smiling at me. I know that things have been different the last couple of weeks and that he's been better, but I'm not sure I trust his smile. It's probably because of Kayden, but nothing about this feels right.

"I heard about earlier, Isabelle. I'm sorry that they said that shit to you."

Of course he knows what happened. I bet Amy couldn't wait to run and tell him all about it. Making the autistic girl cry and run from them must have gotten a lot of laughs. I played right into their hands just the way they wanted me too, even if the look in Dillon's eyes says differently.

"Will you dance with me?" he asks and I flinch at the sound of his voice, something he picks up on because he speaks again. "Belle, you can trust me."

If I want to do what I promised my mom, then it's gotta start now. As much as I don't want Dillon to be the one I'm dancing with, it's just the way it has to be. Letting him take me by the hand and lead me to the dance floor, I swallow down the trickle of fear that's rising to the surface. I focus on the guy leading me, until we're in the middle of the room and he's resting my arms around his neck as the music starts.

I'm still filled with an uneasy feeling and it's obvious to Dillon in how frigid I'm standing. It's when he leans in and speaks that I finally let it go.

"Don't let them get to you, Isabelle. Just focus on me. I'll get you through it."

Kayden

After leaving Isabelle's, I did what her mom said and went home. I showered, dressed, making sure I looked exactly the way I wanted to look when I thought I'd be picking her up. I did everything that way, so that if she did show, she would see that I'm alright.

I must have been standing here like this for a half hour or more, finally reaching a point where I gave up believing she would show. I lost the smile and reverted back to the way I've always been. Something happened when I finally stopped faking it. I actually felt alright. Not perfect or the way I wanted to be, but at least I wasn't feeling completely empty anymore.

I'm not sure what happened, but one second, I'm standing in the corner, my face angled down toward my boots and suddenly it's like there's this pull inside me to look up. I catch a bit of a breeze pass by, thinking that someone ran by me, but when I look up, I start to see what the breeze was all about. It was a sign.

Standing in the doorway, in a dress that looks like it was ripped straight out of a fairy-tale, is Isabelle. Her hair tied back and out of her face, except for two bits hanging down on either side, falling into her cheeks. Her dress is strapless and light blue, the top tight to her body, yet for some reason glowing under the lights above us. The rest falls away from her and as her eyes catch mine, it hits me exactly who she looks like. With the way her hair sits and the way her dress shapes around her, she looks like Cinderella.

She's breathtaking.

Shaking myself to stop from staring, I start to move forward, but before I can even take two steps in her direction, I see him. Dillon comes up from behind her and I watch as his lips move and she responds with a nod. I can't make out what they're saying, but considering she doesn't seem eager to get away, it isn't anything bad.

It's only when she places her hand in his that my blood starts to run hot. I'm reminded of the day in the locker room when I told him she was mine. Seeing her moving across the floor with him, ties me up in knots. It's not supposed to be him leading her to the dance floor. It's supposed to be me.

The knot tightens as he wraps her arms around his neck and she leans into his body as they sway to the music. It's no longer just my blood boiling over now, but my head too. I can feel the urge to rip her away from him driving me and I fight it. As much as I want to act like a Neanderthal right now and take my girl back, I can't do that. I have to let this play itself out.

"Amy's gonna kill her."

Great. Apparently standing here focusing on them, left me open for people to start conversations.

"Screw off, Charlotte."

"Way to be a total asshole, Kayden."

"You know it. Now go away."

"You know what Kay? Screw you! A couple months ago, you couldn't get enough of me, but now, all because of some retard in an ugly dress, you treat me like I've got some disease. I don't, you know, she does."

I'm against hitting girls. That's not to say I've never purposely knocked into someone before in the hall, hell, I did it to Isabelle a lot, but never actually come right out and hit a chick. I'm getting dangerously close to that point right now. Charlotte is seriously pissing me off.

"You really wanna know what you were, Char? A fucking distraction, that's it. You're like every other girl in this school, shallow and bitchy. Sure, your chest distracted me for awhile, but like most toys, it got boring."

"Asshole." She seethes at me under her breath and I laugh. She really thinks calling me that is gonna wound me. She's as stupid as she looks.

"Run along, Char. Amy must be going out of her mind, not having you there to follow her around like the dog you are."

It's harsh and I know it, but it has the desired effect. She turns on her heel after I catch her rolling her eyes and stalks off, leaving me alone again.

The song is changing now, to one with a heavier beat and I watch Isabelle and Dillon. When they make no move to get off the dance floor, even going so far as to start dancing to the song, I know I've had as much as I can take. I'm not sure what his game is, but if it's turning me inside out so I become the jealous asshole, he's succeeding.

I have never wanted to kick someone's ass so much in my life.

She smiles at him as he spins her around and everything shifts inside of me. Up until twenty four hours ago, I thought I was the only person in the world that could make her smile like that. Now I'm seeing the truth. Apparently Dillon can too.

My worst fears are coming true.

I'm losing her.

Belle

I'm not sure how it happened, but I'm actually having fun.

As Dillon swings me around again, letting me dance around him, I'm smiling and laughing and having the time of my life.

When he told me to ignore everyone around us, I did as he said and everything seemed to get lighter. I kept my eyes locked on him or at least his chest and now as it's a new song, I'm doing the same again. I focus on his smile and how amazing dancing this way really is.

There's a set of eyes I can't entirely block out though and after one particular spin, I catch them and they seem to be the complete opposite of what I'm sure is evident in my own. Where I'm happy, he seems damaged, hurt even, and I can't help but feel that I'm the reason why.

When Dillon asked me to dance, I was so sure he was doing it for Kayden that it didn't even occur to me that maybe he was acting on his own. With the scowl on his face now, it all makes sense. I don't stop dancing though. I don't go to him the way I want to. I just do the one thing that's always been so hard to do with him. I look away.

As much as I want to believe that Amy is lying, I can't. There's this part of my brain that keeps going over every single thing that's happened with us and it just seems to bring more truth to what she said. When you spend a long time doing things to someone, not so nice things, why would you change it unless you were playing a game with them?

That's where confusion sets in. I can replay every second of our time together. The way it felt when he kissed me, the struggle he had asking me out and the way his eyes always go soft and tender whenever he's around me. Is it possible to fake that sort of thing? I know actors do it because there would never be any movies if they didn't, but away from the cameras and the insanity, can a real, living, breathing person do that sort of thing?

"Oh no! I'm losing her." Dillon calls across to me and I grin as we continue dancing. He could have easily made fun of me for what I did, but instead he cracked a joke. As off as he makes me feel most times, it's obvious he's not the same guy as before.

Neither is Kayden.

The song ends as I banish all thoughts of Kayden from my head and Dillon leads me off the dance floor and over to where the drinks and food are set up. I'm not sure if he realizes it or not, but I'm not going to be able to eat anything that's set out in front of us.

It's the first real reminder since I got here that I'm not like anyone else. I'm still the freak.

"You want a drink? They got punch, but since a couple of the guys threw vodka in it earlier, I don't recommend it. I think there's soda too."

I nod my head and he makes his way around to the other side of the table, grabbing a soda and popping the top before making his way back and handing it over. The way he does all of this gets to me. He made sure that never once was he out of my line of vision, just the way I needed him to.

Dillon is doing everything right.

I nod my head in thanks, wishing I could just say the words.

"You're welcome, Cinderella." He answers with a smirk. He points up toward the stage and as my eyes follow he speaks. "I gotta help set up the slide show for the Homecoming Court. You gonna be alright on your own for a bit?"

I nod and he smiles again.

"Thanks for the dance, Isabelle. Maybe I can steal another one before it's over."

As I watch him retreat, I think about what he said. Can I really stay for much longer? I know things have been going well so far, but I also know that it's going to start wearing on me.

"Isabelle..."

Oh no. Not now. Not when I'm having such a good time.

I look up and I'm slammed with the intensity of his eyes as they meet mine. Soft, just like before and even in the limited amount of light in the room, the green shines through crystal clear. I feel myself melting the more we just stand locked in place.

"We need to talk about earlier." He says slowly, almost as if he's unsure that he's used the right words. "What Amy told you is total bullshit. I'm not—I'm not playing you, Belle. I would never do that. Not to you."

I want to believe in him so bad my chest physically hurts. I need to believe because with the way he's made me feel over the last few days, the last thing I want to do is go on without him. I'm just not sure I can.

Just like Amy said, he's played me before; he could easily be playing me now.

"Alright ladies and gentleman, it's that time again. It's time to announce the Homecoming King and Queen of Wexfield High, 2014."

Thankful for the interruption, I turn away from him and those eyes that I swear can see straight into me and focus on Principal Daniels. I might not think I can last here much longer, but I at least want to try and get through this part. It's what I really want to see.

It's the one time that a boy and a girl get to feel like the prince and princess of the entire school. It might not be something I'll ever get to experience myself, but at least I can be here for the people that do.

"You might look like a princess, Isabelle Reagan, but if I had my way tonight, you'd also be a queen."

Kayden

Homecoming King.

Well I didn't see that coming, but as surprised as I am by it, I'm even more surprised by who the principal calls out as my Queen.

If there's ever a time when I needed a sign, it was now. I needed something to give me hope again. Hope that I would be able to get Isabelle to believe in me.

As soon as her name is announced, I know I've found it.

Watching as she makes her way toward the stage and more than that, toward me, I can feel her confusion as if I'm the one experiencing it. I don't think she expected this to happen and I have to admit, neither did I. There isn't another girl on the planet that deserves to be Homecoming Queen more than her though. This is her moment and man, do I want her to enjoy every second of it.

Before I know it, she's standing beside me and the principal's talking again. He's talking about us and how our fellow students have put together a package, something that we're sure to enjoy.

It's only when the sound of my voice comes over the PA system that I realize it's not going to be at all what he's expecting. In fact it's going to be something way worse.

"She's nobody, a ghost."

"I can't even get within ten feet of that retard without wanting to puke."

"You shouldn't feel bad for her; you should feel bad for me, having to hang out with that thing as long as I did."

"Since when did high school become Kindergarten? They're letting babies in now?"

"Go ahead man, push her. Ram right into her. She'd probably like it."

"Everything would've been fine if her mom had just done the honorable thing and aborted her."

Just when I think it can't get any worse than hearing my own voice saying these things, all of it spliced together from what felt like years ago, the screen behind us lights up and as I turn, I see her texts sliding up the screen. All of the private things she said, believing I could be trusted with it.

At first, the messages look tame. Her telling me how much she misses me, the hearts and happy faces flooding by the way I'm expecting them to. It's only when the last message makes its way onto the screen that something dies inside of me. It's the text from the night I asked her to tell me how she felt and it's up on the screen, blown up huge, for the entire world to see. Our most private moment exposed.

I'm going to be sick.

I'm afraid to look over at her. I don't want to see how she feels written all over her face. If she'd been a wounded animal that day in the parking lot, she has to be a hell of a lot worse now. The show isn't over though, now there are photos of us being filtered across the screen, my voice with the same repeated lines playing over every single one of them.

There are pictures of us together, when we were happy and then single shots, but the worst one is again kept until the very end, probably because it would be the one to have the most impact. It's a candid shot of the two of us as we're exiting the bathroom, the day Amy and Charlotte burned her, tearing her apart inside and out. The pants she's holding in her hands are noticeably stained, and you can tell by the mess in her hair just how hard everything had been on her.

I remember every single thing that happened that day and not once do I remember pictures being taken. It's obvious by the way I'm ushering her out, I was completely focused on the task and not on making sure we weren't being followed. It's just another way I let her down. I should have known that this was gonna happen.

And I knew just who's to blame for all of it.

Dillon Murphy.

I was right all along. He hadn't changed the way Isabelle thought. He was still the same damn snake he's always been. The difference is, this time; he'd played his part so well even I didn't see through it. He not only screwed with her, but me too.

The screen finally goes dark and of course our blissfully unaware Principal is trying to do damage control, but he doesn't realize that it's too late. Controlling that would have been shutting the shit off the minute the first hateful comment spewed out of my mouth, not waiting until the end.

Idiots.

I see movement out of the corner of my eye and the blue of her dress retreating and as she flies down the stairs, heading for the door. Wasting no time, I chase after her.

Catching her as she makes it about halfway across the gym, I grab her arm and spin her around to face me.

"Isabelle, don't run."

She's crying. I can see them running down her face, one after the other and with each tear that drops, I'm pretty sure my heart rips apart a little more. I know the way all of that looks and sounds, but she has to know I would never have done that to her. I don't think I have it in me to do that to anyone, at least not anymore.

She's shaking her head at me, moving so fast it looks like a really bad exorcist impression. I need to make her stop this. The last thing she needs to do is completely meltdown in front of everyone.

"Isabelle—Stop! Please."

I try to pull her to me and she yanks back on my arms, slipping on the floor and falling down in the process. Before I can reach out my hand to her, another hand comes out of nowhere and tracing it all the way up, I see the very last person I expected, standing beside her.

"Get away from her, you son of a bitch!" I yell. "You did this!"

"What are you talking about, K? Everyone heard you on the tape. You're the one that said all those things. Gotta hand it to you, bro. I didn't know you had it in you to be that god damned cold."

I notice her struggling to get to her feet and again I hold out my hand to her. She grabs onto it, pulling herself up and in an effort to protect her from what's going to happen next, I push her behind me. Before I take my next step though, I hear it.

She speaks.

"You said it...all of it."

It stops me in my tracks and as I turn toward the sound, toward her, that's when it happens. Dillon's fist connects with the side of my face and I stumble. Concerned with her and making sure that she doesn't get hurt, I push her again. I see the look of complete freaking horror on her face as she's taking everything in.

Blocking him before he can level me with another punch, I get my bearings back and rise to my feet. Ducking as he swings at me, I use the only tool I've got left and I kick him as hard and as quickly as I can. Stunning him exactly the way I hoped I would, I'm on him before he can even get a chance to adjust to the change. Rushing my body at his, I drop him to the floor and even though his hands are raised in a weak attempt to block me, I level him with punch after punch, until they all start blending together.

I can feel my energy draining, but I don't stop. I can't. He's had this coming for far too long and I don't give a shit if we're in the middle of the homecoming dance or not, he's going to pay for every damn thing he's done.

As I raise my hand up in the air, I feel someone attempting to hold me back and not thinking, I spin around, my other hand ready to swing and take them down. One direct hit. It's only when I hear the scream that I realize it wasn't a teacher or even the Coach that I hit.

It's Isabelle.

"Fuck!"

Climbing off Dillon, content that for the moment he won't be getting up, I slide across the floor toward her. It's only when a hand comes out in front of me that I stop. Ms. Taylor is looking straight at me, her eyes as hard as steel, her hand directly out in front of her, as she's bent over the only girl I've ever loved.

"Stay away from her, Kayden. You've done more than enough."

She leans over Isabelle and says something I can't quite make out before using her weight to pull her up. I'm on my knees in the middle of the floor, watching as she's lifted up into her favorite teacher's arms and escorted out of the gym. It's only when she's completely out and I know she's safe that I'm able to move again and when I do, I turn right back to Dillon.

His lip is broken open, bleeding, and I can already start to see his left eye changing colors from the punches I leveled him with. I'm tempted to rail on him again, but something stops me. Looking at him now, he reminds me of something that I've been doing everything in my power to block out.

He's as broken physically as I am, but that's not what hits me hardest. It's the realization that through all the brokenness, he reminds me of someone.

Me.

Chapter Twenty-Two

Belle

"Isabelle, are you alright?"

That's such a silly question. Of course I'm not alright. She was in the gym just like I was. She saw what happened to me. How can anyone be alright after something like that?

"I—want—to—go—home." I answer, my voice quivering after ever word.

Ms. Taylor got me out of the gym as quickly as she could and straight into the girl's washroom, even though it's the last place I want to be. I didn't have the energy to stop her, so I went along with it. Now I'm locked in the stall alone, trying to calm myself and she's on the other side worrying about me.

"As soon as you're done, I'll take you home sweetheart. Don't you worry about that."

Her words don't offer much comfort. Telling me not to worry is pointless. That's all I'm doing right now. I'm worrying about calming myself so I don't ruin my dress, worrying about Kayden and what's going to happen to him for what he did to Dillon. I'm worried about how I look to this teacher who seems to care about me. I'm just worried about everything.

"Can you call my mom?" I ask, my voice evening out though it comes out more of a whisper then I intended.

"I'll do that as soon as you're done."

I slide the lock off the door and ease my way out, still shaky on my feet, but able to walk if it means getting out of here faster.

"I'm done. Can we please go now?"

"Absolutely."

She walks ahead of me and pushes the door open, allowing me the chance to walk out before holding on to my arms and guiding me toward the front of the school. I hold my breath and close my eyes as she guides me, only releasing it the minute we're safely outside.

I know she means well, doing this for me, but I hope she realizes that after she drops me off tonight, she won't see me again.

The minute my mom hears about what happened, she's going to keep me home and this time, I'm going to let her. I wanted to do right by her, letting her finally go back to work instead of having to stay home with me and look where it got us. After tonight, I'm not sure I'm ever going to be okay again.

Sitting in the warmth of Ms. Taylor's car, I close my eyes and will the voices that have been flooding my head, to hush. I need quiet now. I can't take much more of the Kayden rage show on repeat. Not only am I hearing his pre-recorded words on a loop, but I'm also hearing everything he said leading up to it.

Amy told me the truth and Kayden proved it.

His wish for me to be Homecoming Queen came true, which means, he knew about the montage they would be playing. He'd probably been the one that set it all up. Despite the angry way he turned on Dillon, who is also to blame, it had still been his voice saying those hateful things.

I was a game to him.

Did I know Kayden said mean things about me? Yeah, but the things on the tape tonight, were definitely not what I thought he was capable of saying. He'd done it though and no matter how hard he tried to deny it, he couldn't.

"Do you want to talk about it?"

Shaking my head, I hear her sigh and I wonder just how much pity she feels for me right now. She might be a special needs teacher and she might even care a little more than the others, but I'm pretty sure right now all she feels is pity and sadness.

"Isabelle, what happened in that auditorium tonight, it wasn't your fault. You did nothing to deserve it. It should never have happened at all. I do not want you beating yourself up over this."

Easy for you to say. You're not the one everyone makes fun of and calls retarded.

"You're an amazingly strong, talented and beautiful girl. That is what I want you to remember when I drop you off tonight. What happened is not a reflection on you; it's a reflection on them."

I just want her to drive faster, so I can get home, run to my room and never come out again. Can't she just see that and make it happen already?

"Isabelle, I feel that I brought this on and for that, I'm deeply sorry."

Well that's new. How does she figure any of this is her fault?
"Why?"

"A few weeks ago, I spoke at length with Kayden about you. I showed him the writing assignment that I had you do. He asked me questions about you and the struggles you have. I gave as much factual information as I know, but I fear that after what happened tonight, I did the wrong thing."

She talked to Kayden about me? When? He asked her about my autism? Why would he do that?

The questions keep coming at me and I shut my eyes again, trying to focus on something, anything that will stop the influx.

"I thought he was one of the good guys." She says and I can't help agreeing with her. I thought the same thing, even though history should have been enough to tell me otherwise.

"What did he ask you?"

"He asked me what I knew about Autism, more specifically, your particular diagnosis. He asked about strengths that you have and weaknesses he might not have been aware of, that kind of thing. There was something more though."

"What does that mean?"

"He seemed genuinely concerned with doing right by you. In fact, I don't believe I've seen a student so determined before. He claimed he was tired of doing everything wrong, so learning was going to be his first step."

"The first step to what?"

Even thinking like this is making the ache in my chest worse. I don't want to know what his game was. I already know the end, but with the way she's describing it, it's like there's more to it and I need to know, even if it hurts.

"To making things right, at least that's what I assumed when he sat with me. You walked away from him and he wasn't entirely sure how to deal with that."

I know the day she's talking about. It's the day I overreacted and walked away from him at lunch. I thought he was planning something with her and it hurt that he was keeping it to himself. I guess I should be happy I have answers now.

She pulls up into my driveway and I unbuckle the seatbelt, fully prepared to say goodnight and duck inside as quickly as possible, but before I can reach the door handle, she speaks again.

"I know it's probably not the right time to say this, but Isabelle, I don't believe it."

"Believe what?"

"I saw his face the day he came to see me and I'm having a hard time reconciling that Kayden, with the one tonight. I don't think he had a hand in this."

Understanding what she means, but not sure I can agree, I thank her for driving me home and slide myself out of the car. Waving once as she backs out of the drive, I turn toward my house, the lights from the living room guiding me forward like a beacon.

As I slowly make my way up toward the door, there's only one thought running through my head.

Despite what my mom believes, sometimes regrets are a good thing.

Kayden

I am seriously fucked up right now.

After they carted Isabelle out of the gym, Dillon and I were kicked out. Worst part of all was them stripping me of my crown. Poor bastards actually think something that frigging stupid matters to me.

Apparently they take beating the ever living shit out of each other in a room full of people seriously. Who knew?

There was a minute or two when we got kicked outside by Coach that it looked like we were gonna wail on each other again. At least that's what I wanted to do the minute the doors closed. The problem with that is, if I go at him again, I'd be beating on him for shit that I did. Sure, he put it out there, instead of being the decent guy he'd been pretending to be, but that was my fault too.

I knew Dillon was a complete douche. I mean, I taught him everything I know. Add that to what he already had stored away from before and he was a walking time bomb for this stuff. I knew it and still chose to believe in him.

It's actually her fault when you think about it. If it hadn't been for her and her oh-so-trusting attitude wearing off on me during our time together, I would've remembered what a complete dick Dillon Murphy really is and that shit tonight wouldn't have happened. Yeah, that's much better. It's all Isabelle's fault.

No, see, that's not right. That's the anger and alcohol talking.

It's not her fault at all. None of this is her fault. All she did was fall for a complete asshole. Can't say I didn't warn her.

God, I screwed this whole thing up. I had one of the best human beings in the world wanting to be with me and I had to go and blow it all to shit. I craved the popularity so damn bad that I forgot where I came from. I used her, making fun of her, in order to make myself look better. All I did was make myself look like the chump I really am.

She's so much better off without me. I'm just not sure I'm all that better off without her.

Walking away from Dillon, his laughter at my back not even registering, I had one set goal in mind of where I wanted to go. Somehow though, I didn't end up following through. I might be the world's biggest dick bag, but I know better than to drive when I'm like this. So leaving my car in the parking lot, I start walking. I was going to walk to Isabelle. I needed to see her, explain what happened tonight.

I ended up at the liquor store instead.

I sat there for over an hour, drinking straight from the bottle and now I'm attempting to do what I wanted to do earlier. I know showing up at her house, drunk off my ass no less, is probably not the way to go, but it's not like I can just walk home. Dean sees me like this and I'm dead for sure.

With as pissed off as Coach was when he threw us out on our asses, I'm not even sure I'm gonna have a spot on the team come Monday. I screwed up with Isabelle and screwed up my full ride to a college of my choice all in a half hour time span. I am the king.

Well, I was, until they took it away from me.

Ha, I'm so messed up.

If I know Coach, he called Dean already. So going home is not happening. I've already had my beating for the day. He can take his anger and shove it, or use it on some more of the house. With the way it's looking now, there probably isn't a spot in the place he hasn't completely destroyed in his drunken fits. It's amazing the place even stands at all.

So Isabelle's house it is. Her mom likes me. I'm pretty sure; even drunk I can charm her enough to get in the door. Who doesn't love sweet and respectable Kayden?

Except you're not sweet and you damn sure aren't respectable after what you did to her daughter.

You know, I can't even remember when I said all that shit they got me on tape with. I'm not denying I said it because I know my own voice, but I've been making fun of her for so long, it could have been three years ago and I wouldn't know. Gotta hand it to him though, he nailed all of the primo material. I couldn't have picked better than that.

I told Tim that her mother should have aborted her for crying out loud. How much worse can you get?

I just hope she didn't tell her mom exactly what I said about her, otherwise, I'm definitely not making it past her front door tonight.

Finally reaching her driveway, I try to keep myself as steady as I can.

"Isaaaaaaaaabelleeeeeeeee!"

It's slurred and I swear I cracked a couple times, but it came out loud enough to have an effect. Where they had been no light before, there is now. Right where her living room is, it brightens and I know that I've been heard.

Making my way up the rest of the driveway, I take her steps, one at a time, until I'm standing directly in front of her door. Pressing my finger down hard on the doorbell, my body sways back and forth as I wait for someone to get a clue and answer.

When the door opens, I expect it to be her mom. There's this part of me that wants to see her angry face and be yelled at for what I did tonight. I need to be screamed at. I think I actually need it as badly as I need Isabelle herself.

It's not her mom though. It's her.

Her face is still stained with tears and even in my haze I wonder if they're new or just left over from before. Even though she's standing in front of me, her eyes are locked on the ground, not even acknowledging that I'm standing here. Seeing her like this pisses me off. I walked all this way to talk to her, the last thing I need is for her to look anywhere but at me.

"You, you need to look—at me!"

Like magic her head lifts and for a split second I think I'm actually going to have those pretty blue eyes aimed in my direction, more than happy with whatever expression shines in them. I'd gladly take her anger, sadness, hell, even laughter if it meant she would just look at me again.

She doesn't afford me that luxury though, instead looking toward my house across the street, her eyes dull and lifeless. I move toward her and the minute I do, I regret it. Instead of cowering the way I expect, she pushes her body into mine until I stumble backward off her front step. Before I can react, she shoves her arms into me, again making me stumble. With one more shove, as hard as I think she can push, she gets what she wants. I fall flat on my ass on the ground in front of her.

I start laughing hysterically and that's when I see it. Her face scrunches up and she starts crying.

I'm sick of seeing this girl cry in front of me. All I've wanted since the day I found her in the parking lot is for her to smile. I felt like the luckiest son of a bitch walking the earth the day she smiled at me for the first time. Now I'm back to doing what I've been doing to her for eight years now. I've turned her back into the wounded bird she'd been when I saved her.

Something is seriously wrong.

Focusing on the day I saved her, calling her a wounded bird, it's all wrong. I'm the one that's wounded and she wasn't the one saved that day. I was. The life I'd been living had gotten old, so when the opportunity presented itself, I saw an opening and I took it. She saved me and she has no fucking clue.

"Belle…"

Trying to focus my eyes on her, I realize as the haze lifts that she's not standing in front of me anymore. It's only when I feel the softest hands in the world run across my face, I know why she's not where she was.

"Goodbye Kayden."

Those lips of hers, so soft, I imagine it's what lying on a cloud feels like, come to rest on my forehead and before I can reach out, grab her and make her stay with me, she's on her feet again. Her back is to me and she's walking away.

I'm completely blasted off my ass and I probably won't remember all this in the morning, but I do know one thing I'm never going to forget, no matter how much I drink tonight or where I go from here.

I'll never forget the sound of her voice as she tells me goodbye.

Chapter Twenty-Three

Belle

The strangest thing happens to me when I hear Kayden yelling from outside.

Mom gets up from the sofa, more than ready to go to the door and handle it, but I don't let her. I stand in her way, blocking her and don't back down until she sits down. When she'd gotten to the door after the game, I had no problem letting her take control, but something is different this time.

She can't do this anymore.

I'm seventeen years old and just like Ms. Taylor told me before she dropped me off, I'm smart and I deserve better. For so long I've stayed in this comfortable little place inside of myself where none of their words could touch me. Somewhere along the way, the walls I constructed broke down because I became flooded with all the awful words, taunts and physical pain they put on me.

That can't happen anymore. It's time to face it, this time without any walls up and put an end to it once and for all, whether I can speak the words or not.

When I opened the door and came face to face with him, I wasn't sure what was going to happen. I know I wanted to get rid of him, get him back home where he belongs, but anything else, I didn't plan. The first thing I noticed about him wasn't his eyes or the way he's dressed, but how he smelled.

People make fun of me all the time for the accidents I have and as hard as having them is for me, I do understand what people find funny about it, even if it's mean. It's why one of the things I heard on the tape, didn't hurt me as much as it should have. Going to school with me really is like going with someone in Kindergarten.

Kayden, smelling like he bathed in alcohol for the past three hours, might be worse than all of my accidents combined. It's such a strong scent that I have a hard time even looking toward him because of the way it floats toward my nose. If I breathe that smell in for too long, I'm actually scared I'll end up being the one that's drunk, not him.

He yells at me to look at him and something inside me snaps. I'm not sure if it's just everything that's happened these past few weeks or the glazed over look in his eye as he's yelling, but I've had enough.

I start pushing at him, shoving as hard as I can, trying to get him away from me. I want him away from the house, away from my mom and Tristan, who despite everything he's heard tonight, still loves Kayden almost as much as I do. I want him back in the house of horrors he lives in across the street and I never want to see him again.

When he finally falls, that's when I break. I know I want him away, but seeing him on the ground that way, I worry that I hurt him. He laughs so loudly there's a second where I think I'm watching the hyena exhibit at the zoo and not a real person. That's when the stupid tears start falling. There's something about the way he's laughing and it's aimed at me that rips me apart inside.

We're no good for each other. We never have been. I was going to use my time at the dance to tell him that and it's there again, the need to do it. He's sitting on the ground in front of my house, drunk, because of everything I've put him through. It's further proof that he deserves someone better.

I need to let him go.

So when I slide down onto my knees and touch his face, I do the only thing I can do, in order to do the right thing by him. I lean into his forehead, close my eyes and place my lips to his skin, saying my own private goodbye, before standing and saying the words out loud, the way they need to be.

What I've been suffering with all of these years, not being able to talk, almost seems like it's lifted in that moment. I have no fear about the words I'm about to say. In fact, for the first time in a really long time, they seem like the right ones. My heart isn't beating out of my chest; it's slowed to a dull crawl. I'm secure with this, knowing it's what needs to be done. There can be no looking back.

"Goodbye Kayden."

It's only when I've walked completely away from him, back into the safety of my house with the door shut behind me, that I wipe the tears from my eyes and make my way up the stairs to my room. Where I might have looked through the window to make sure he got home safe before, I don't do that now. I can't. This time, a goodbye has to mean goodbye, even if it hurts me deeply to do so.

"Are you okay, Belle?" I hear my mom call up the stairs.

"No, but I will be."

Kayden

I don't know how long I laid out there on her lawn, but after staring up at the sky for what feels like hours, letting the dizziness pass, I finally start taking the steps to get up. Her last words to me are firmly planted in my head and with them running on repeat; I start stumbling across the street.

It's time to face Dean.

No one knows this, but I dread this part. Coming home every day after practice or even just after school, I take my time driving down the street, so I can prolong it as long as possible. I hate coming face to face with him. Walking in the door and seeing his dead eyes looking through me, shows me a truth I really don't want to see.

This is my future.

The way Dean is, slumped over in his bed or hanging off the sofa, while he's sleeping off another bender in his boxers. That's what I have to look forward to if I don't do something drastic to change it. I thought nailing a scholarship would do it, hell, I even thought getting together with Isabelle and spending all of my free time over there, would be what changed the road I'm on, but it's not. No matter what I do to change it, this is always going to be my path.

I'm destined to become Dean.

As expected, the minute the door cracks open, I'm met with a pair of angry brown eyes. This time though, the normal glaze I'm used to isn't there. I'm not sure if it's because I'm so wasted that my eyes are playing tricks on me, but he doesn't look drunk.

He walks toward me and I notice there isn't a sway in his step like usual. He's completely straight and from the look in his eyes, growing angrier by the minute. I would prefer he was wasted; it would make this go a little smoother. There's nothing worse than an angry, yet sober Dean. He's twice as dangerous then.

I'm not sure if it's the alcohol talking or what, but I start laughing again, even more hysterically then I did earlier with Isabelle. Dean not being drunk has to be some sort of sick joke right? The guy hasn't been sober more than a day in the last six months. It's a trademark thing for him. Who is he trying to impress being the sober one now?

"Glad you think this is funny."

"You're sober, it's hilarious."

He smirks at me, which normally would scare the shit out of me because I know what's coming, but this time it doesn't. I don't feel anything. I guess that's what happens when you've lost everything that had any real meaning. You become numb to what's left.

It happens so quickly, I don't have the time to adjust and suddenly my back is up against the wall, his hand pushing into my chest, locking me in place.

"You think you're such a smart, son of a bitch, yet every single thing you do is stupid. You're no better than that stupid mute bitch across the street!"

The anger inside of me rises the minute he mentions Isabelle, but the liquor I drowned myself in before has left me so off kilter, I don't have it in me to fight him on it. Any other time, I'd have no problem shutting him up, but I really am completely empty. I've got nothing left.

"I didn't bust my ass to get you on the team just so you could blow it all for a crush on a retard."

He lands the first blow, following it up immediately with another one straight into my stomach until my body starts sliding down the wall. He releases his arm and watches me fall to the floor, the smirk now a full grin. He's pleased with himself. Bringing people pain or at least causing me pain brings him enjoyment like nothing else.

I feel the kicks next, as he levels me with one after the other, my brain losing count after the fifth or sixth one, all of them blending together until I can barely tell them apart.

Picking me up off the floor, he lifts me in the air until I'm standing on my feet, swaying a little, but steady enough that I'm not going to fall unless pushed. He starts screaming at me, his words coming so quickly, I can't make any of them out, his hands shoving into my chest until I'm stumbling backwards.

I hear the sound of the glass smashing before I feel the impact. It's when I start feeling the stinging pain in different parts of my body that I realize exactly what's happened. He shoved into me so hard that I feel backwards and smashed through the glass table. It now lays in pieces, some of them digging into my back, my legs and arms. I feel the dampness on my body and I know that not only did I break straight through it, but it broke me open in the process.

I know I should try and get up, that I need to fight back before he decides to do something even worse, but I can't. I've got nothing left to fight for.

Fighting with Dillon probably screwed my chances on the team and the scholarship I wanted so badly. My own words about Isabelle ruined any shot I have at a future with her. There really is nothing left. I'm completely alone, the same way I was when Mom split, leaving me with Satan incarnate.

Closing my eyes, blocking out whatever Dean is going to do next, I let the darkness pull me under and just like times before, the last thing I see before it completely drags me down is Isabelle as she walks toward me, smiling.

Belle

Something doesn't feel right. I've got this sick feeling in my stomach. It's been there for over an hour and no matter what I do, it doesn't go away.

I thought it was because of everything that happened tonight, but even when I'm not thinking about all of that, it's still there, turning me inside out. I tried taking medicine, hoping that would fix it, but it did nothing to help. I closed my eyes and tried to sleep, something I'm sure my body wants more than anything, but all I do is toss and turn, the sick feeling growing even more.

When I've finally had more than I can stand, I go downstairs, but when I reach the bottom step, I just stand and watch the picture in front of me. Tristan's on the sofa, curled up in my mom's arms, the TV playing some superhero movie, but neither one of them is paying attention. Mom's head is turned into his and he's blocked by her body so I can't make out where his face is, but I think he might be asleep.

It's a peaceful picture, one I've seen a million times before, but one that gets to me now more than ever. Despite everything that I have to deal with, at the end of the day I still get to come home to this. To a mother, that despite her own failings, loves unconditionally and who will do anything to keep her kids safe and protected.

There's no darkness, pain or fighting here. There's just love.

We have stress of course, every family has that, but here, the way it's dealt with is just so different than what I've seen and read about. The stress doesn't break us; it seems to make us stronger.

Watching them this way, it makes me think of the people that don't have this. It makes me think of him, despite the fact that he's the last person I want to focus on. He had this, at least a little before his mom left, but it wasn't quite the same. Now, he doesn't have it at all and even though I never want to see him again, my heart breaks for him.

Leaving him outside on the lawn and walking away, I have no idea where he ended up and it's scares me. No matter how upset I am, I know what's going to happen if he goes home and not even Kayden deserves that. I should have brought him in, instead of leaving him out there.

Maybe I didn't do the right thing for him after all. Sending him home to Dean is never going to be the right thing.

Placing my foot down flat, the floor creaks under the pressure and the peaceful picture of my family shifts, my mom turning her head toward the sound and locking eyes with me.

"It's alright, Belle." She whispers, giving me all the proof I need that Tristan is indeed asleep in her arms. "Go ahead, just be careful."

She knows what I want to do and I don't have to say a word. This is another reason I'm so glad that she's my mom. It's been proven that there are people in the world that, because of their own issues, can't handle when things are hard. She's not like that at all. I think in some way, I was put with her because of how strong she is, even at her weakest point. She could have given up at any time, sent me away somewhere, but she didn't. She stayed right by my side, fighting for me every step of the way.

Grace Reagan is the strongest person I know.

"I will. I won't be long."

I'm not sure what I'm going to do, but once I've traded out my slippers for the sandals and put my jacket on, I know that I've got to do it.

Kayden Walker may be everything that he's claimed to be right from the beginning, but he's still a person underneath all of it. A living, breathing person that deserves better then to go home every single night and fear what might happen. The sick feeling inside of me, it's because of him and until I see for myself that he's okay, that Dean hasn't hurt him, I won't feel right again.

Not bothering to look both ways, content that at this time of night, the street's going to be quiet, I run across and it's only when I get to his door that I know why the pain in my stomach is so strong.

I hear what sounds like bottles smashing, then the yelling, but it's not Kayden. It's all Dean. I would recognize that angry, gruff sound anywhere. Even though I've seen his brother in the peak of his rage before, it doesn't sound anything like this. I'm about to knock on the door when I hear the moan. It's not loud and just as quickly as I hear it, it's gone. It's just Dean yelling again, but I know the moan was from Kayden.

Shaking off the fear, I turn the knob and push the door open with my hand once it clicks. It's then I see the damage that's been done.

Dean's standing in front of the bar, his face red, eyes empty and dead, blood covering his hands. If he heard me open the door, he doesn't acknowledge it. His gaze never leaves the floor in front of him. Following it, I see what he's looking at and the sick feeling in my stomach grows so big, my being there can no longer be a secret.

Trying to catch it before it happens, I cover my mouth, but it's no use. The soda from the dance and the crackers I tried eating come flooding out and when it hits the floor, Dean finally turns to me.

"Don't you know how to knock or do they not teach you that in the retard class?"

His words cut me, but not enough to stop me. No matter how scared I am, how much I want to cower in the corner and cover my ears, I can't do it. Kayden needs me.

Sliding my hand into my pocket, I feel the cold metal of my phone, but instead of pulling it out and doing what I should, I start moving toward him.

The glass table that only a few weeks ago had been standing upright with bottles and cans all over it, is now a bunch of broken pieces and shards all over the floor. On top of it all, is the only boy in the world with the power to hurt me. Except this time, he's the one broken and hurting. I need to get to him, make sure he's still breathing and then I need to get him out of here before Dean can do any more damage.

"What do you think you're doing?" He screams at me, as I bend down on the floor as carefully as possible, trying to avoid the small shards of glass I see sticking out of the carpet. Doing what my mom taught me, I lean my head to his chest. I'm met with the steady beat of his heart and even though it's weak, I feel the air from his nose as it tickles my skin.

"You hear me stupid? What the fuck do you think you're doing?"

Spinning around, I level him with a look that I hope says everything I'm not sure I can say. I've never felt this way in my life. I've felt a lot of different things before, but this is new to me. I actually want to get up right now and hit him, not stopping until he's the one on the floor barely breathing.

Kayden is his brother. He should be protecting him from stuff like this, not be the one causing it. He should know better. He's ten years older. He's an adult, just like my mom. If she can handle everything that's been thrown on her, then why can't he? Why is beating on the little brother that loves him, the right thing for him to do?

Sliding my phone from my pocket, I dial 9-1-1 and put the phone to my ear, praying they answer before Dean takes it from me. As soon as I hear the operator's voice, it's like a block has been lifted and I start talking, even though I know that any second it could be over. Nothing is going to stop me, not even Dean.

Giving them the address, I listen to the operator as she tells me things to check and do, to make sure that until help comes, Kayden keeps breathing. The altercation I expect to come from the older guy behind me doesn't, as I continue doing everything she tells me to. It's only when I turn around and face him again, that I really get a good look at him.

He's standing completely still, the anger in his eyes gone, replaced with something I'm not familiar with. Whatever it is though, as long as it keeps him where he is and away from his brother, I'm okay with it.

"You can talk…" he says, the gruff tone of his voice significantly lower than it had been when I got here.

"Yeah, imagine that."

Turning back to Kayden, checking his pulse as I hear the sirens in the distance, I lean in as close as possible, resting my head on his chest. I let the beating of his heart calm the fear welling up inside of me. It's only when I see the flashing lights flood through the room that I raise my head and again, focus on the person now standing to the left of me.

"I'm going to make sure you never hurt him again."

Chapter Twenty-Four

Kayden

When I passed out, I thought that was it. I was just waiting for the end to come.

As it turns out, me being ready to die means squat, because I'm still here. I'm a little more broken and bruised then before and my head hurts so bad, I'm pretty sure it's going to explode any second, but otherwise I'm exactly the same.

When I woke up, I was in the hospital; there were a couple of cops leaning against the wall and a lady in a white coat over me. When I saw the white, I thought it might be Heaven, but that was quickly thrown out the window the minute she started prodding at me.

Angels don't probe you, aliens do.

Shortly after she finished with me, the Doctor came in and filled me in as much as he could on what happened to me. For the most part, I already knew it had something to do with Dean, but hearing all the injuries I had, that was a bit of a surprise.

I told the cops as much as I could about what happened, even telling them what happened earlier in the night, so that in some way they'd know he wasn't entirely to blame for it. I'm the one that went home drunk, knowing what would happen. I brought it on myself and I wasn't going to make light of it. Not anymore.

It's then that they told me something I didn't know. If hearing about my injuries surprised me, this damn near blew me away completely.

Isabelle is the one that called 9-1-1. She's the one that told them exactly what happened when they showed up and she's the reason that I made it to the hospital instead of eventually bleeding out on the floor. I have no doubt that if she hadn't done that; Dean would have just continued his assault until I was dead.

As ready as I was to die after everything that happened, I'm glad that it didn't get to that point. I wasn't suicidal, just broken.

They've got Dean in custody and regardless of what I told them about my drunkenness, they're pressing charges anyway. Child endangerment is something they threw around, as well as child abuse. I'm three months away from turning eighteen; there isn't a part of me that's still a child, but apparently, none of that matters to them. He's finally going to pay for what he's been doing to me all of these years and it's all because of her.

What she was thinking coming over to my house, I don't know, but I can imagine what would be happening now if she didn't. Whatever her reasons were, I'm never going to be able to repay her.

They released me today, two days after everything and it's been hard coming back here. I thought I knew what I was going to find the minute I opened the door, but there's no amount of preparation I could do that could have readied me for the scene in front of me now.

Where I expected to see my blood, the broken table, shards of glass, I see nothing. The brown carpet is gone and there's a white one in its place. It hits me as I stare at it in shock that when my mom bought it years before, it had been white. It's only after all the parties, fights and other general insanity we've lived, that it turned brown. Where the glass table had been, a wooden one now sits and there's nothing on top of it, but a couple of books and magazines.

The bar's completely wiped down, the mess from before gone and as I make my way over the fridge, opening the cupboards as I go, I see that all of the food that had been thrown around or emptied all over the house, is now placed neatly in lines, along with the dishes.

Everything is the way it should have been. The way that, from the time mom split, I wanted it to be. If I didn't know the real horror that had taken place here, I would have thought I walked into a whole different house. Not just any random house either, a real home.

You don't have to be genius to know who did this. There's only one person in my sad existence that would have cared enough to make this happen.

Isabelle.

Despite calling it in and making sure the police knew everything that happened to me, she hadn't come to the hospital once in the two days I was there. She didn't call, even though I stupidly tested the line in the room a few times to make sure that it worked, so she could. I'd given up on ever hearing from her again by the time they let me out.

I know why she didn't come. She'd been making sure that when I did get released, I had a clean house to come back to. Isabelle and her mom no doubt, wanted to be sure that I had a home, the one thing I never thought I would ever be afforded again.

Wondering if they did the same to the bedrooms, I grab a soda from the fully stocked fridge and make my way down the hall toward my room.

Pushing the door open and scanning around inside, I see that what they did with the front of the house, they also did in here. There's a whole new set of sheets and blankets on my bed, and everything has been moved around in a way that makes me think they wanted to make it easier for me to get around, should I need it.

I had my shit all over the place before and liked it that way. I knew where everything was, even though it was usually in a pile all over the floor. Now though, the TV and the stand are up against the wall, I can actually see my carpet again and all my clothes, CD's and other crap is mysteriously out of sight or straightened in the shelves that now cover my walls.

Seeing all the work they put into this room alone, I want to run across the street and thank them, but after everything I put her through, I can't do that. I can still remember what happened earlier that night, the goodbye crystal clear in my head. So as much as I want to thank them for everything they've done, I can't.

It's better for her if I keep my distance, even though it's the very last thing I want to do.

Belle

I'm pretty sure someone in the office has lost their mind.

The morning announcements came on like usual, but when they were over, the strangest thing happened. Instead of hearing the cut off noise when they turn the P.A system off, music starts playing instead. Normally it wouldn't have registered with me because I tune it out, but it was so familiar that I couldn't ignore it. Not only was it a song I knew, but it was by my favorite band.

"The Mess I Made" by Parachute is playing clear as day through the entire school and looking around at all the other kids in class with me; I can see that they're also pretty surprised with it.

It's not that we've never heard music over the system before, because we have, but usually it's lower and in the background, someone's voice speaking over it. The cheerleaders use it when they're promoting events that they're putting on. This is different though. There's no nasal voice speaking over it, no announcement being made. It's just the song.

I've been back at school for two days now, despite my claims that I didn't want to come back. After talking things through with my mom the night I found Kayden, we both decided that no matter what happened at the dance, it would be best if I finished out the year. Where I had been scared at first, it's gotten easier and now I don't even know what I was so afraid of to begin with.

Nothing's really changed being back, but it does seem that where Dillon and the others went out of their way to hunt me down before, they're silent and only shooting out names from a distance now. It's like what happened at the Homecoming Dance never happened. I fell back into my old routine of walking the halls like a ghost again and they left me alone.

Today is a different story altogether and I know why. It's because today's the day he comes back. Kayden Walker. The boy I found bloodied and broken in the middle of his living room floor, has been released with a clean bill of health and is ready to make his comeback.

I'm not sure how much people know about where he's been, but since I haven't said a word since the night I told the police everything, if people do find out, it isn't going to be because I told them.

As happy as I am that he's back, I'm not looking forward to seeing him in the halls again. I'm not sure how he's going to react to me now, especially after saying goodbye to him the way I did three days ago. Part of me hopes he just falls back into his old routine too, so we can go back to normal, but something tells me that won't be the case.

When everyone finally cleared out of his house, I talked my mom into helping me clean it up. I didn't expect her to want to help, considering everything that happened, but she jumped into it even more than I did. After taking me to Home Depot, grabbing shelving units and other things we were gonna need, she grabbed some sheets and blankets from our closet and we made our way over.

Within a few hours we had the entire place cleaned and ready. His room had been completely transformed and looked so comfortable, I wanted to climb on his bed and relax in it for awhile. I only hoped that when he came home, he felt the same and it didn't make him feel worse.

As the bell rings, signaling lunch, I slide myself out from the desk and start packing up my bag. It's been getting colder lately, so going outside has been hard, but it's something I definitely need to do today. I'm afraid that if I stay inside like I have been the last two days, I'm going to run into him and that's just not something I'm ready for yet.

As soon as I get out into the hall, the music starts up again. This time, it's a different song, but it's the same band. If I didn't find it strange before, there's no denying it now. This time, it's "Drive You Home" by Parachute and despite not really believing it could be true, I can't help but think all of these songs are speaking directly to me.

What are the odds that my favorite band, is the one someone continues to play through the P.A system? It could easily be one of the football players trying to screw around with the cheerleaders, but something tells me it's more than that.

"So, did Ms. Owens drink before she came to work today?"

I can't help but laugh at the question. Eric, after weeks of keeping his distance from me, is finally back in my life and despite not understanding it before, I couldn't be happier for it. I missed him. I hated that everything that happened with Kayden pulled us apart. He appeared at my side the morning I came back and he hasn't left since.

He's a lot of the reason I adjusted back so well. Having him there with me, it kept me calm. I might have thought I deserved to be completely alone before, that no one could deal with my issues or accept me as I am, but I'm learning that it's so much better having a friend. It's even better when it's one that gets it like Eric.

"Probably."

"Who knew she liked this sort of stuff."

I shrug and he laughs and just like every other time we've been this way in the last two days, I'm okay. I know that people are still making fun of us, but unlike before, I don't focus on it. In a few months, we'd all be moving on from here and even though the ignorance might never entirely go away, at least these people would.

"Isn't this your favorite band?"

"Yeah..."

There it is again, the nagging feeling that something with this music just isn't right. If even Eric can pick up on it then there has to be more to it.

"Meeting at the tree for lunch? He asks, breaking away from the dissection and back to what's most important.

Food.

"Yeah, so go grab your lunch and I'll meet you out there."

He smiles at me and turns back the way he came and as I watch him retreat, I start thinking about how much things have changed in such a short amount of time. Despite it all, I only have one person to thank for all of it.

Kayden.

Kayden

It's amazing what you can accomplish when you sell someone a sob story like the one I sold Ms. Owens this morning.

It's not that anything I said is a lie, because it isn't. I just relayed everything that happened to me over the last few days and what I needed to do. She bought into it so quickly; I almost didn't have to finish the story at all.

Having nothing but time on my hands yesterday when I came home, it came to me and I put it together step by step. I could close my eyes and see it taking shape, which meant that despite knowing it might fail, I still had to see it through. I've never seen something so clearly in my life.

Despite the chaos in my head from the concussion, I'm determined to make my comeback count. By now, I'm sure the entire school knows what happened to me and that I wasn't out because of the alcohol poisoning. I'm ready for all the looks and whispers though. If Isabelle can come back after everything that happened the night of Homecoming, I can do it too.

It's time I face my secret head on instead of running from it and letting it change me, the way I have been for too damn long.

I've spent the last eight years using my mother leaving as an excuse for my behavior. For the way I treated people and the anger that ran so easily through my veins, but that's all it is, an excuse. I've been using them forever and it's gotta stop. I became an asshole, not because of my mom or even Dean. I did it because it was easier than being the good guy.

Isabelle changed all of that, whether she realizes it or not. That's why this comeback I'm making today is for her, just as much as it is for me. It's my chance to come back and change the way I've been. Start over fresh. It's time for me to be the good boy my mom knew I could be. It's time for me to prove just what kind of person Kayden Walker really is and this time, make it stick.

The first step in doing that is reaching out to the person that made me realize it. Who despite seeing the darkest parts of me, the things I've done and said about her, still acted like the little life preserver she is, reaching out in a way that only she can do and saving me.

Before school started, I made sure to get permission from all my teachers to leave early in an effort to catch her reactions to the stunt I'm pulling. I'm pretty sure a lot of them thought I lost my mind, but they gave me what I needed. I was able to stand outside her classroom, far enough away so she couldn't catch me and see her reaction to the first song as it played right after the announcements.

I also caught her reaction to the second one, though seeing how close she's standing with Eric as it happens, bothers me more then I want to admit. Even if she doesn't want me back in her life the way I so desperately want to be, at the very least I want her friendship again. It doesn't mean I have to like seeing her interact with other guys though.

Ducking out of the hall before she can catch me, I head back to the office and the minute I slide through the doors, Ms. Owens is smiling at me.

"You want this next one going outside, right?"

I nod and smile and she motions me over. I look out the window and I'm shocked with how close her favorite tree is to the office. I've spent time out there with her before, but never realized just how visible we would have been to everyone on the other side.

"What you're doing, Kayden, it's a good thing."

"I sure hope so. I really don't want to screw this up again."

"Isabelle's a lucky girl."

See, that's something I don't agree with. I'm doing all of this because I'm the lucky one. I got to spend my entire childhood with the most beautiful girl in the world. I am by far the luckier one and I won't let anyone believe otherwise.

"I'm the lucky one, Ms. Owens."

She smiles at me before pointing to the machine in front of us. "When you're ready, just push that red button and the song will play. I've already set it to the outside speakers."

I nod, thank her and take a seat on the windowsill. I'm going to sit here and wait until she comes out.

It's when I finally see her making her way toward the tree a few minutes later, Eric right on her heels that I know it's time. The minute she sits down, her back completely up against the trunk of the tree, I push the red button just the way Ms. Owens told me to.

Let the games begin.

Belle

Okay, now I know something's up.

No sooner do I sit down at the tree then the music filters out through the loud speakers and with the way Eric's looking at me now, I'm pretty sure he's realizing the same thing. The first time could be looked at as a fluke, maybe even the second time too, but this time, it's different. I know this is geared at me, there's no way it can't be.

It fills me with a horrible feeling inside. There is only one person that knows anything about what this song means to me and I haven't seen him all day, even though he's supposedly back.

Is the security I felt coming back just a dream? Is this another sick plan by Dillon to get to me and break me the way they did at the dance? Does Kayden even realize what's going on or is he as big a part of it as the other stuff that's been done to me?

I've been doing so well the last few days. In the times when the anxiety is too much to handle, I make sure that I take myself away from everyone and do what's needed. I haven't had an accident or cried. In fact, nothing bad has happened at all. I've been perfectly fine.

This music thing though, if I focus on it too much, will break me. I know it.

"Don't think about it, Belle. Sure, it's 'the' song, but that doesn't mean anything."

As thankful as I am that Eric's here with me, he's not helping. Telling me not to focus on it is only going to make me do the opposite.

"There's only one person besides you that knows about that song, Eric and I only told you about it like two days ago. There's no way it isn't meant for me."

The song in question is "Kiss Me Slowly" by Parachute, the go-to band for whoever's doing this stuff today and it's pretty obvious why it's getting to me. The only reason Kayden even knows about it is because it came up in one of our text conversations, which just makes me wanna scroll through my phone and find it.

"Isabelle, don't do it. You're gonna make yourself crazy."

"Can't get any crazier then I already am." I answer, before sliding my finger across the screen and going into the messaging app. Running my finger up the screen, I pause the minute I see the familiar words.

K: What are u doing right now?

Me: Not telling you that. It's embarrassing.

K: I swear I won't tell or laugh at u.

Me: No Kayden.

K: Wanna know what I'm doing then?

Me: If you want to tell me.

K: Trying to find the perfect song.

Me: For what?

K: U

Me: I told you what my favorite song is.

K: I know that. Not what I meant.

Me: What do you mean?

K: It's stupid. Forget it.

Me: "Kiss Me Slowly" by Parachute

K: Is that a song for u?

Me: No, it's a song for you.

K: Ty.

K: I wanted a song that I could listen to when we're not together so I wouldn't miss you so much, okay?

K: That song is perfect.

I never did answer him back that night. I'm not sure why I even told him the song to begin with, but I can see now that when they stole my texts, they got that one too. There's no other reason for this song to be playing now. It's the only thing that makes sense.

"Eric, I need to get out of here."

Not waiting around for him to try and talk me out of it, I get up and make a mad dash for the inside of the school, praying that when I finally do get inside, the music will have stopped. I want to escape it and the memories it brings up, once and for all.

I feel like I've gone back in time as I make my way into the school and down the familiar hallway that's going to lead me to my destination. I've taken this exact route three times in as many weeks. Despite everything I've been through since, how much stronger I've gotten; here I am doing it again.

Before I reach the safety of the bathroom, I'm cut off. Four people appear in front of me and as I raise my head to meet their eyes, my whole body turns cold. Nothing's really changed at all. I've been living in a dream world.

Amy, Charlotte, Tim and Dillon are all standing in my way and none of them looks all that pleased to see me.

"Isabelle," Dillon says first, taking a step forward. "I think it's time we had a little chat."

Chapter Twenty-Five

Kayden

There's one aspect of coming back that I definitely wasn't looking forward to and seeing what I am in the hallway now, I'm reminded of why I dreaded it so much.

I haven't heard from or seen Dillon and the others since Homecoming. I didn't want to see them, but considering the way things used to be, I expected to run into more than one of them the minute I got to school.

I'd been lucky though because until now, I avoided them all. It looks like I'm not going to be able to do that anymore. They're blocking Isabelle from being able to enter the bathroom and just like every other time they get within two feet of her, I want to rush to her side.

Backing as close as I can against the lockers, I keep myself out of their view, but not completely hidden so I can't see what's happening. I can make out Isabelle, feeling the tension in her body from here. I know she's been dreading this moment as much as I have and I'd give anything right now to sweep in and get her out of there.

Unfortunately I can't do it because if I do, she's going to assume I'm here to finish what they're starting, even though it's the farthest thing from the truth. She believes that I'm the one that put together that shit at the dance and there's no way I can make her see differently, at least not yet.

The way Dillon is sneering at her makes me sick. I should have finished what I started at the dance that night, even if doing it would have made everything worse. The hold over the school he's had for the last four years has to end and if I have to be the person to do it, then so be it.

Things need to change.

"You haven't seen Kayden around, have you?"

I watch her shake her head and I sigh. Of course he's doing it this way. He's going to bring me into it right away, so when it's over, he's not the one that gets the blame, I am. He's purposely doing everything he can to ruin everything I set up this morning and I've never wanted to kill him more.

"Yeah that's right, he's been avoiding you. With the smell coming off you right now, I can't imagine he's been able to escape you entirely."

"D, did you see that? She just rolled her eyes at you man!" Tim yells before laughing. "Retard grew a set."

"Is that what you're doing, Isabelle? Trying to show us how tough you are?" Dillon asks, his voice so viciously sweet, I can feel myself getting a toothache from here.

"Maybe I need to take her into the bathroom and show her how tough she really is." Amy joins in and it takes everything in me not to move forward. There is no way in hell I'm letting them do that to her.

"I'm thinking you might have to."

"Listen retard," Charlotte cuts in. "Whatever silly little ideas you've got in your head about Kayden and you, forget them. He's back now and he wants nothing to do with your sorry ass. The game's over. He's with me now."

Despite wanting to let her handle this, I've heard more than enough. Before I can come out from my spot, I'm pulled backward and a hand comes across my mouth. It's a weak attempt to keep me silent, which means it can only be one person.

Eric.

"I know you want to stop it, but if you do, you'll push her away." He whispers and I can't help but agree with him. With everything I've been doing today in an effort to soften her, the last thing I wanna do is set it right back to the start again.

"Then you stop it." I hiss back. "She won't hate you."

"Like I can stop those guys!"

"Where's your backbone man?"

"Wasn't born with one." He answers back, his face deadpan.

"Funny."

"I try. That stuff on the P.A, that's you right?"

I nod and he smiles, which with what comes out of his mouth next, confuses the hell out of me.

"Are you doing it to hurt her?"

"No. The opposite actually."

"Thought so."

"So why even ask?"

"Because even though it doesn't seem like it, I'm her friend."

"You got a funny way of showing it. Where the hell have you been for the last month?"

"Staying clear of Hurricane Kayden."

Well shit. I wish I'd known that before. If I had any clue that the reason he completely bailed on Isabelle had to do with me, I would have fixed it. With my track record though, I probably would have made it worse.

"Look, as fun as this little chat is, you see what's happening as well as I do. I need to stop it."

"Give it a couple more minutes."

Now he's got my attention. What does he know that I don't? What could Isabelle possibly do in the next two minutes to stop what Dillon and the others have planned for her?

It's only when I turn back to check on them that I see what he's getting at.

Isabelle doesn't need me at all.

She's got this.

Belle

I'm smiling and despite the fact that there's nothing about this situation that's funny, I can't stop.

The minute Amy mentioned taking me in the bathroom, there was a second where I felt my heart speed up and I worried about what would happen next. When Dillon agreed with her, it got a little worse. It's only when Charlotte opened her mouth that everything changed.

It's no secret that she likes Kayden; even to someone like me, it's completely obvious and kind of sad. Even if everything that happened between us was a game, I think I know him well enough to know that the last person in the world he wants is Charlotte. She's needy, pushy and way over the top. As popular as Kayden is, he's content staying under the radar. She's the complete opposite, which means they would never work out.

It's because of this that I know what to do and despite being afraid, I'm not going to let it stop me.

"If he's yours, where is he now?"

Tim breaks first, laughing and Charlotte shoots him a look of death before Dillon joins in.

"Holy shit, the retard can actually speak."

"Thanks, Tim."

His face scrunches up at my words and I know I've confused him. That's the thing about these guys that until lately, I never knew. They might be intimidating and downright scary, but if you look hard enough, you can find a failing in them. It makes them just like everyone else.

"Thanks for what?"

"For proving that Neanderthals still exist."

"What the—"

The smile from earlier quickly turns into a laugh as I realize, he didn't understand any of what I just said. He's definitely not the bright one of the group.

"What confused you? The word I used or the fact that you are one?"

"Amy, I think you need to take this mouthy bitch into the bathroom and show her what happens to people that talk back to us."

"Yeah Amy, do it. You see how well it worked out for you the last time."

This is the most I've spoken since I started here almost four years ago and despite knowing that, I can't stop. I've been waiting years to stand up to these people, the ones that spent their entire high school existence making my life a living hell. Now that I can do it, there's no way I'm stopping, no matter what they threaten me with.

"You take one step in her direction and getting suspended will be the least of your worries."

Spinning around at the sound of the voice, I see him and he's not alone. Eric's walking right beside him.

"There you are baby! I knew you'd show up!" Charlotte calls out and the hall is filled with laughter, as Eric starts and Kayden quickly follows it up with one of his own.

"Yeah, I bet you were banking on it. That is why you're doing all of this, right? You figured I'd come running?"

Turning back and seeing all their faces, I realize he's right. They cornered me because they wanted face time with the very person walking up behind me now. The thing is, by the time I finally fought back, they'd lost hope of him ever appearing.

"You want me, you got me."

"Kayden…"

I don't want him doing this. He just got back, the last thing he needs to do is get into a fight, especially over me. Everything that happened with Dean should have been the end of it.

"Isabelle, I can't believe I'm gonna say this because it's weird, but please, shut up."

I want to be hurt by his words, but with the smile he's wearing, coupled with the softness in his green eyes as they're directed solely at me, I can't be. He's not trying to be mean this time. He's just being Kayden.

He turns back toward Dillon and the others and his expression quickly changes. Gone is the softness in his eyes. Now he just looks annoyed. Almost as if this is the last thing he wants to be doing on his first day back.

"You know, I've been trying to figure it out and it just never made sense to me. There's always been this unwritten code with us. We pick people, throw them around, talk shit about them, making them feel like shit under our shoes, but we always steer clear of the Special Ed kids."

Dillon's eyes go wide, like his secrets are being exposed and I'm confused by it. It doesn't seem like such a big secret. Honestly, it's something I was thankful for until they chose me to target. So what's with the look now?

"At least that's how it was until you chose to single her out. I didn't get it at first, but I do now."

"Well don't keep us in suspense man; we're dying to know what your retard loving ass thinks."

"Tim, say that word again. I dare you."

Tim's mouth instantly shuts and Eric laughs, probably as amazed as I am at how right I was with my earlier statement. He does seem to follow commands easily, almost like a dog obeying its master.

"You chose Belle to get to me. I still don't understand why, but it's obvious that it's what you wanted. That's why you gave me the choice a few weeks ago isn't it, Dillon? Choose another victim or you'd continue to harass her? You planned on continuing anyway, you just wanted her to hate me at the same time."

I can tell by the look in Dillon's eyes that he's been caught. Whatever plan he put into motion weeks ago is being pulled apart at the seams and he can't talk his way out of it. I had no idea that's why Eric was chosen, but now that I do, everything's clear. I really was a game all along, but not to Kayden.

I was a game to Dillon.

"Every frigging step you made was to try and bring me down. I thought it was her, hell, I think she thought it was her, but it was never about her was it? It was always me."

Dillon nods and I feel sick. There are so many things I blamed Kayden for; even knowing deep down, he had no part in. All the while it was him they were after. They really wanted to hurt their friend.

"It ends now."

Dillon takes a step forward and there's a moment as he moves in on Kayden that I think they're going to end up fighting again, but just as soon as I think it, I watch Kayden take a step back, closer to me and he makes his position clear.

"I said it ends now and I mean it. We all know I can easily take you down, but that isn't going to solve shit. I'm done."

He turns his back, his eyes again leveled in my direction and he smiles, but only the one side of his mouth lifts. There's an uncertainty in his eyes, like he's unsure what he's supposed to say or do next and as much as I want to guide him. I can't.

"This is never gonna be done, K. I told you. When you least expect it, I will end you."

"I'm on the edge of my seat Dillon, really I am. You want me, I'm not that hard to find. What I'm talking about is the torture, not only to Eric, but Isabelle too. It's over. If I hear or see any of you near these two, or any other kids the way you were with them, suspension or expulsion from this hellhole will be the least of your worries."

"Is that supposed to scare us?"

"I don't really give a shit what it does, but try me and find out."

Turning his body, this time moving until he's positioned directly in front of both me and Eric, he points down the hall.

"Let's get out of here. It's over."

We both turn and start moving away from Dillon and the others even though we can still hear them arguing with each other. It's only when we've made it far enough away that they'll be unable to hear us that Kayden speaks again.

"Eric, can I talk to you for a sec?"

Kayden

He wasn't supposed to be a part of my plan, but with the way he seems to care about her and the way he smiled at me when he heard it was me rigging the P.A system, he's the only person that can help me with what comes next.

I have no doubt that the mess with Dillon is nowhere near over. I also know that despite my threat to him about leaving Eric and Belle alone, he'll still find ways to get around it. I'm banking on him doing that. I meant what I said about backing away from the fighting. I'm done with it, but it doesn't mean I can't get him back in other, smarter ways.

She's wary of me, since I stopped in the middle of hall and called for Eric instead of her. Pretty sure that's gotta come as a shock, but I can't worry about that right now. Everything that happens from this point forward has to have my entire focus. If it works the way I hope, it all comes back to her happiness anyway, so I can handle her being pissed for a little while.

Hearing her speak only solidifies what I'm doing here. There may have been a point, a few weeks ago where she actually needed me there to protect her, but I always knew she could take care of herself. That all she needed was strength and her voice. She proved that to me today, talking down to those assholes that until a few weeks ago, I called my best friends.

My mom, during one of the times she spent ripping my dad apart used to complain that there's no woman alive that needs or wants a Walker. Walker boys are defective. We would break the person we love down, until they were only a shadow of their former self. I believed that for a long time. It's probably why I stayed silent with Dean for as long as I did. If he was no good, it meant I was no good, so all we had was each other.

She was wrong. I know that now and it's because of Isabelle. I can be good for someone, even if I screw up along the way. I can be that good boy she said a girl like Isabelle deserves and I've finally got the chance to prove it.

I can't take back everything that I said about her, the things I did over the last eight years, but I can spend the next eight minutes, hours, days and months making up for it. I finally see what I've been refusing to all along.

It's okay to have differences, to not be like everyone else around you. It doesn't make you weaker or less worthy than anyone else that might appear normal. It is what it is. You're just different. At the end of the day, we all want the exact same things in life and I think Isabelle and I are living proof of that.

"What do you need, Kayden?"

"Remember what you said earlier about me getting involved?"

"You mean, when I told you to hang back and give her a chance? Yeah, I do."

"Well I've got one more thing planned, but it's not until later. I'd do it on my own, but I think that after what just happened, she might not trust it. If I ask you to help me, will you do it?"

"You swear this isn't gonna turn into something like Homecoming?"

"I'll sign my promise in blood if that's what you want. This isn't a joke."

"That's gross. You don't need to do that. What do you need me to do?"

"Get her to the gym at 3:45. I want her there right at that time."

"Why?"

"Everyone will pretty much be cleared out by then and what I'm planning, I sort of need privacy for. Well, present company excluded, if you don't mind missing your bus."

"All you need is her in the gym at 3:45?"

"That's it. I got the rest from there."

"Alright, I'll do it, but on one condition."

Despite everything I put this kid through and everything I believed about him, I've gotta hand it to him. He could easily be afraid of me right now, but he's not. He's just doing what I should've been doing all along.

Looking out for her.

"Name it."

"This time, whatever you're gonna do, make sure it's for keeps. You might be able to threaten those guys into leaving us alone, but you won't bully me. If you hurt her, I'll hurt you."

"Deal."

Epilogue

Belle

The rest of the afternoon passes by in a blur and thankfully it's an uneventful blur. The musical interruptions stop after the broadcast outside at lunch. The strange thing is, even though I know it was Dillon trying to get to Kayden, I found myself missing it.

Moving from class to class, everything quiet even though I'm surrounded by noise, I start believing that I imagined the whole thing. With the way I stood up for myself, a move that in the last three years I've never done, I've got no other explanation for everything that's happened today.

I don't see Kayden again and I struggle with how that makes me feel. I know I was scared to come face to face with him, but with everything that happened when we did finally come together, the fear's been replaced by something else.

Love.

No matter how out of my way I go in order to avoid it, run from it or even deny its existence at all, it doesn't change the truth.

I am in love with Kayden Walker.

It's that love that makes me search for him down every hall, around every corner, even though something tells me he doesn't want to be found. It's that love that makes me hound Eric for information. There's an overwhelming urge to know what the two of them talked about that for whatever reason, I'm not allowed to know.

There's only one part of admitting how I feel that bothers me. If everything that happened was designed by Dillon and not

Kayden, the way I originally thought, then why isn't he searching me out? If everything he said during our few weeks together was real, the way he made it sound, then why isn't he here now?

Love might have the power to heal, but it also has the power to hurt, which is what it's doing to me.

I don't want Eric to be the one he's talking to. I want it to be me, though deep down I realize I don't deserve his words. I did the exact thing to him that everyone has been doing to me for years. I suppose it's not all that surprising that he's going out of his way to avoid me, despite talking to my friend earlier.

I judged him. I took everything that happened and assumed he was behind it, instead of believing in the person that I'd gotten to know. I made a horrible mistake and it's one I'm not sure I can ever take back.

For all the acceptance and understanding that I crave, I sure didn't extend it to the one person that deserved it most. The world can't be expected to change and adapt to anything it perceives as different, if we don't first do it ourselves.

How many times has that been drilled into me, not only by my mom, but my teachers too? One easy lesson and somehow I'd completely forgotten it, in favor of being just like everyone else.

Realizing all of this though, it doesn't make the hurt I feel at being ignored any easier.

"You need to come with me."

"Excuse me?" I ask, as Eric grabs me by the sleeve, attempting to drag me a completely different way than the one I actually need to go.

"Ms. T wants to see us in the gym." He answers, as if it's something I should have known.

"Why?"

"I don't even know."

Now I know something's going on. If Ms. Taylor actually wanted to see us, she would have given Eric a reason and he's got an even better memory then me. There's no way he wouldn't remember what it is. I call bullshit on his *I don't know*.

"Try again, Eric."

"Would you just trust me and come?" he whines before shooting his best sad eyes at me. "It's supposed to be a surprise. She's been putting it together for awhile or something, but god, don't tell her I said that. She'll kill me."

That's another thing he's good at. Being over dramatic. This explanation makes more sense though, so removing his hand off my shirt, I motion for him to move and follow along behind the moment he does.

The entire time I'm walking, I try and figure out exactly what kind of surprise my teacher could be putting together for me. My birthday is in the spring, so it can't have anything to do with that and there's really nothing else that jumps out. I think about asking Eric, knowing that if I ask enough of the right questions, he'll break and tell me, but with the hurry he seems to be in to get me there, I'm not so sure I want to stop him.

I'm not big on surprises. There are just too many variables to consider and usually even just thinking about it is enough for me to shut down. Ms. T knows this better than anyone, so why she's doing this doesn't make sense to me.

As we finally round the corner and the gym comes into view, I see her standing outside the door, her face wearing the same welcoming smile she has every day when I walk into her class. Seeing her this way settles the worries that have been building the entire way here.

"Alright, well here you go. I'm out of here. I gotta catch the bus."

The minute he mentions the bus, it hits me. That's my only way home. If I'm not out there to catch it, same as Eric, then I'm going to be stranded here for the hour or more it'll take until my mom gets off work.

"Wait!" I call out. "How am I supposed to get home?"

"Don't worry about that. Something tells me, you'll get home just fine." Ms. Taylor answers easily.

Okay, now I'm confused and the only person that I could get answers from is completely out of sight. I could ask her what she means, but before I can open my mouth, she motions for me to go in.

"Isabelle, I know how you feel about surprises, but go in. I promise you, it's not going to be as bad as you're imagining."

She has no idea the scenario's I've got running in my head right now. I can see the accidents, the tears and me falling completely apart so easily, it's like it's happening in real time even though I'm standing here, completely safe and dry.

Have I mentioned I really hate surprises?

"Go on, dear."

Closing my eyes, taking a few deep breaths to calm the heartbeat that's threatening to beat itself to death inside my chest, I move forward slowly, until I'm all the way through the door and standing a few steps inside the gym.

It's when I open my eyes that I see it and more than that, I see the person standing in the middle of it.

Kayden is standing in the middle of the gym, dressed, not in the clothes I saw him wearing earlier, but in a suit and as my eyes lock completely on his, he does the one thing that up until now he's never done.

He takes my breath away.

Kayden

There was this moment while I stood here waiting that I actually thought Eric ditched me and she wouldn't show up. In fact, the longer it took waiting for Ms. Taylor to open the door to signal she was here, I worked myself up so much, I'm pretty sure I've got grey mixed with the blonde in my hair. That's how much I'm relying on this to work out right.

It was hard to put all of this together with only a half hour to work with, but somehow I did it. It might not be an exact duplication of the dance, especially since she won't be appearing in the Cinderella dress and I'm in a suit instead of the ruined tuxedo, but it's as close to perfection as possible.

The lights from that night are filling the room with stars. There's a bottle of soda and soup from the deli, sitting on the table off to the left. It's as close to her favorites as I could manage and I really hope that when she does show, she's surprised by it. I've even got the tunes, though it's definitely not the system they used for Homecoming. It's a beat up old boom box that Coach had hidden in his office. Since it plays CD's though, it's everything I can possibly ask for.

Everything is ready. The only thing missing is her.

The door opens and I can hear Ms. Taylor's voice coming through, the low tone telling me that Isabelle's here and she's on the other side of the door. After a few minutes, where I start to wonder if she's ever going to make her way in, she finally steps inside. Her eyes are closed, but she's walking toward me just the way I imagined her doing in my head.

There's an excitement level in me, seeing her move that I've never known before and if I thought it couldn't get any stronger, I'm wrong. As she opens her eyes, it feels like an explosion goes off in my chest at the sight of her, as she takes it all in.

"Umm…"

I actually expected her initial reaction to be something worse. When Ms. T agreed to help earlier, she explained, in excruciating detail, all of the ways that she pictured this going wrong. She warned me about Isabelle's fear of surprises and that I needed to prepare myself for whatever the fallout might be. I'd taken it all in and prepared myself as much as possible, but in her typical way, she goes and does something I never prepared for at all.

"Belle, are you okay?"

She moves closer to me, her head moving up and down in a nod and it scares me. With the way she talked so easily in the hall earlier with Dillon, the last thing I want is for her to revert back to silence now, especially if I'm the reason why.

"What is this?"

"What does it look like?"

"It looks like Homecoming."

"Then I guess you have your answer, don't you?"

"Why?" she asks and I'm actually stumped by the question. Not because I don't have an answer for her, because I do. I'm stumped that she's even asking me at all. Does she really not get why I would want to do this for her?

"You don't know?"

She shakes her head and I frown. With the way she looked at me in the hall, I thought she might have been on the same page as me. That she missed me as much as I did her and wanted to fix everything that I stupidly broke, but now I'm not so sure. For the second time in as many minutes, I'm scared I'm doing the wrong thing again.

Shit, I suck at this part. Explaining how I feel, why I do the things I do, what she means to me. I mean, she's the one that dropped her feelings on me first, because I choked the last time we were like this. I can already see that I'm going to blow it before I've even started.

I can't just leave her hanging. I've done that for far too long already. Even if I can't get the words to come out right, I have to at least try. She's standing here now, giving me a chance, despite all the crappy stuff in our history. I owe her the words, even if they're not as perfect as I want them to be.

"In my life, I don't have a whole lot of memories that end happily, but the ones that I do have and can easily pull up in my mind, Isabelle; they all have you in them."

"I don't understand."

"I know, but I'm going to try and explain okay?"

"Okay."

"The first real memory I have, is one of the first times I was old enough to remember being at your house. We must have been about three, maybe four. I came and sat down beside you while you were playing and it's like, even then, you knew I wasn't anything special because you just ignored the hell out of me."

I stop, allowing myself to recall the moment as clearly as I can in my head and unable to control it, I feel the smile spreading across my face.

"It bugged me so much. I tried everything I could to get your attention and nothing worked. Then one day, you finally looked up, those big blue eyes of yours pointed right at me, an annoyed look on your face. I swear, it was like the best thing ever. I didn't even care that I annoyed you. The only thing that mattered was—I finally got your attention."

"I don't remember that."

"I figured that. Isabelle, I don't think you're supposed to remember these things because they're my memories of you. I don't want you to either, because they're so important to me that I don't want to share them. Not with anyone, not even you."

She smiles and I'm just frozen in place. It's actually the perfect time for her to do it since this is another memory I have that I need to share.

"Once I got you to look at me, the next step was getting you to smile for me. I tried over and over to get you to do it and nothing ever worked. Half the time, I just upset you so much you'd cry and I'd end up having to go home. One day though, I decided that I'd tickle your feet, I mean everyone smiles and laughs at that right? So I did it and sure enough, you smiled and I never really knew how important it was at the time. Remembering it now though, I see it."

"You see what?"

"When you smile at me Isabelle, it's like I've being hit by lightning. Once you do it, time freezes. All motion just stops. It's as if the smile keeps me still. Some of the happiest times in my life are when you smiled at me. Then and now."

"Okay."

It's not the answer I'm expecting, but considering she's still standing here with me, I can't ask for much more. I've got so much work to do, repairing everything that I broke. It can't all be fixed with a few pretty words and a perfectly decorated gym. As long as she's staying though, I'm fighting.

"The point I'm making with all of this is, every good thing that's happened in my life up until this point, has in some way revolved around you. Getting you to notice me, you smiling at me, the way my name sounded the first time you ever said it, the way it still sounds, even today. The softness of your lips when they're pressed on any part of me, the cute little faces you make when you're texting me. How perfectly your hand fits in mine. It's always been you."

"Kayden..."

"See what I'm saying?"

"Kayden, stop please."

The plea in her voice stops me cold. Is this where she tells me that she's heard enough and turns to walk away?

"I spent so long locked in my own head that I really don't know how this is gonna sound, but I need to say some things before you continue. I can't take listening to you tell me how happy I make you, not after everything I've done."

What she's done? Huh? What the hell is she talking about? She hasn't done anything but believe in me and from where I'm standing, that isn't a bad thing. She's the reason I'm even here at all.

"I'm sorry, Kayden. I'm sorry because I really believed you were playing some kind of game with me. I believed that what happened at Homecoming was your fault. I did the one thing that I want everyone else to stop doing with me. I judged you based on the way you were, not the way that you are. You were nothing but sweet, tender and loving with me and I believed the worst in you. I let you down."

"Are you done?"

She nods and I reach out to her, taking her hand, placing it against my own and linking our fingers together.

"You have nothing to be sorry for. It's hard not to believe the worst in someone when they spend eight years proving they're the worst human being alive. What happened to us, Isabelle, that's on me. I said all the things you heard at Homecoming and there's nothing I can say that can ever take them back. The only thing I can say is, I was an ignorant, blind asshole who isn't deserving of even five minutes of your time, let alone five weeks."

"Kayden..."

"Isabelle, I love you."

I've gone over in my head a million times how I was going to say it the first time it came out. It's not exactly the way I imagined it, but I refuse to take it back. It's the truth and that's what all of this is about. Telling her the truth and giving her the night she missed because of the horrible things I did.

"You wanna know why I did all of this?"

"Yes, I do."

"I did all of this because there's only one thing I'm sure of anymore and that is, I love you. I think I've been in love with you since I was three years old."

"You're in love with me?"

"Yes."

"You put all of this together for me?"

"Yes."

"Kayden..." she whispers and I see the tears start to fall from her eyes. I start to think I've made everything worse until she speaks again, stopping my heart. "What took you so long?"

This girl, I swear—will be the death of me.

"I needed someone to show me the way."

It's when I pull her into me, feeling her body connect itself to mine that it hits me. What I said before is true. It's always been Isabelle. There has never been another girl that the minute our bodies meet, can make me feel this complete and as long as I live, there never will be. She's it.

I hear it then, clear as day, even though the way we're holding each other, her face buried in my chest, it comes out muffled.

"I love you, Kayden."

Here's the thing. It doesn't matter if her face is buried in my chest or she's on the other side of the world from me. As long as she's the one saying the words, I'm always going to hear them clearly because she's not just speaking to my head.

She's speaking to my heart.

"Isabelle?" I ask, not wanting to ruin the moment, but remembering there's still one more thing I haven't done.

"Hmm?" she murmurs as she breaks away from my chest and looks up, meeting my eyes dead on.

Pointing toward the stereo on the stage, I take her hand and guide her toward it. Pushing play, I wait until the music starts and then I look at her. Her eyes go wide, but the smile remains as the realization takes hold.

"It was you?"

"It was me." I answer with a grin.

"Why?"

"You owed me a dance."

The End...

Count On Me Playlist

Face Down by The Red Jumpsuit Apparatus
Bully by Shinedown
A Beautiful Lie by 30 Seconds To Mars
Wrong Side of Heaven by Five Finger Death Punch
Broken by Lifehouse
Invisible by Hunter Hayes
Drive You Home by Parachute
The Reason by Hoobastank
The Only Exception by Paramore
Count On Me by Default
Ready When You Are by Trapt
The Mess I Made by Parachute
Only One In Color by Trapt
All That I'm Asking For by Lifehouse
She Is Love by Parachute
Kiss Me Slowly by Parachute
(Kayden & Isabelle's dance)

Authors Note

There are three subjects touched on within this story that I would be remiss if I didn't mention now that the story has been told. Autism, Bullying and Child Abuse are very real issues that millions of people across the globe struggle with daily.

No child on the Autism Spectrum is the same as another. The experiences that the fictional character of Isabelle deals with throughout the story may not be what your child or even you have experienced. As the mother of three children on the spectrum, I took as much care as possible in making sure this story adequately explained and showed the true wonder that is our children, but it is not an exact science. If I have offended you in any regard with the making of this story, you have my utmost apologies. This is only a small part of what autism really is and I hope it can be viewed that way.

If you would like more information regarding Autism, please visit http://autismcanada.org/ No website can take the place of a medical professional. If you suspect you, or your child may be on the Spectrum, please seek medical advice.

Bullying is something that has been around as long as time but has recently been on the rise. If you or anyone you know is being bullied for being you, I want to tell you that you are not alone. Do not suffer in silence. As hard as it can be to speak up about what you're suffering with, please do it. No one deserves that. If you want to reach out and aren't sure where to look, please visit http://www.pacer.org/bullying/. There is information and people there that are more than willing to help. Also, talk to your parents, friends and other trusted individuals. Please remember that it's not you, it's them. Never give up, never give in. You'll get through it.

If you or someone you know is suffering with child abuse, please do not hesitate to call Child Help National Child Abuse Hotline at 1-800-4-A-CHILD (1-800-422-4453). There are people there 24/7 that are more than willing to help you or those that you know and care about. You do not have to suffer alone anymore.

Acknowledgements

This book would not have been written if it wasn't for my real life Isabelle's. Caleb, Noah, Raine and Bella, thank you for showing me, each and every day just what is so great about this world. You never cease to amaze me and I will love you, forever and always.

If it wasn't for my Daddy and his never ending supply of love and acceptance for both me and his grandchildren, I'm not sure this book would have seen the light of day. So thank you Dad, for showing me what true love and acceptance really is.

As always, there's my best friend, Joey. Without him, there would be no me. Thank you for pouring over this story, both in the beginning stages and the end. More than that, thank you for showing me that there are real Kayden's in the world. It is my hope, as my children get older; they have someone in their life that touches their lives the way you have touched mine. I love you.

For Will: You have shown me a tremendous amount of support and that, coupled with your friendship is what I hope to carry with me for years to come. Thank you for being a friend to me and also for being a fan. It means more than you will ever know and it's a sure bet that support is what keeps me writing.

Theresa Troutman. It's been said that writing is a lonely existence, but you've proven that wrong in the short time since I met you. Thank you for your constant words of encouragement, support and more than that, your friendship and expertise. It means the world to me, just as you do.

To the parents of special needs children, the world over. Even though this book is primarily a work of fiction, there will be traits you'll recognize in your own children. It is my hope that making the story the way I did, I have shown that our children are not what they have been made out to be, but so much more. Each and every one of you has my utmost respect and adoration for everything you face each day, all in the name of love for your children. Never give up, never give in and continue to fight always. Those beautiful children love you for it, as do I.

To the people that spend their hard earned time and money on this story. Thank you from the bottom of my heart. It means more than you will ever truly now. This story was a labor of love and I hope you enjoy the story and characters as much as I did writing it.

About The Author

Melyssa Winchester is a mother of four from Toronto, Ontario, Canada. When she's not knee deep in adolescent awesomeness, she's falling in love, one book boyfriend and girlfriend at a time. She is a lover of all things romance and will forever believe in a real and try happily ever after.

When she's not off being a mom or writing you can find her doing one of two things. Reading or buried under the covers watching Supernatural, Sons of Anarchy or Veronica Mars.

Melyssa is currently working on Before The Light Book #1: Hold Onto Me (Michael's Story) that follows the lives of the characters from the Love United Series before they came together. She is also hard at work on a standalone title Shades of Blue and plotting many more upcoming projects for the future.

You can find her on the web, either at her personal site, Facebook (which she just might have an obsession with) or Twitter (@WinchesterBooks) where she talks incessantly about her kids, her writing and all things book boyfriend related.

Other Works by Melyssa Winchester

LOVE UNITED SERIES
1. Holding On To Heaven
2. No Surrender
3. Wanted
4. Stairway To Heaven
5. A Light In The Dark (Coming April 2014)

Coming Soon:

BEFORE THE LIGHT
(Love United Series of Novella's)
1. Hold Onto Me (Michael's Story)
2. Absence Of Light (Ryan's Story)

TAKE ME WITH YOU

ALL MY HEART
(Kayden and Isabelle's future story)

SHADES OF BLUE